THE CASE OF THE RELUCTANT WITNESS

THE SIXTH CHRONICLE OF A LADY DETECTIVE

K.B. OWEN

MISTERIO PRESS

For Nancy Samson, with gratitude

The Case of the Reluctant Witness
The Sixth Chronicle of a Lady Detective
Copyright © 2022 Kathleen Belin Owen

Published in the United States of America

Cover design by Melinda VanLone,
BookCoverCorner(dot)com

ISBN: 978-1-947287-36-5

CHAPTER 1

nce again, I read through the telegram from Chicago.

FLORA AT GRETA'S NEEDS SAFE ESCORT NYC
DA'S OFFICE EXPECTED TUES 12TH FOR
TESTIMONY. YOU ARE CLOSEST OFFICE
WILL COMPENSATE YOU.
~FRANK

I bit my lip. How had he known where to find me? Though we still worked together on the occasional case—he, too, was employed by the Pinkerton Agency—I hardly kept him apprised of my movements.

"Not bad news from home, I hope?"

My long-time friend, Cassie Leigh, attempted a peek over my shoulder at the note—no easy feat, as she was at least a head shorter than I am. She and I were a study in contrasts.

1

Where she was dark-haired and dark-eyed, I was pale blonde and gray-eyed. Temperamentally speaking, we differed as well, which made for an unlikely friendship, to say the least. While I was not especially nurturing—I tended to expect the worst from others—Cassie possessed a generous-hearted disposition, often prompting confidences from relative strangers. Such a trait had proved invaluable in my work.

"A case." I passed her the note. "I'm reluctant to accept it, though."

She smoothed the paper. "Understandable—we've only just arrived. Your mother would be most displeased."

Displeased was putting it mildly, given Mother's view of my "sordid" profession. Her term, not mine.

My parents had learned the particulars of how I earned my living only last summer, when a cousin had urgent need of my sleuthing skills. Papa had been sanguine about the news. Mother had not. On the bright side, the case had ended nine years of family estrangement. Now we had more of a family détente.

"I have another reason to decline." I pointed to the sender's name.

Cassie's nose twitched in annoyance. "Frank? Why is he asking *you?*"

I shrugged. "I suppose because we're family, at least in name. Flora is Frank's sister. And we're not far from South-brook, where his great-aunt Greta lives."

"I've never heard of the place."

"The town is near New Haven, about half a day's train ride from here. But I hesitate to become embroiled in Frank's family troubles." I drew a breath as my chest constricted, an unpleasant but all-too-familiar sensation. It happened either when I was laced too tightly, or my estranged husband intruded upon my life.

She peered at me, her delicately arched dark brows drawn in a frown. "Have you given thought to your father's offer to arrange for a quiet divorce? Then you'd be free of him completely."

I suppressed a snort. "I doubt a piece of paper would keep him from bringing me his problems." Frank had already made clear he was determined to stay involved in my life.

Take me back, Pen. I'm a changed man.

Had he changed enough? Did I truly want him out of my life completely? Those were questions for another time. Meanwhile, I should send a reply to give him time to find someone else. I exhaled, and the tightness eased.

Cassie left me alone to compose my answer.

I struggled with two different opening sentences before finally deciding upon a third—surprising, as saying no to Frank should be easy by now.

Perhaps I hesitated because cases didn't come my way as often as they did for my male counterparts at the agency. I was hardly positioned to infiltrate a criminal gang by working in the mines or to confront striking steelworkers with the business end of a rifle—though I was sufficiently adept at wielding one. My cases tended toward problems that require what my employer termed "a woman's touch"—catching hoisters, fare skimmers, blackmailers, and the occasional murderer. I didn't imagine the latter was what William Pinkerton had in mind when he hired me, but when people are determined to misbehave, there's no help for it.

I'd nearly finished my reply when a soft knock on the library door interrupted my thoughts. My mother's seamstress poked her head in. "Miss Penelope?"

"Yes—come in." I set aside the paper.

She gestured to the blue-silk dinner gown draped over her arm. "When you're free, miss, could you please try this on? There are sure to be alterations needed." She eyed my tall, angular frame—not at all the standard for feminine beauty these days.

Of all the tedious activities women are regularly subjected

to, trying on female apparel is among the worst of them. "Thank you, but I'm not in need of another dinner dress."

"Mrs. Hamilton's orders, miss. She insists upon you being suitably attired for tomorrow evening's affair."

I blinked. "Affair?"

"You don't know? There's to be a large dinner party in your honor. Several old friends of yours are coming." Her lips twitched. "Including that handsome gentleman you used to see—Mr. Frasier. He's widowed now, you know."

I was well aware of Leonard Frasier's widower state, having unexpectedly encountered him a couple of years ago while on a case.

Mother had obviously returned to her matchmaking ways.

"Oh! Was it to be a surprise?" the seamstress asked. "I do hope I haven't spoiled anything."

Time for a change of plans. I glanced back at my reply to Frank and crumpled the sheet. "No, not at all."

The next day saw Cassie and me stepping aboard the express train for Southbrook. We settled into seats as far from the drafty doors as we could manage—not only because of the chill on this dreary March day, but to evade the thick coal smoke that lingered at the back of our throats and made our eyes water.

"What do you know about Flora and Greta?" Cassie asked, once she'd caught her breath and tucked away her handkerchief. "Have you met them?"

I nudged my satchel out of the way of passing feet. "I've only met them once—ten years ago, just after Frank and I returned from our elopement. He wanted to introduce me to what little family he had left, his sister Flora and his great-aunt Greta." I winced as I recalled that meeting. It had been a frosty reception. The woman had flat-out accused Frank and me of currying favor to coax money from her. We didn't stay long.

"What's she like?"

"A haughty woman, with a perpetual scowl and a sharp tongue." I buttoned my jacket up to the collar with a shiver. "She must be in her seventies by now. Quite wealthy."

Cassie's eyes brightened. "Frank's family doesn't come from money. She married well, I suppose?"

"Indeed, though the match was rather unconventional. She was a music hall dancer in her youth. A rich man named Marlowe—much older—became enamored of her, and they married."

"Really? That's not usually how the story goes."

"True enough." As it turned out, Greta had more than a comely face and figure—she also possessed a keen business sense. "After her husband died, she opened one of the most exclusive hotels in the area, the Marlowe House. She lives on the topmost floor of the hotel. Quite comfortably, if memory serves."

A little boy, perched in his mother's lap upon the bench across from us, began to squirm and wail.

"Has Flora lived with her all this time?" Cassie raised her voice to be heard.

The mother flashed us a sheepish look and handed the child a peppermint stick, which settled him down into sticky silence.

"She was living there when we'd first met," I answered. "Barely old enough for her come-out back then. Later, she married a fellow named...ah yes—Richards." I watched the blurring view through the window and wondered—why wasn't she with her husband? What was her value as a witness?

It was obviously no routine matter. Frank had referenced his sister's safety, and he never paid extra for unnecessary words in a telegram. Did he anticipate someone trying to interfere? I always carried my double-barrel derringer with me —compact enough to fit in my reticule—but it lacked significant firepower. Or accuracy. I generally didn't need it. My wits, my lockpicks, and a sturdy pair of legs served me better.

If only Frank had given me more to go on. How typical. I tried to ignore the queasy feeling in my abdomen, equal parts annoyance and worry.

∾

We took a cab from the station to the hotel, situated in the commercial section of town.

"Southbrook is older than I realized," Cassie said, as we rattled along a bone-jarring cobblestone street before turning onto the smooth, macadamized main thoroughfare.

"This building appears particularly ancient." I pointed to a turreted mansion—its gilded sign proclaimed it to be a boys' academy—across the street from our destination.

Marlowe House, though newer than the boys' academy, was an impressive edifice. It was built in the grand tradition of French-Empire architecture, boasting an iron-trimmed mansard roof, stone pavilions flanking each wing, and more arched windows than I had time or inclination to count.

The tunic-attired footman attending the door hurried over to help us alight on the slippery pavement—it had been drizzling all morning, and the skies were only now clearing. "Good afternoon, ladies. Is this all your luggage?" He reached for the two cases and single valise the cabbie had unloaded at the curb.

I handed the cabbie his fare. "We're here for a short visit."

Cassie's mouth curved in amusement, no doubt imagining, as was I, how many cases and trunks the fellow was usually saddled with by patrons of the fairer sex.

"Follow me, please."

The interior was no less grand, with a leaded glass skylight illuminating the parquet floor and grand sweep of the mahogany staircase. Groupings of plush, rose-velvet chairs and cherrywood occasional tables were tucked beneath windows. As dearly as I would have loved to sink into one of them after hours of sitting upon hard benches, I followed Cassie over to the check-in desk.

The clerk was a slender little man with silver-rimmed spectacles and hair slicked down along a precise middle parting. I could smell the macassar oil from here.

"Good afternoon," he said. "Do you have reservations?"

"We do not." At his frown, I asked, "Will that be a difficulty?"

"We have an out-of-town theater company staying on for a second week. But I seem to remember—" He bent over his appointment book, thumbing through several pages. "Ah! Yes, a cancellation. Just the one room, however."

"That's fine," Cassie said. "We can share."

"You'll also have to share a hall bath with several other ladies." He paused, as if waiting for our objection. When none came, he went on, "Your room is in the old wing, you see."

"That won't be a problem," I answered.

"All right, then. Your names, please?"

"I'm Mrs. Wynch." Although I generally used my natal name of Hamilton since my separation from Frank, it seemed prudent to give my married name while dealing with Greta and her staff.

Cassie flashed me a brief frown. "And I am Miss Leigh," she said to the clerk.

"Sign here." He passed over a pen. "How long will you be staying?"

"Only a few days, I expect," I said. "Until Friday morning at the latest." The sooner we got Flora to her destination, the better I'd feel.

Once we had signed the register, he reached over his

shoulder for the key, then hesitated. "Wait—you said *Wynch*? You are a relation of Mrs. Marlowe, ma'am?"

"Not a blood relation. I'm married to her grandnephew, Frank. I was hoping to see her, in fact. And Flora as well—I understand she's staying here?"

He pursed his lips. "Do they know to expect you? Mrs. Marlowe made no mention of you or the other lady."

"An unexpected change in plans brought us to town." I'd questioned my decision at least a dozen times today, and it wasn't even tea-time yet.

Tea-time. My stomach grumbled. I hadn't realized before now that I'd been too preoccupied to eat this morning.

"They aren't on the premises now. I don't know when to expect them. They are very busy ladies, you know." His pointy nose twitched in disapproval, but whether it was at ladies being busy with activities outside the home or Cassie and me distracting them from those activities, I couldn't say.

"Come now, Barnaby," said a brisk male voice, nearly at my elbow.

I hadn't even heard the fellow approach. I turned for a good look at the narrow-shouldered, youngish man of middling height.

"You know they're at the theater," the fellow went on. "No need to be so circumspect." He gave us a slight bow. "John Davis, at your service, ladies. I'm one of the Pierson Players."

"Oh, how exciting," Cassie breathed. "I've never met an actor before. The Pierson Players—is that the theater company the clerk was speaking of?"

He inclined his head. "One and the same."

Upon closer inspection, I realized he was older than he'd appeared at first glance—perhaps his middle forties—evidenced by the gray flecks in his dark pencil mustache and the crinkles at the sides of his deep-brown eyes. It was the energy of the man, in both voice and movement, that belied his years.

He gave us an equally careful perusal—I suspected this one missed little—as I introduced Cassie and myself, along with our purpose. Our public one, at least.

"Ah," he said with a nod. "I didn't imagine you two were blood relations to Greta and Flora—I pride myself on noting family resemblances—but I'm sure they will be delighted to see you. I'm heading to the theater myself. You're welcome to ride with me."

"You have performances on a Tuesday, sir?" Cassie asked.

"Merely rehearsals—a new comedy. Flora is in the production, and Greta is her acting coach."

"Flora is an actress?" I asked incredulously. Again, I had to wonder about the lady's absentee husband and what he had to say about it.

Davis hesitated, teeth tugging at his mustached lip. "Let us say that she's…new to the business. Hence the necessity of a coach. She plays a minor character, though recently she also became understudy to the new leading lady."

"That seems quite the promotion. How did that come about?" I asked.

He rubbed the back of his neck. "Miss Templeton—the former lead—had an accident."

"Oh dear. What happened?" Cassie asked.

"She fell and wrenched her ankle—quite badly. She's confined to bed."

Cassie clucked her tongue. "How unfortunate."

"It's a hazardous occupation sometimes." He fell silent and smoothed his mustache, as if considering the philosophical ramifications of such an undertaking.

"I can imagine." I resisted the urge to roll my eyes. Theater gossip was not what we were here for. "Shall we go?"

The theater was only two blocks away, but Davis insisted upon us taking a cab. Perhaps he thought our constitutions couldn't withstand the exertion.

Upon arriving at our destination, he led us around to a side door.

"This is where I leave you. I'm needed backstage. Be as quiet as you can before the lights come back on."

The door led us inside to the ground-level *parquette*, with seats arranged in sections forming an arc in front of the stage. Even in the dim light, one had the impression of immense space. Brass-railed balcony boxes loomed at the sides above us, and I could just make out the ornate gilt ornamentation framing them. Our nostrils were assailed by the scents of sawdust, fresh paint, and beeswax polish.

A rotund little man with a clipboard leaned against the stage apron, watching a man and a woman upon the stage. The spotlight overhead picked up tiny specks of dust motes drifting to the floor.

Neither gentleman was known to me—the one standing on stage was notably handsome in that lustrous-eyed, tousled-dark-hair, sculpted-jaw sort of way that no doubt predestined him for the footlights—but I recognized the lady at once. Flora appeared much as I last remembered, with soft, pale-blonde hair pulled back in a charming chignon, a delicate chin, and a diminutive, graceful form. There were deep shadows beneath her eyes, though I couldn't tell if it was from the harsh spotlight, fatigue, or something related to my mission.

We made our way toward the silhouettes of a dozen or so people who were scattered in the middle section.

"Down in front," a voice hissed.

Cassie and I scrambled into the nearest chairs.

"Is that Flora on stage?" Cassie whispered in my ear.

"Yes."

"Where's Greta?"

"I can't tell—it's too dim. Perhaps backstage? We'll have to wait for the lights."

We watched the scene playing out before us—the story of

a woman concocting an elaborate plan with her butler to catch her husband at infidelity, though all the while the butler was her husband in disguise. Supremely farcical, but there was no accounting for popular tastes.

Flora was doing passably well, only fumbling a line here and there.

"She seems to enjoy the stage," Cassie whispered in my ear.

It was true. The lady's features were animated, her voice strong—though perhaps rather monotone.

The screech of a door at the back of the theater caused heads to swivel—and no wonder, as the sound called to mind a cat's tail being trod upon. One of the ladies in the row ahead of us caught my attention.

I'd recognize that heavy-browed glare anywhere. Greta Marlowe.

Her gaze slid past us, without recognition.

I tried to see the subject of her scowl, but all I could make out in this light was a trim-figured young lady, perhaps in her twenties.

The man with the clipboard waved at the arrival in irritation. "Kay—finally. You're late."

"Sorry," she called, shrugging off her coat as she hurried down a side aisle toward him. "I wanted to make sure Viola was settled in her new quarters before I came."

"I see." The man softened his tone. "We've had Flora run through lines in your absence, so I suppose it was useful."

"Can we take a break?" the dark-haired man on stage asked.

"Already?" The other man sighed. "All right, everyone, we'll make it a brief one—return promptly in twenty minutes. We're already behind." As the lights came up, he frowned at the fellow on stage. "Barrett, you in particular have a great many lines to get through." Then he called toward the backstage area, from where I could hear the shuffling of feet—

workmen, no doubt. "Would someone please oil the door hinges?"

Greta climbed the steps along the side of the stage, with unusual agility for a woman of her advanced years. But I shouldn't be surprised. Even from this distance, one could see the trim curves of the dancer she had been in her youth.

"I'll be back," I murmured to Cassie and jumped up to follow.

"Mrs. Marlowe?" I called, overtaking her on the steps.

The lady squinted up at me. The years had been kind and had left her some remnants of beauty—hair white, yes, but full and sleekly tucked in an elegant up-do, blue eyes still clear beneath salt-and-pepper brows, cheeks smooth and slightly pink.

"Who are you?" she asked.

Flora, who had been moving toward us, hesitated.

"Frank sent me," I said.

Greta froze, then her brow cleared. "I know you. You're his wife." Her lip curled. "What is it—low on funds again?"

I stiffened my spine and tipped my chin. As the daughter of society's most respected blueblood matron, Honoria Hamilton, I was more than capable of matching this woman's haughty air. "He has sent me to collect Flora. As you are no doubt aware, there's a district attorney who requires her as a witness."

Her mouth formed a wordless *O*. Flora must have heard something of what I'd said, as she now stood with clasped hands.

I pressed my advantage. "Do you wish to continue the conversation here or somewhere more private?"

CHAPTER 2

The dressing room was quite small, but at least it had a door. Not that it closed fully. The jumble of petticoats, boots, and a rack of stage weaponry made sure of that. To make matters worse, the steam heat was on full blast. It wasn't that cold outside. I hoped we wouldn't be here long.

Greta made tight-lipped, perfunctory introductions as we were seated.

I inclined my head toward Flora in greeting. She had Frank's heavily lashed, hazel eyes, though no trace of the defiant Wynch jaw that Frank and Greta each possessed. I would soon learn, however, that the young lady possessed the Wynch stubborn streak I was more than familiar with.

Flora smoothed her skirts. "I know we've met before, Mrs. Wynch," she began politely, "but my recollection of you from a decade ago is rather vague."

"Understandable. But do call me Pen. No need for formality among family relations."

"Barely family," the old lady chimed in tartly, "when you and Frank never trouble to write."

"I don't recall you communicating with us, either," I said. What did the old lady want, an oath of fealty? "However, let us address a more pressing topic. Frank sent me here to accompany Flora to New York City. It would be best for us to head there by the end of the week and get her settled."

Greta abruptly stood, stepped around the rack of weaponry—at first, I'd wondered if she sought a sword to brandish at me—and fully shoved the door closed. I don't know how she did it. Sheer force of will.

"I'm not going." Flora's expression grew mulish as she folded her arms.

I ignored the petulant display. "What exactly is it the prosecutor wants of you—to identify someone? Did you witness a crime?"

Flora waved a dismissive hand. "I have nothing of value to contribute to their case. I don't even understand why they are requiring it—I don't know anything. The play is far more important. I must remain here."

"From what I understand, your role in the production is a minor one. I'm sure they can make do."

Flora stiffened. "Minor? You don't know what you're talking about. No role in any play is minor."

I blinked at the ferocity of her tone. This one obviously viewed the stage as hallowed ground.

"Besides," Greta interjected, "after what happened to Viola, the director needs Flora more than ever."

"Who's Viola?" I asked.

"Viola Templeton, the original leading lady," Greta said.

"Ah, yes," I said, recalling John Davis's account. "She fell."

"Fell?" Greta's voice held a hard edge. "It was far more serious than that. The trap door beneath her gave way during rehearsal yesterday. A faulty latch."

"It was only Barrett's quick reflexes that saved her!" Flora added breathlessly. "He grabbed her before she tumbled ten feet to the basement below. She could have...died." She shuddered.

Greta patted her hand consolingly. "And now, Kay Finnerty—Viola's understudy—is assuming the lead."

"Kay Finnerty...that's the young lady who interrupted the rehearsal?" I asked. Between defective trap doors and squealing hinges, the theater needed some long-overdue repairs.

"Yes. I'm Kay's understudy now," Flora said, her voice suffused with self-importance.

"I heard about that, too," I said. "However, since trap doors don't give way on a regular basis, I'm sure the director can spare you."

Silence.

I dropped it for the moment. "What case are you to be a witness for?" I asked. "Frank omitted the details." Which still rankled, but at least we were making progress now.

Flora and Greta exchanged a long look.

"Well?" I prompted, keeping a firm check on my temper. Why must people dither so?

Greta patted the young lady's hand. "You may as well tell her."

Flora sniffed and groped for a handkerchief. "My husband. He's to be tried for counterfeiting bank notes."

I sat back in surprise. That explained Flora running off to her great-aunt and seeking a new career on the stage without consulting her husband. And yet....

"Doesn't spousal privilege protect you from being forced to testify against your husband?" I asked. A similar situation had nearly thwarted a case I'd worked on several years ago.

Greta Marlowe let out a heavy sigh. "Flora is not legally Humphrey's wife."

I got the gist of the sad story before a stagehand came knocking. The break was over.

Flora jumped up, hand on the knob.

I stepped in her way. "We haven't settled when we're leaving for New York. When is the last performance here in Southbrook?"

"Saturday evening," Flora said tersely.

"Well, then, we shall take the Sunday train," I said.

She glanced at Greta, who gave a reluctant nod.

"All right." Flora wouldn't meet my eye as she escaped from the stuffy room, but Greta had a deep enough scowl to suffice for them both as she brushed past me.

I went in search of Cassie amid the maze of curtained alcoves, plywood dividers, and storage racks overflowing with stage props. She was standing beside a dark-haired woman on the nearer side of thirty, who carried a voluminous burgundy gown over her arm.

This one seemed familiar. Where had I seen her before?

"Pen!" Cassie gestured to the lady. "You remember Rose? Rose Harper, from the academy glee club."

I couldn't quite place the name, but I extended a hand nonetheless. "Nice to see you after...so many years."

"Hard to believe we were once so young." Rose squinted up at me, an amused smile tugging at her lips. "Seems you've grown even taller since then. I would not have thought that possible."

Now I remembered her—one of the academy's charity-scholarship pupils. She'd developed an inexplicable resentment towards me in those days, which had taken the form of needling remarks about my height.

I shrugged. Such comments had ceased to be hurtful long ago. Someone had to be tall—it might as well be me. "As you can see, anything is possible."

Rose blinked.

Cassie, who got along with everyone and had been better friends with Rose back in the day, missed the under-currents of the interchange. "She's now the theater's seamstress and boards at Marlowe House. Isn't that a happy coincidence?"

"Yes indeed," I said absently. My thoughts were decidedly elsewhere—namely Flora and our unwelcome delay.

"That will afford us more time together during our stay." Cassie squeezed the seamstress's hand. "It will be wonderful to catch up."

Rose gave a quick nod, though her enthusiasm didn't seem to match my friend's. "I understand the two of you are in town to visit with Flora and Greta. How long are you here?"

"Until Sunday," I answered, ignoring Cassie's puzzled frown. Indeed, that had not been the original plan. But that was an explanation for later.

I knew I'd made the right decision in acquiescing. We had the time to spare. Besides, what was I to do, cart the young lady off in manacles? Still, uneasiness prickled at the base of my neck in a way that augured an impending headache.

"Ah. Then you'll be able to attend one of the performances," Rose said.

Cassie and I exchanged an amused glance. Based on what we'd seen thus far, we wouldn't be running out to buy tickets.

Behind us came the sound of voices as players returned to the stage.

Rose shifted the gown in her arms. "I must get back to work."

"We'll leave you to it, then," I said, already edging toward the door. "Goodbye, Rose. It's, um…nice to see you again."

Cassie and I stepped outside.

"Shall we risk walking back to the hotel?" I eyed the overcast sky and clutched my coat more tightly to my chest against the stiff breeze. "I don't believe the rain has finished with us."

Cassie hung onto her hat. "It isn't far—I think we can make it. Besides, it will give you a chance to explain why we're leaving Sunday instead of Friday."

"It was the best way to placate Flora." I explained the

young lady's reluctance to serve as a witness and her refusal to miss the performances. "We'll still have plenty of time to get her there," I finished.

"I suppose that's fair," Cassie said. "I imagine dealing with the authorities is a disagreeable prospect."

"Even more disagreeable in this instance—she's giving testimony against her husband."

"How awful! But wait—" She hesitated. "I thought a wife couldn't be forced to testify against her husband."

"That's true. However, it turns out Flora's so-called husband doesn't believe in the custom of marrying only one wife at a time. The first Mrs. Richards is still alive…and they are not divorced."

Cassie made a face in distaste. "Flora has been living with him all this time and…? Oh, dear. Poor girl."

We waited at the corner for a large stagecoach to rattle past. One of its wheels hit a water-filled rut and doused us with icy-cold water that left us gasping.

"Ugh." Cassie brushed at her coat. "I suppose walking wasn't the best idea."

I grimaced in agreement.

Once we were across the street without further incident, she asked, "What sort of trouble is he in?"

"Flora said he's an engraver by trade. At some point, he fell in with a counterfeiters' ring. He was caught making bank plates."

She clucked her tongue. "Sounds like a horrible man. Did Flora know what he was up to?"

"She claims ignorance, which I have difficulty believing."

Cassie unfurled her umbrella as the first drops began to fall. "She must know something pertinent. Otherwise, the prosecutor's interest in her makes no sense."

"Exactly. Based on my experience, wives—bigamous or not—generally know what their husbands are doing. Whether or not they turn a blind eye to it is another matter."

"Speaking of experience, did you tell Greta and Flora that you're a Pinkerton?"

"Not with those flimsy dressing room walls, and people coming and going backstage. I don't know if they would have believed me anyway." Greta continued to regard me with overt skepticism, as if she still expected me to ask for money.

"Flora has trying times ahead," Cassie observed.

"From the authorities seeking to coerce her testimony, yes, and perhaps—" I hesitated.

"Perhaps what?"

"There may be others who won't want her talking to the district attorney."

"You mean, someone might try to harm her?" Cassie stopped dead in her tracks. "Oh, Pen—we aren't bodyguards."

"I know, I know," I said soothingly. "There hasn't been any trouble so far. Greta assured me that only Frank and the prosecutor know Flora's whereabouts."

"What about her husband?" she asked. "He would know where to find her, too. What's his name again?"

"Humphrey Richards. Yes, it's likely he knows where she is, but he's in prison and not able to communicate with any confederates." I didn't volunteer the fact that it isn't impossible for inmates to send messages outside the confines of prison walls.

Cassie gathered her cloak tightly around her in a protective gesture, which caused the umbrella to tip—nearly spearing an outraged pedestrian before I could grab it.

I could see the signs of rising panic and hurried to stave it off. "We'll be fine, dear, don't worry."

"The delay is risky," she protested. "You know, as well as I, that time is our enemy here. And what if Flora does perform before the public? Her name will be in the papers then."

"She hardly seems ready to enrapture audiences," I said wryly.

"This isn't funny." She choked down a sob.

Oh, dear. There was only one remedy for my friend's alarm —a tactic I'd used on other occasions.

"Well then, there's no reason for you to remain here," I said evenly. "Why don't you head back to Chicago tomorrow? I'll join you at home as soon as I've finished."

Cassie drew herself up to her full height—which meant the tip of her nose reached my chin—her dark eyes snapping in defiance. "Don't be ridiculous. I'm staying."

I suppressed a smile. My friend may complain about the risks involved when she helps me with a case, but she's never backed down from one yet. "Thank you, dear."

The grand dining room at Marlowe House was more than large enough to accommodate all the guests who cared to dine at the same hour. A long table bisected the space, with smaller table groupings scattered at the periphery. The décor was tastefully done—at least in my mind, as I am not fond of the Victorian style of gaudy excess. The flocked wallcovering was a muted olive and cream with flecks of rose, the latter color repeated in the draperies, tablecloths, and an enormous Turkish rug. The entirety conveyed understated affluence.

Many of the actors I'd seen at the theater were seated at the large center table, with Greta presiding over them as queen of her domain. She was dressed in a red brocaded silk tonight, charmingly trimmed with gold fringe at the bodice and sleeves. Her eyes sparkled as brightly as the diamonds on her fingers, which flashed with each fluid gesture. One could take the lady from the stage, but not the stage from the lady.

Cassie and I chose a quiet table to ourselves, next to a deep bay window that afforded us a view of the street below. As it was already dark, the corner streetlights had come on, giving the bustling outdoor scene a cozy glow.

"I didn't expect a busy thoroughfare at this hour." Cassie unfolded the pristine-white linen napkin beside her plate.

"The hotel undoubtedly does a good business, being so strategically placed. I wonder how Greta manages the running of both the lodging and the theater."

"She co-owns the theater with someone else," a female voice chimed in. Rose stood beside our table. "Do you mind if I join you?"

Before I could formulate an excuse, Cassie held out a menu and gestured to a chair. "Oh yes, do join us."

Rose waved off the menu. "Thank you, but I know the offerings by heart. I recommend the bourguignon."

After we placed our orders, I returned to the previous topic. "You say Greta shares ownership of the theater?"

"That's right. Al Chaffee had a different partner years ago, back when it was called The Starlight. The way I heard the story, the partner ran off with all their money. I don't know the details—it was before my time. Greta put money into it, became the majority owner, and renamed the theater in her husband's memory. But it's Al who runs everything."

"That's just as well," Cassie said. "I imagine hotel operations here keep her busy enough."

Rose shrugged. "I don't think Greta's much involved in running the hotel, either. She has staff for that."

Must be nice to simply own things and have everyone else do all the work for you, I reflected.

We were quiet for a while, sipping from our water goblets and picking at the dinner rolls—a bit dry, but palatable. Much like our present conversation.

However, if there's anything people are inclined to talk about, it's themselves. "How do you like working in the theater, Rose?"

She brushed crumbs from her fingers—this one liked to take her time—before answering. "It suits me, especially as Mr. Chaffee lets me run things my own way. I'm in charge of the entire costuming end of the operation, and I've recently taken on responsibility for the stage props as well. Acting troupes such as the Pierson Players have costumes and props of their own that they place in my keeping, but they also borrow from the theater inventory." She gave a deep, dramatic sigh. "You have no idea what a challenge it is just to ensure no one leaves with things that don't belong to them."

"Do you have staff to help you?" Cassie asked.

"We have carpenters for the sets, and Mr. Chaffee's daughter Sally helps with sewing." She craned her neck to survey the room. "The Chaffees must be dining in their rooms tonight."

"They live here?" I asked.

"Yes—since last year. It's more convenient to the theater than where they were before."

Cassie reached for her salad fork. "It sounds as if Marlowe House is more of a boarding establishment than a hotel."

"Rather a mixture of the two. Rent isn't cheap here, but fortunately my rate is discounted because I work at the theater." Rose inclined her head toward Greta, now tipping a crystal goblet to her lips. "She does quite well for herself."

As our food was brought to us, Rose said, "I was wondering—would you two care to join me in an excursion tomorrow?"

"Where to?" Cassie asked.

"The Arboretum—we're borrowing potted plants for the stage set. I could use some help in making selections. A couple of men will collect the plants later, so there's really no effort on our part, and it's pleasant to stroll through the greenery on a late-winter day."

Cassie, the avid gardener in our household, perked up. "I would love to."

"I would have to stop at the telegraph office first." I wanted to update Frank on when Flora and I would arrive in

New York City. I gazed out the window again to the street below us.

"That's no problem," Rose said. "There's one right on—is something wrong?"

I hesitated. "Could be nothing. A man across the street has been lingering in the same spot for a while."

Cassie leaned cautiously toward the window, taking care to stay out of sight. "Ah—tan raincoat and tweed cap?"

"That's the one."

"Let me see," Rose said, impatiently standing up to lean across the table.

"Wait—he might see you," I said, but it was too late.

"He's gone," Rose said.

CHAPTER 3

$\mathcal{T}$he bourguignon was indeed excellent, and I observed others partaking of the same. As the guests got up from their seats after the meal, it was obvious that things were done a bit differently at Marlowe House. There was no after-dinner separation of the ladies to the parlor and the gentlemen to their port and cigars. Instead, the entire group congregated in the well-appointed music salon, taking turns at the piano for ballads and popular songs in which most of the company—myself included—joined in.

"Definitely an improvement upon stilted conversations over tepid tea and dry biscuits," Cassie murmured in my ear. "Instead of talking of concerts, we're practically in the midst of one."

I chuckled. "Should any actors apply for lodging back home, perhaps we should consider them favorably." Cassie and I ran a humble boarding house in a quiet neighborhood in Chicago—a section of the city that was home to grocers, plumbers, clerks, and the like. No sign of a theater anywhere. But it provided us with the means to meet our expenses in between my detective cases, for which I was grateful.

I stood. "They've finished laying out the after-dinner sweets and coffee. Do you want anything?"

"Coffee, please," Cassie said. "It smells heavenly, even from here."

I had more than coffee in mind, however, in visiting the buffet. I wanted to see if our watcher had returned, and the table was situated beside the windows overlooking the same street.

The burgundy silk curtains had been drawn, so I side-stepped a caddy of petit-fours and discreetly applied my spoon to the side gap. My pulse quickened. There he was.

"What, ho, my dear lady!" a boisterous male voice called. "Waiting upon the arrival of an admirer, perhaps?"

I wasn't as discreet as I had supposed, apparently. I kept my expression neutral as I faced the acting company's leading man, Barrett Ward, a lean-built fellow nearly a head shorter than I.

"Nothing of the kind." I set the spoon upon the saucer. "I merely wanted to see if the moon was out tonight."

He was nearly as handsome up close, where the whiteness of an impeccably tied cravat—monogrammed with a *W*, as were his cuffs, I noticed—set off to advantage his dark-brown, wavy hair. Proximity, however, also allowed one to see the jowls beginning to form along that chiseled jaw and the reddened nose of the habitual drinker.

He ducked his head in a playful gesture. "My apologies for teasing you. It is a custom of mine—puts new actresses at their ease, you see. You may know me—Barrett Ward, at your service, Miss—?"

"Mrs. Wynch," I said. "And yes, I already know who you are, Mr. Ward. I had the opportunity to observe you in rehearsal today."

"Did you, now?" He tilted his chin upward in pride. "Then you know I have the lead role." He put a hand to his chest in mock-humility. "I play the part of Maxwell Jones, the long-suffering husband at the hands of a mischievous wife. How do you like our little comedy?"

"Um, well," I hedged, "I'm in no position to critique it, as it is unfamiliar to me."

Ward's shoulders sank a bit before he recovered his good spirits. "Nat Pierson has just finished writing *She Did Him Wrong*, so no one's familiar with it yet. But once you have rehearsed with us this week, all will become clear." He clasped my hand and gave a little bow over it. "I'm so glad Nat has hired a woman of your, um...height. I told him that a lady more—Amazonian, if you will—would be perfect for the role of Prudence. Though our Mary will not be pleased, as he had promised her the part—"

"Mr. Ward," I said sharply, pulling my hand away, "you misunderstand me. I am not part of the company." *Amazonian*, indeed. The cheek of the man.

"Oh—I beg your pardon." He blinked. "Then why were you at rehears—ah, that's right. You are a relative of Greta Marlowe's?"

"Indeed."

The fellow who had escorted us to the theater earlier—Mr. Davis—approached. With a polite bow in my direction and a murmur of apology, he said to Ward, "They're gathering players for *Euchre*."

Ward's eyes brightened. "Excellent! I'll win back last night's losses and then some. Chaffee's here already?"

Now was the time to make good my escape. "If you'll excuse me."

I brought our coffees over to Cassie. "Here you are, dear. Cream, no sugar."

"Excellent." She watched me over the rim of her cup as she took her first sip, eyes sparkling with amusement.

"What's so funny?" I asked.

"I noticed the leading man was paying you some attention,

at least until Mr. Davis showed up. Did you know he's Barrett Ward's valet?"

"Davis?" I settled myself into the seat beside her. "Didn't he say he's one of the actors?"

"He serves in both capacities."

"I didn't notice anyone else in the company with a personal attendant."

"Ward is the only one—rather insisted on it. I hear it has created resentment among some."

"Ward does think rather highly of himself," I murmured. "But the fellow's remarkably short on common sense—he thought I was a member of the company. Can you believe it? Tried to ingratiate himself."

"Perhaps his fondness for the ladies overrides his good sense." Cassie shifted for a better view of the room. "There he is with that woman who was injured—Viola Templeton. She's quite lovely, isn't she?"

I covertly observed the lady in question as she reclined on the divan with her wrapped foot propped upon a cushion. Several of the players had gathered their chairs around to keep her company, and no wonder. She was indeed a beauty, with a creamy complexion only nature can provide. Her emerald silk dinner dress would have cost our month's household budget, but there was no denying that the shade complemented her titian hair and green eyes.

Ward stopped by the group only briefly, however, no doubt moving on to his card game.

Cassie clucked her tongue. "Poor Miss Templeton. To lose her role over a freak accident."

"She doesn't seem to be suffering at the moment. I'd say she's enjoying the attention."

"Surely, we can grant her a bit of diversion," Cassie admonished. "It's unquestionably tedious to spend one's recovery in solitude."

My friend's generous heart served as the perfect foil to my

cynicism, the better angel over my shoulder, so to speak. But expecting the worst of human nature had been my bread and butter these past few years. Sad to say, it had served me well.

I took a last sip of my coffee and stood. "I'm heading upstairs. I have some things to take care of."

"Really? We've already unpacked."

I bent close and dropped my voice. "Our man across the street has returned, wearing a different coat and hat now."

Her breath hitched. "You're sure? Do you think he's after Flora?"

"That remains to be seen. If so, it's likely to occur after everyone has retired. I have some preparations to make in the meantime."

"Do you need any help?" She started to rise, but I put a hand on her shoulder.

"Stay and enjoy the company, dear." There was nothing she could do for me, and lively entertainment didn't come our way that often.

Cassie's dark eyes clouded in worry. "Fetch me if you need anything. And do be careful."

Caution was top of mind as I went up to our room, locked the door behind me, and checked my hiding place for derringer, lockpicks, and logbook. All were undisturbed—it was a habit of mine to lay nearly invisible strands of my own blonde hair atop the items before I left the space unattended. In a room of this size, there weren't many hiding spaces, should someone care to make a search. At least I would know if the items had been discovered.

I changed out of my mauve satin dinner frock into a dark dress of quiet worsted that I liked to wear for reconnoitering. After recording the day's events in my log—including a dissatisfying, vague description of the man watching the building—I tucked my gun and my two most useful lockpicks into the deep pockets I had sewn into my skirt, restored everything else to their place of concealment, and went exploring.

Marlowe House was comprised of five levels and two wings, and likely a below-ground cellar, which I had yet to determine. The street level contained a library and front parlor, along with most of the utilitarian spaces necessary for running a boarding establishment—a reception area with check-in desk, clerk's office, and cloak room, along with a kitchen, housekeeper's suite, and servants' quarters. Judging by the size of Greta's staff, however, not all lived in. Next was the first floor, which offered additional communal rooms—a dining room with an adjoining pantry and a spacious music salon. The second and third floors were comprised of guest bedrooms, washrooms, and linen closets. Cassie and I had a room in the older wing of the third floor, where the bedrooms shared a hall bath at each end. I hadn't seen the newer wing yet, but Rose had described those guest rooms as well appointed, with a connecting bath for each.

Greta and Flora resided in a suite of rooms that took up the entire fourth floor. Which meant that, if Flora was a target —a big *if* at this point—I wouldn't have to worry about an intruder climbing in directly through a window to get to her. However, I wanted to determine how many doors led to Greta's suite of rooms and how they were secured. After that, I'd examine the street access to the hotel.

I took the main staircase to the fourth floor. The sounds of piano music and lively voices drifted up. I still had time.

Along one side was a railing-enclosed gallery that over-looked the main staircase that started on the floor below. The doors leading to the suite itself were brass-knobbed, solid oak. Plainer, painted wooden doors stood at the ends of the corridors to my left and right. The service stairs for each of the wings, I guessed.

The double doors to the suite were locked. I crouched for a closer look at the mechanism. The lock was new. I wasn't sure whether I had a pick to fit it. A casual intruder likely would not.

But were we dealing with a casual intruder? I shook off the prickle of unease that settled at the base of my neck and checked the doors at each end of the corridor. Those had no locks and, as I'd supposed, led to servant staircases. I stepped inside the right-side stairwell, its wooden steps narrow and worn. The stairs continued up beyond this floor, likely to access the roof. I ignored that for now and started downstairs, my heels clattering against the creaking wood. An intruder would have to climb the steps in his stockinged feet, and even then, I doubted he'd be completely noiseless.

I'd reached the third floor when a female voice called out. "Hello? Can someone help me?"

I pushed open the door to see the actress I now knew to be Kay Finnerty hunched in a nearby doorway to what must be her room, her face white.

"Miss Finnerty, what's wrong?"

"I've tried to ring for the maid. No one has come," she said thickly. "Can you—" She ran inside, where I heard sounds of retching.

"I'll get someone," I called to her and hurried across to the other wing to find Cassie, hoping she'd returned to our room by now.

I also hoped Miss Finnerty hadn't had the beef.

Cassie was indeed in our room, getting ready to retire. After a brief description of Miss Finnerty's predicament, she shrugged on a dressing sacque and hurried to help, which freed me to get back to the task at hand.

I continued down the staircase and reached the ground level without further incident. I cracked open the door. A short corridor led to the library.

The steps continued down to what had to be a cellar. I wished I'd brought a lantern. The gas light fixtures ended here, and the bottom of the stairwell was a pool of inky darkness. Chill air seeped beneath my skirts.

I took a breath. Onward.

I discovered that, thankfully, the cellar wasn't pitch black. The streetlights outside provided diffused light through a casement window set high into the back wall. Although the window was large enough for a man to fit through, it had rusted shut long ago.

I continued to explore the room, the musty, damp chill filling my nostrils. I clutched my shawl closer. The cellar was primarily used for the storage of canned goods, tools...even a discarded laundry mangle. A deep metal barrel stood in the corner, perhaps once used for fresh-water storage before the days of indoor plumbing. There was another door at the far end, mechanical sounds coming from within. The door opened into a narrow boiler room—more of a closet. I stuck my head inside for a quick check. Nothing untoward, except for the terrible clanks and groans coming from the equipment. No wonder they built a closet around it. Greta should really have someone attend to that.

There were no other ways of ingress save the coal chute hatch, which was locked from inside.

With one last survey of the noisy, dank, miserable space, I gratefully climbed back up the stairs. The gathering had broken up at this point.

I continued to the fourth floor. Time to speak with Greta and Flora.

A young maid opened the door at my knock.

"My name is Mrs. Wynch," I said. "I wish to see Mrs. Marlowe. Will you tell her I'm here, please?"

She blinked in confusion, then left the door ajar as she hurried to talk to her mistress. I took that as permission and stepped inside.

Greta emerged through an inner door to my right, struggling to tie the sash of her peach silk dressing gown. "Relation or not, Penelope, you cannot simply walk into my private quarters uninvited."

"I do apologize for the intrusion."

A door on the opposite side had opened slightly.

"It's urgent," I went on. "And confidential." I nodded toward the maid.

Greta dismissed the girl.

"You can come out, Flora," I called. "This concerns you as well."

Once the three of us were seated around the bright fire in the hearth—I was still thawing out from my time in the cellar and particularly grateful for its warmth—I explained the presence of the man on the street corner.

Flora paled.

Greta patted her hand. "Now, now, dear, it is probably nothing. Likely a lay-about. A town of this size has many such men."

I crossed to the window and shifted the curtain slightly. "I don't see him now, but it's best to be cautious. Do you typically lock the outer doors to your suite at night?"

Greta stiffened. "Yes."

What about your inner bedroom doors?"

Greta frowned. "No—why should we?"

"Well, do so tonight, just as a precaution. Who is responsible for securing the street level doors and windows each evening?"

"Our desk clerk, Barnaby," Greta said. "He locks up before he heads home." She checked the mantel clock. "That was a couple of hours ago. It has already been done."

"I would like to be sure."

Greta shrugged. "Suit yourself."

Flora shifted impatiently. "This is all so…melodramatic. No one is after me."

"I would not be so sanguine. Your husband was an active participant in a counterfeiting scheme with unscrupulous men."

Flora flushed. "Humphrey may have been mixed up with such men, but I was not. I left him as soon as I figured out what he was up to. I doubt his confederates even know I exist. That is why I want no part of being a witness."

Figured out what he was up to. Flora's first slip-up today. "So you knew?" I asked. "How did you discover his scheme?"

Greta stood, her expression grim. The audience was over.

Barnaby had done his job well—no easy feat, considering the sheer number of first floor windows. All was secure, including the front doors and kitchen door in the back. Checking the latter had earned me a puzzled look from the scullery maid who was still drying pans.

The hotel was quieting down for the night. I lingered over a book in the library until I was sure the staff had either gone home or retired to their rooms.

As I considered the best place to keep watch, I finally settled upon the corridor just outside Greta's suite of rooms. It seemed prudent to stay close to the two women rather than guess exactly which street-level window or door our intruder might break into.

I eyed the street from the fourth-floor windows once more. A thick fog had rolled in. The streetlamps could barely penetrate it.

I concealed myself in an alcove that held a spacious linen closet. As I waited in the dark, my mind turned over the possible goals of our unknown loiterer. I understood the skepticism of Greta and Flora—if the mere assassination of Flora was the object, why not stage a street accident or accomplish the deed with a single rifle shot?

I was certain of one thing, however—Flora knew more about her husband's operation than she was letting on. Clients had lied to me countless times over the years, of course, but it was nonetheless exasperating.

Frank would have to give me the answers I needed. I'd

send him a message in the morning to that effect, as well as to apprise him of recent developments. It would be gratifying to be able to say I'd caught an intruder, though I didn't want to get ahead of myself.

I shifted upon the stool I'd appropriated from the closet and checked my pistol once more. It was going to be a long night.

~

I'd lost track of how much time had elapsed before a sound caught my attention. I strained to listen over the pulse pounding in my ears.

Yes—soft creaks, but where they were coming from made no sense. They seemed to be…above?

The roof.

Mercy, I hadn't considered the roof at all. But with flat-roofed downtown buildings this close together and second-story men for hire, it was entirely possible.

Only one stairwell led all the way up to the roof—the one in the old wing at the other end of the corridor. Weapon in hand I hurried towards it, my footfalls silent in the slippers I'd opted for. They weren't suitable for chasing miscreants, but that had never been my plan.

I had just reached the door when it slowly swung toward me. I flattened myself in its shadow and waited.

He was so intent on his mission that he passed my position without checking over his shoulder. Even in the gloom I could see he was young, perhaps his early twenties, shorter than me and slightly built, but obviously agile. His hair was blond, straight, and worn past his collar. A scarf obscured the lower part of his face. It was too dark to see his eyes.

I watched from my place of concealment as he crouched at the doors to the suite and applied a lockpick. As I was depending upon the element of surprise and couldn't approach without being seen, I'd have to wait until he'd gone through the outer doors before trapping him inside. I hoped Greta and Flora had heeded my warning and secured their bedrooms.

Greta's lock was giving him trouble. On two occasions, he rummaged in his pocket for another pick. After several minutes, I heard a click and a soft sigh of satisfaction before he let himself in and shut the doors behind him.

Time to move.

I crept noiselessly across the thick carpet runner and put my ear to the door to listen. No help.

I slipped in and closed the door softly behind me, groping to slide the inner bolt with the hand not holding the gun.

Where was he?

Suddenly, a form loomed, followed by a flash of metal wielded by a pale hand. I put up a protective arm and gasped as the knife slashed the sleeve—my second-best shirtwaist, to boot—and sliced into my flesh.

He stepped back and raised the knife again. I fired.

In the gloom I couldn't tell exactly where I'd struck him— I'd been aiming for his chest, but he'd moved incredibly fast. His shocked grunt assured me I'd hit him somewhere. He was still on his feet, however. He shoved me to the floor and pushed through the doors.

I was vaguely aware of commotion behind me and lights coming on, but I paid little heed as I scrambled up and ran after him.

He'd wisely chosen to flee the way he'd come—the roof— no doubt realizing the risk of encountering a gauntlet of servants and guests while descending four flights of stairs.

I raised my skirts high to take the steps two at a time, but by the time I reached the top, I knew the chase was done. The last glimpse I had was of his silhouette as he scrabbled across the flat roofs.

CHAPTER 4

"*Y*ou've made a fine mess of things, Penelope," Greta said tartly. "Why Frank decided to send his wife instead of coming himself, I will never understand. Now the fellow has gotten away." She swept a dramatic hand to encompass the Persian carpet in the foyer. "And there's blood on my new rug!"

We were gathered in the parlor of Greta's apartment, joined by Cassie, currently tending to my wounded arm. My years in this business had given her plenty of experience in such matters, poor girl.

I made the necessary introductions while two maids busied themselves with cleaning up the carpet.

I could only hope that not all the blood was mine. If I'd wounded the fellow sufficiently, he'd be unable to try again.

"What's important now," I said, "is that we determine his identity, his purpose, and whether he was acting alone. Why hasn't Flora joined us? I have questions for her."

"I gave her a sleeping tonic to settle her down, poor child. Your questions can wait. She needs her rest. With Kay ill—"

"You know about that?" I asked sharply. I winced as Cassie dabbed at a tender spot.

Greta shrugged. "Of course. My staff keeps me well informed. Naturally, it's an unfortunate occurrence, but Flora must assume the lead role now. She has a busy week ahead."

Flora must assume the lead role... How suspiciously convenient. I kept my thoughts to myself...one problem at a time. "You were tending to Miss Finnerty earlier," I said to Cassie. "How is she?"

Cassie made a face. "Poorly, when I left her at midnight. If her condition hasn't improved by morning, a doctor should be called." She tied off the bandage at my elbow and gently pulled my stained, tattered sleeve over it. "A doctor should check your wound as well. You might need stitches. I fear it will open and start to bleed again."

I shrugged. "Better my arm than my heart."

"A doctor?" Greta protested. "We cannot have word circulating about this. It would alarm the guests."

Cassie stuck out a stubborn chin. "I don't care who is alarmed. I insist that a doctor see Pen in the morning."

I hid a smile. No one gets between Cassie and the person she's trying to protect. "I'll find a way to account for the injury without causing talk," I said to Greta.

The woman muttered something under her breath.

"Now then," I continued, "since Flora is unavailable, you will have to do. Tell me what you know about her situation. What would have precipitated the attack? Flora obviously hasn't told us the whole story."

Greta glanced over at the maids in the foyer and called, "Leave that for now. Bring tea for us. Strong and hot."

Perhaps the woman was softening towards me at last. All it took was a gash in the arm.

Once they had gone, she sat back with a sigh. "I don't quite know where to begin."

"I can tell you myself," came a weary voice behind us. Flora, blonde hair fraying from its braid and night robe slop-

pily gathered around her thin frame, stood in the doorway
She appeared childlike, fragile.

She waved off her great-aunt's objection and perched
upon the ottoman. "The sleeping draught did nothing for me.
I'm too worried, I suppose." Her glance flicked over to Cassie,
who was tidying up the bandaging supplies. "I saw you this
evening, but we haven't been introduced."

"The lapse is mine," I said. "This is a dear friend from
Chicago, Cassie Leigh. Cassie, I'd like you to meet Mrs. Flora
Richards, Frank's sister." My words, the formula for ballroom
dances and dinner parties, sounded absurd under present
circumstances. And of course, introducing Flora by her
married name seemed equally absurd.

Greta shifted uneasily. "Now that your arm has been
tended to, Penelope, I think it best if we talk privately. This is
a family matter."

"Cassie is the soul of discretion," I said.

"Besides," Cassie chimed in, "I often help Pen with her
cases."

Oh dear. So much for discretion.

"Cases?" Flora said distractedly. "What do you mean?"

It was bound to come out. Whether it helped my interaction with these two or not, there was no help for it now.

"I'm a detective, like Frank," I answered. "He and I work
for the Pinkerton Agency." Without thinking, I rubbed my
bandaged arm, then winced.

Flora bit her lip. "The police sent a Pinkerton after me?"

"No, no—Frank asked me to escort you as a personal
favor, since I happened to be close by. He was worried about
your safety. Now we can see his concern was well founded."

Her delicate chin quavered.

I pressed my advantage. "I need the entire story this time.
It's the only way I can determine how best to protect you. So,
let us start at the beginning. When did you arrive here?"

"A few weeks ago."

"Was Greta expecting you?"

Greta answered for her. "I've wanted Flora to leave her husband for a while."

I sat back in surprise. "Really? Because of his criminal activities?"

"I had no knowledge of anything of the kind," the old lady snapped. "Though I'm hardly surprised he's involved in shady dealings. He's a heavy-handed brute. I'm sorry to speak so bluntly, dear," she added, flicking a rueful glance at her great-niece, "but you were miserable for years."

"Was it his arrest that finally decided matters for you?" I asked Flora.

"I left before then. Aunt Greta had told me the Pierson Players were coming to town, and she was sure she could get me a place in the company."

"Nat Pierson is a good friend of mine," Greta interjected.

I barely paid attention to that. "When did you find out your so-called husband had been arrested?"

"Do not call him that," Greta snapped. "Gossip will start circulating among the staff. Flora does not deserve the scandal that would be thrust upon her."

I lifted a shoulder. "As you wish." Perhaps the preference was understandable—properly married to a criminal and a brute, rather than having lived in sin with one. "I shall rephrase. When did you find out about *your husband's* arrest?"

"Last week," Flora said. "The assistant district attorney—someone named Sanderson—sent an official to interview me and sign a document. That was the first I knew of it."

"And it was the first we learned of the existence of another Mrs. Richards," Greta added with a scowl.

A thought occurred to me. "How did the prosecutor's office know not only where to find you, but of the first wife's existence? Did your husband tell them?"

Flora gave a snort. "Humphrey would never give any policeman the time of day, much less anything else."

40

"They must have been checking into his background," Cassie suggested.

"I suppose," I said. "Let us continue. Someone interviewed you—what did you tell him?"

"Only the truth," Flora said. "I knew nothing of Humphrey's business activities. His engraving shop was in town. Customers didn't visit our home or send correspondence there. And I was not inclined to meddle. Humphrey could not abide me sticking my nose where it did not belong."

One of the maids returned with the tea, and I suspended my questions until the girl had deposited the tray and left us alone. Greta poured and passed around the cups.

I took mine gratefully. The tea was just the bracing jolt I needed. "Here's what I really want to know, Flora. What have you held back from the authorities?"

"What makes you think I have?" she answered tartly.

"Besides an intruder breaking in with a knife," I said, "there's the fact that the district attorney wants to interview you in person, at his office. That's likely a prelude to testifying in court. He must be convinced you know something more."

She fussed with the sash on her dressing gown, not looking at me.

I drank my tea, letting the silence stretch. The ticking mantel clock and the *ting* of a spoon were the only sounds to fill the void.

"You're right, of course," she said finally. "I haven't been entirely, *um*, forthcoming."

Cassie reached for my cup and refilled it, knowing—as she often did—when we were going to have a long night ahead of us.

"I didn't exactly *lie* in my statement." Flora's voice took on a plaintive whine. "Humphrey did *most* of his work in his shop in town. But...he *did* have a workshop set up behind the house so he could continue work when he had a deadline. And *sometimes* people visited him there...*occasionally*, I could see who it

41

was, and...*perhaps*, I'd overhear a few things." She stopped as if on cue, taking a dainty sip from her cup and diffidently nibbling a ginger crisp.

"Go on," I prompted. Flora's dramatic pauses might play on the stage, but it was wearing on my patience. Also, my arm was beginning to throb. If we were at home, Cassie would have dosed me with a fingerful of brandy in a mug of hot milk, then ordered me to bed.

I settled for a long swallow of cooling tea.

Flora resumed her narrative with an aggrieved sigh. "A man by the name of Jimmy visited every night for a solid week. I could tell he made Humphrey nervous. My husband doesn't have the best of tempers to begin with, but he was especially on edge then."

"Can you describe the man?"

"Shortish, with wide shoulders and a thick neck. He was bald. I didn't see his face all that well, but his nose was quite prominent in profile."

Not our prowler tonight, that's for sure. "Jimmy—what? Any idea of his last name?"

She shrugged. "I never heard a surname, just a nickname. Humphrey was talking to someone—I don't know who—complaining that 'Jimmy the bagger' had better stop coming around if they wanted him to finish on time."

Jimmy the Bagger? I bit my lip. I knew the name. The description fit, too.

Greta leaned toward me. "You know who she's talking about?"

"It sounds like a fellow named James Bagnard, known colloquially as Jimmy the Bagger." I grimaced. Nasty fellow, and quick with his fists. Frank and I had had the misfortune of encountering him eight years before. "When he isn't in prison, he works as a strong man for counterfeiters and bank sneaks. Last I knew of him, though, he'd been sent up to Sing-Sing. I have no idea who he's working for these days."

"It wouldn't be difficult for the authorities to find out," Cassie pitched in helpfully.

"You should not have withheld something so crucial," I said. "Did Jimmy realize you'd seen him?"

"Of course not," Flora snapped, but even Greta was looking askance by this point.

Cassie frowned at Flora and pointed out what we were all thinking. "If no one was aware that you saw this Jimmy the Bagger, how do you explain the break-in tonight?"

Flora folded her arms in defiance. "It might be a simple coincidence—or perhaps a thief, in search of valuables."

"Our intruder was hardly after the good silver," I said dryly, "which is in the dining room three floors down. Someone hired the fellow to attack you, either Jimmy himself or whoever he's working for."

Flora subsided into a moping silence.

Greta rested a be-ringed hand on Flora's arm. "We must turn our energies to protection now."

"The best way to accomplish that," Cassie said, "is for Flora to leave by the earliest train tomorrow, with Pen and me accompanying her. Once she has told the district attorney all she knows, there will be nothing the criminals can do about it."

I nodded my agreement. "I'm sure the Pinkerton Agency has a safe house in the area that we can use until you meet with the prosecutor."

"And miss my only chance to play the lead in *She Did Him Wrong*?" Flora's eyes took on a hard glint. "Absolutely not." She pouted at her great aunt. "There must be another way. It's only a few more days."

"I have an idea," Greta said.

"And what is that?" I was sure I wasn't going to like it.

"The fellows from our carriage house can take turns keeping watch inside the hotel at night. I have a couple of sturdy men who will suit."

"What about the daytime hours?" Cassie asked.

"I'll be perfectly safe then," Flora said. "Too many people are underfoot at rehearsals for that to be an issue."

Greta nodded her agreement.

"If I go along with this notion," I said, "Flora must agree to take the first train to New York City on Sunday."

"Yes, of course," Flora said placidly.

CHAPTER 5

WEDNESDAY, MARCH 7

J slept until mid-morning and would have missed the doctor's visit to Marlowe House if not for Cassie, who woke me, helped me dress, then practically dragged me down to the library where he waited.

As we were descending the main staircase, I asked, "Has everyone left for rehearsals already?"

Cassie nodded. "About half an hour ago."

The doctor was warming his hands by the fire and stood politely as we entered the library.

"Here's the friend I was telling you about, Doctor," Cassie said, steering me over to a reading table where a medical bag had been deposited. "Mrs. Wynch."

He took my hand with a slight bow. "Dr. Byrd, ma'am. Let's see how we're doing here." He pushed back my sleeve and began unwrapping the bandage. "Miss Leigh was rather vague about how you came to injure yourself. Would you care to explain?"

I glanced over at Cassie, who gave a slight shrug. I was on my own.

"It happened last night," I began. "I was getting out of a hired conveyance. I stumbled in the dark and caught my arm on a raw metal edge of the door mechanism. I didn't realize the full extent of the injury until I got inside. Miss Leigh dressed it for me."

The doctor gave an absent-minded nod. "She did a fine job, under the circumstances."

Once my arm was completely unwrapped, I could see how deep the cut was. At least it was only seeping now.

The sight didn't seem to bother the doctor at all, who turned my arm gently this way and that in the light of the table lamp. "Make a fist."

I did so.

"Keep your hand clenched and flex your wrist for me."

I complied.

"No tendon damage," he said.

"That's good," I said.

"Is this the only place you were injured?" He pushed my sleeve up farther, beyond the elbow.

"Yes."

He frowned. "You seem exceedingly accident-prone, Mrs. Wynch." His finger lightly traced the cluster of fading scars at my upper arm—a souvenir of a previous misadventure. "How did you do *that*?"

"Lawn tennis," I retorted. "I don't see how it is your concern, Doctor."

The man rolled his eyes. "Lord save me from athletic females."

As he cleaned and dressed the wound, I asked, "How is Miss Finnerty faring?"

He reached for the bandage scissors. "She'll pull through, but her recovery will take a few more days."

"What brought it on?" Cassie asked. "It seemed awfully sudden."

"Likely something she ate. Although Mrs. Marlowe strenuously objects to the notion, she has instructed the cook to go through the larder in search of any tainted items."

"No one else got sick," I said, "so it must have been something unique to what Miss Finnerty consumed."

"Obviously," he said curtly. "But I've agreed to leave it to the kitchen staff to resolve. Accidents happen. For the good of the hotel's reputation, it's best that tales not circulate."

"Yes, of course."

"Well then, that should do it." He proceeded to pack up his bag. "Be careful with the arm, change the dressing if it gets soiled or bleeds through, and generally observe how it heals. If you have any issues—or further mishaps"—his lips curled slightly—"my office is right down the block, next to the boys' academy."

I stood. "Thank you."

He hesitated before taking his leave. "If I may make a suggestion, ma'am—take more care in the future when getting out of, *ahem*, dark carriages. And perhaps, generally speaking, a more sedentary pursuit would be in order. Knitting, for example."

It was then that I knew he hadn't believed my story for a minute. But I was grateful for his discretion.

I inclined my head. "I will keep that in mind."

We returned to our room after the doctor left. Cassie gathered her hat and gloves.

"Where are you going?" I asked.

"Out with Rose to the arboretum. Remember, we promised her yesterday. I assume you aren't well enough to come. I'll make your excuses."

"On the contrary, I'll be fine." Besides, I still owed Frank a telegram. I reached into the armoire for my navy walking suit. "I want to make a stop at the telegraph office on the way."

"You're sure you're up to it?" Cassie's brows pulled in a frown.

"Of course. Wait for me downstairs. I won't be more than a few minutes."

Maneuvering with my tender arm was awkward, however, and the simple act of dressing was a slow, frustrating process. Although I was anxious to hurry downstairs so as not to keep them waiting, I stopped to make sure my lockpicks and logbook—my derringer is always with me these days—were hidden from prying eyes. Though I fumbled a bit, I eventually managed to lock the door.

Cassie and Rose waited out on the sidewalk while I went in the telegraph office to send my message to Frank. I stood at the counter to compose the note, hesitating. How to succinctly convey the incidents of the past day and night without revealing confidential information?

Finally, I wrote:

F RELUCTANT TO COOPERATE. PREVIOUS COMMITMENT DELAYS OUR DEPARTURE SHOULD STILL ARRIVE IN TIME.
UNEXPECTED VISITOR LAST NIGHT NEED BACKGROUND INFORMATION ON F'S HUSBAND SEND SOONEST MARLOWE HOTEL PRIVATE MESSENGER IF POSSIBLE.

I read it over, still not satisfied. But it would have to do.

I passed it to the clerk, along with my payment. "Please send it right away."

With a long-suffering sigh, he dropped it in a tray and handed me a receipt.

The arboretum was a refreshing place to visit on this gloomy March day. The earthy pungence of soil and greenery, mingled with the scents of rose and orchid, lifted my flagging spirits.

Though Cassie was inclined to linger among the orchids, Rose prodded us towards the section containing the ornamental shrubbery.

"Here's what I'm considering for the garden scene." Rose pointed to a long, raised bench filled with boxwood.

Cassie grimaced. "It seems so...large."

"Difficult for stagehands to maneuver," I agreed.

"I know," Rose said, "but we need to convey a sense of greenery without having to move a lot of little things to set up the scene to follow, which is in the drawing room."

Cassie pointed to a trio of potted trees. "These are sufficiently dense when grouped together, and they're of varying heights to add more interest."

Rose bit her lip. "Mr. Chaffee warned me about having too many things for his men to move."

"It's not so many," Cassie pointed out. "And if you put them on small, wheeled caddies, they'll be a lot easier to move than one large one would be, which would require several men to shift."

"I do see your point." In a rare outpouring of warmth—the lady had been rather reserved since our arrival—she clasped Cassie's hand. "I'm so glad you could accompany me." She checked the watch pinned to her jacket. "Let me just make the arrangements with the proprietor. You're welcome to stay," she added, no doubt noticing as Cassie eyed the displays wistfully. "I have to get back to the theater. There are sure to be costume alterations, with Flora now assuming Kay's role."

As Flora was shorter and more petite than either Viola Templeton or Kay Finnerty, I had to agree. Rose would be taking in a number of seams.

We said our goodbyes and Rose left us.

I touched Cassie on the sleeve. "If you don't mind, I'm ready to return to the hotel now."

Her gaze flicked to my cradled arm. "Of course."

As we got our bearings at the street corner, we saw Rose ahead of us, walking in the direction of the trolley stop.

I was assessing an upcoming gap in the traffic to cross the street when Cassie said suddenly, "Who's that man talking to Rose?" She pointed.

I sucked in a breath at the sight of a slightly built, lean man with longish blond hair. *Our intruder.* Today he was stooped slightly, favoring his right side. "That's the fellow who broke in last night."

"Talking to Rose?" Cassie asked incredulously. "But she seems to know him."

Indeed she did, and the fact that she was wiping her cheek on her sleeve indicated their conversation was a distressing one.

"Wait here." I hurried toward the street corner.

A trolley car had pulled up to the stop. Rose turned away from the man to climb aboard. He took a few hesitant steps toward her. My haste, however, had caught his attention. Our eyes locked briefly, just before a passing cart blocked my view. I picked up my pace, weaving between pedestrians to reach them, but by the time my sight line had cleared, the man was gone, and so was Rose.

"What now?" Cassie asked, finally catching up to me.

"We'll continue on to the theater to talk to her." I tried to ignore the throbbing in my arm.

"Are you sure you're up to it?"

I shrugged. "The sooner we talk to her, the sooner we return."

But Rose wasn't at the theater, even though she should have arrived ahead of us.

"She may have thought of another errand and changed her plans," Cassie suggested.

"Perhaps. I can't help but wonder, though, if her change of plans is the result of her encounter with that man."

We lingered backstage another half hour before giving up.

"I want to stop at the telegraph office on our way back to the hotel," I said, "on the off chance that Frank sent an answer already."

But we were just as unlucky there.

"Nothing yet, ma'am," the clerk said. "We'll be sure to deliver any reply to Marlowe House as soon as we get it."

"We're not making much progress today," I muttered, as we walked along the block toward the hotel.

"We'll have plenty of time to question Rose at dinner tonight," Cassie said encouragingly. "We must be patient."

As patience was not a virtue I could lay claim to, I chafed at the delay of two crucial items I needed: Frank's telegram and information from Rose.

I suppressed a sigh. In this line of work, one got a great deal of practice in waiting.

Cassie put the room key in the lock. "Why don't you lie down for a while?"

"Good idea."

She flung the door wide.

I stepped through, then stopped short. "Someone has been in here, and it wasn't to clean."

She brushed past me. "How do you—? Ah yes, I see." She nodded toward the bureau, where folded edges of fabric peeked out from a few drawers.

We checked our belongings.

"Are you missing anything?" I asked, pulling out the lowest bureau drawer to examine the recess beneath. My logbook and pouch of lockpicks appeared undisturbed, thankfully. All the hairs in place.

"Everything's here," Cassie said, "but my journal and personal correspondence have been rifled through. Don't worry," she added quickly, "I never write down anything about your cases."

"I'm grateful for that," I said. "I'm not missing anything, either."

"Why us?" Cassie asked. "What were they after?"

"Good questions." I restored the bottom drawer. I'd have to consider an alternate place. This one wasn't secure any longer.

I examined the door lock. "No fresh scores or scratches that I can see."

"Are you sure you locked it on your way out?" she asked.

I made a face. "I did have difficulty with it."

She flashed me a sympathetic glance. "I can imagine."

"Whatever way they got in, we've only been gone a couple of hours."

"Far easier for an insider to slip in," she agreed.

"It shouldn't be difficult to determine who was around during that time. Most of the acting company is at the theater. I'll inquire among the staff downstairs."

Cassie and I were about to part ways at the library door when I noticed Viola Templeton within, ensconced upon the settee. A pair of crutches were propped within easy reach and an open book rested in her lap as she stared at the fire, obviously lost in thought.

I'd been wanting to speak with her, so I elected to take advantage of the opportunity. The staff inquiry could wait.

"Good afternoon, Miss Templeton," I said, as we entered. "I don't believe we've been introduced. I'm Mrs. Wynch." I nodded toward Cassie. "And this is my friend, Miss Leigh."

The lady extended a hand. Her grip was surprisingly firm for a woman, and I suppressed a wince as she yanked on my tender arm. "A pleasure to meet you." She frowned. "Are you feeling quite well, Mrs. Wynch? You're rather pale."

A sharp woman.

"I'm fine, thank you." My injury was not generally known. I wanted to keep it that way.

We settled into chairs across from her. "I was sorry to learn of your accident," I went on. "Are you feeling better?"

She shifted her bandaged ankle upon the pillow with a

grimace. "Improvement is slow in coming, unfortunately. I wish I could better manage the crutches. I've been relocated to the housekeeper's suite on this floor, so I don't have to manage the stairs. Except for the evenings," she added, "when someone helps me to the dining room and the music salon." Her eyes flashed defiantly. "I refuse to huddle in some servant's miserable little room without respite the entire week."

"I hope you are comfortable down here," Cassie said sympathetically.

"I am not," she said shortly. "The accommodations leave much to be desired, let me tell you. I'm right above the boiler room, which makes all sorts of clanking and knocking noises." She wearily rubbed her temples. "I was up all night."

"The Pierson Players seem plagued with bad luck lately," Cassie observed. "First your accident, and now Kay's illness."

Miss Templeton's face briefly creased in a scowl. "Yes, I'd heard about the poor girl. I'm unable to check on her, obviously, but the maid says she was able to keep down some broth this morning. That's something. She's still too weak to get out of bed."

"It doesn't look promising for her to perform tomorrow," I mused aloud.

Miss Templeton raised a delicate eyebrow. "I doubt Flora would relinquish her newfound role so easily, even if Kay were fully recovered. And Greta would no doubt use her friendship with Nat Pierson to make sure of it." She hesitated, then shifted uneasily. "I apologize for speaking out of turn. I forgot she's your relation."

I waved a dismissive hand. "I'm the first to acknowledge that Greta Marlowe, *um*, knows her own mind. However, I have the impression you might mean something more." I leaned closer. "Do you believe Kay's illness was deliberately brought about?"

Miss Templeton, startled, dropped her book. Cassie retrieved it.

The lady murmured her thanks. "I'll give you my honest answer...*if* you promise to keep it confidential. I know what happens when someone gets on Greta Marlowe's bad side."

"Oh? Do you speak from personal experience?" I asked.

She shrugged. "This is my third season with the company —we return here every year—so I have some familiarity with the woman. And rumors circulate in our little group."

I decided to stick to the topic at hand rather than chase rumors. "What, then, is your 'honest answer,' Miss Templeton? You can count upon my discretion."

"And mine also," Cassie chimed in.

"Very well." Still, she reflexively glanced at the door and dropped her voice. "One of the parlor maids—Meg—is a gossipy sort. If my experience as an invalid has taught me anything, it's that there is nothing so appealing as a captive audience. I hear all sorts of talk." She made a face. "One hardly knows how to credit the veracity of it—I even heard a tale of there being a commotion on the fourth floor in the early hours this morning." She paused expectantly.

I kept my expression neutral. "Really? I heard no such rumor. Were you aware of a commotion last night, Cassie?"

My friend lifted a noncommittal shoulder. "It's news to me. I slept soundly."

Miss Templeton blinked in confusion.

"You were about to tell us what Meg said," I prompted.

"Ah, yes." She smoothed the pleats of her hunter-green-and-gray-plaid skirt. Quite fetching on the young lady, even if her friends were not on hand—male or otherwise—to appreciate the ensemble. "When Meg brought my tray this morning, we got to talking about Kay. I said something about how I hoped it wasn't catching, and that's when she told me she feared the chicken divan had made her ill."

"How so?" Cassie asked.

She thought something smelled off about the dish, and after Kay got sick, she wondered if a spoiled ingredient had been used."

Cassie waved a dismissive hand. "It sounds more like a kitchen accident than deliberate poisoning. Dr. Byrd suggested something similar."

"Perhaps, but Meg told me Greta visited the kitchen during the meal preparation last night and tended to a couple of the pots on the stove. According to the maid, she rarely does that, unless they are short staffed."

"What exactly was she doing?" I asked.

"Meg was too busy with her own tasks. All she knows is what I told you."

Interesting. Aside from the fact of the cook putting up with such behavior—my mother's cook would have chased her out with a cleaver if she'd dared step into the kitchen for any purpose other than reviewing the menu—I had a difficult time imagining Greta toiling over a hot stove. Those fringed sleeves of hers might catch fire.

"Was Kay the only one to have the chicken divan last night?" I asked.

Miss Templeton nodded. "It's a known favorite of hers. No one had a problem with the beef."

"Did the maid talk to anyone else about it?"

"Only the cook, who reproved her sharply for voicing the notion that their mistress was responsible. However, after the doctor came and questioned the kitchen staff, Cook went through the entire pantry and found a few questionable tinned goods that she threw away."

"If Greta is responsible," I said, "do you believe it was accidental or deliberate?"

"It doesn't matter what I think. What do _you_ believe?"

Cassie shook her head. "It would be the height of cruelty for Greta to make Miss Finnerty ill so that Flora could assume the lead. Others could have been sickened as well."

The lady lifted a shoulder but didn't answer.

"Flora's good fortune was only possible to begin with," I observed, "because you had already suffered a mishap of your own. Can you tell us exactly how it happened?"

"Neither Greta nor Flora had anything to do with my injury," Miss Templeton declared. "They weren't even in the theater at the time."

"Still, I'd like to hear about it. We'd heard mention of a faulty latch," I prompted.

She blew out a breath in disgust. "Be careful what backstage gossip you listen to. The latch wasn't defective—it simply had not been fully secured after the workmen finished storing the old sets under the stage."

"There was an investigation?" Cassie asked.

Her lips twitched. "Hardly something so official. Chaffee and Pierson inquired, of course—one cannot have players falling through the floor on a regular basis. No one admitted the error. Stern warnings were given."

"We heard Mr. Ward saved you from falling," Cassie said.

"Yes. He grabbed me just as it gave way. I'd hate to consider what would have happened if he had not."

"How fortunate," Cassie said.

Miss Templeton grimaced. "While I don't think much of Barrett's acting ability—he's rather grandiose—I *am* grateful to him."

"Has the doctor said how long until you recover?" I asked.

"He's rather vague on the subject. But our company will be heading to Philadelphia on Monday for a three-week run of Pierson's new play, and I'm determined to join them."

Judging from the set of her jaw, I didn't doubt she would. That should make it easier to coax Flora away from the allure of the footlights to testify in New York.

But we had other problems to resolve in the meantime.

"How pleasant to have the library to ourselves," I

observed, in what I hoped was an unremarkable shift in topic. "Is the entire company at the theater today?"

"Naturally," the lady said. "There's a great deal of work to be done the day before an opening night. Besides rehearsals and running through lines—Barrett is notorious for learning his at the absolute last minute, which makes Pierson nervous—we have costume fittings and whatnot."

"That does sound like a lot of work," I murmured sympathetically.

"Doubly so, as the play is new. If it had been *The Sweethearts* or *The Banker's Daughter*, we can practically do those in our sleep, having performed them repeatedly these past couple of months."

"The entire company has been at the theater today?" Cassie asked, smoothing a skirt fold.

"Except for Kay and myself. Oh, and Mr. Davis."

"Ah, yes—Mr. Davis," I said. "I understand he's Mr. Ward's valet as well as a player in your company. How does he manage both?"

"He plays in minor roles nowadays. I think he volunteered to serve as Barrett's valet to appease him and do Pierson a favor. They go back a long way, you know—they co-founded our playactors' group."

"And Mr. Davis has been here all day?" I asked, returning to the topic.

"Not exactly. He left for the theater a little while ago." She frowned. "Why the interest in everyone's comings and goings? I thought you were here to visit with Greta and Flora."

"That was the original plan, of course," I lied smoothly. "However, they're so busy nowadays. I hadn't anticipated Flora's involvement in your play."

"No one had," Miss Templeton said shortly.

CHAPTER 6

$\mathcal{I}$ left Cassie and Miss Templeton in the library and sought out Barnaby. His post at the reception desk could prove a useful source of the hotel's comings and goings. I also wanted to see if there was an answer to my telegram.

The greasy-haired fellow leaned forward solicitously as I approached. "Hello, Mrs. Wynch. What can I do for you?"

"I'm expecting a telegram. Has anything come?"

"Nothing yet, ma'am. Something else?" he added, as I lingered.

I might as well take the plunge. It wouldn't be a bad idea to put our would-be searcher on notice.

"I did wonder…what staff has access to our room? When we returned this afternoon, we noticed that our things had been disturbed."

"Is anything missing?"

I shook my head.

"Nonetheless, we should inquire further." He gestured to a point beyond my shoulder. "Mrs. Young, would you mind stepping over here a moment?"

Brisk steps behind me accompanied the request, and I

found myself face to face with the housekeeper for the first time.

She was an angular-framed woman with iron-gray hair, piercing eyes, and a downward-turned mouth that made you want to apologize in advance for whatever was sure to have offended her. Important qualities in one charged with running a household of this size, no doubt.

As Barnaby made the introductions and explained the issue, her expression hardened into a scowl. "None of my girls would dare do such a thing. You must be mistaken."

"Hardly," I retorted. "The disturbance was obvious. Our drawers were pushed in crookedly, their contents protruding from the sides. My skirts had been pulled out of the armoire and shoved back in. We do not leave our rooms in such a state."

Worry creased the housekeeper's forehead before it smoothed. "Are you missing anything?"

"No, but it's clear that someone sifted through our belongings. Our door was locked. The lock doesn't appear to have been tampered with."

"Indeed? And what would a lady such as yourself know about locks?"

Oh ho, she was a sharp one, too.

"One reads the papers," I said dismissively. "Such knowledge is not so extraordinary." I nodded toward the enormous ring of keys hanging from the waist of her blue-serge apron. "Who else besides yourself has a key to the guest rooms?"

She stiffened. "I did not enter your room for any purpose whatsoever, Mrs. Wynch."

"That is why I'm asking about *others*, Mrs. Young."

She bit her lip as she thought. "Meg is assigned the old wing. She is given a key while she works, then turns it back in. Perhaps she was responsible. I'm sure there was nothing nefarious about it—mere carelessness. I'll have a talk with her. If you'll excuse me." With a frosty incline of her head, she walked away.

I didn't believe her for a minute.

I woke up from a restorative nap to the sounds of footsteps on the stairs and voices in the hall beyond. The cast must be finished for the day. Time to speak with Rose.

Thankfully, the pain in my arm had lessened a bit. I changed into my dinner frock with only some awkwardness, reapplied pins to my chignon, and retrieved my shoes. I was careful to lock the door behind me, for all the good it would do.

Rose's room was one of a set near the stairwell. I knocked, waited, knocked again. Checking the corridor first, I put my ear to the door. No sounds of movement within. I tried the knob, which turned easily.

My decision was made. I slipped in and surveyed the room. It was a bit more spacious than ours and featured a small sitting area, where a sewing basket sat beside a worn maple rocking chair. The space was tidy—bed made, slippers tucked neatly beside the bed skirt, the floor swept.

I opened the drawers, the armoire, and the trunk at the foot of the bed. I wasn't quite sure what I was looking for—a letter from a friend or family member, perhaps? A clue to the man she so obviously knew.

Strangely, there was not a scrap of correspondence, not even a personal journal.

The sounds of voices at the far end of the corridor reminded me that I shouldn't linger. Perhaps Rose had gone directly to the parlor for a cup of tea. I hurried downstairs.

Several ladies, dressed for dinner as I was, were seated near the hearth. Cassie sat a bit apart from the group, contentedly knitting beneath a bright lamp.

"Ah, Pen," she said at my approach. "Feeling better, I hope?"

"Most certainly. The rest was much needed." I sat beside her. "Have you seen Rose?"

Her face creased in a troubled frown. "No."

"Seen who?" A tall, buxom lady with a cheerful countenance and fluffy brown hair approached the hearth. I recognized her as Mary Reid, the woman Barrett Ward had referred to as not *Amazonian* enough for her part in the play.

"Rose," I said. "Have you seen her?"

"I wish I had," she said ruefully. "I need her to let down the hem of my costume. She left the theater with an armful of dresses—none of them mine—before I had a chance to talk to her. I thought she was coming back here to work on them in her room. She does that sometimes." She grimaced. "When the workmen are underfoot backstage, the racket and dust can be a nuisance."

I could believe it.

"So, she did show up at the theater today," Cassie murmured to me. "It must have been after we'd given up waiting."

But where had she gone before then?

I politely gestured to the empty chair beside us. "Do join us, Miss—it's Miss Reid, correct?"

"That's right." The lady unceremoniously plunked herself in the chair, which creaked in protest. "And you are—?"

As I introduced myself and Cassie, her face brightened in recognition. "I've heard of *you*, Mrs. Wynch."

"Oh?" I said warily.

"About you and Barrett Ward, I mean," she clarified, which did not, in fact, clear up the matter at all.

"Mr. Ward and I have the barest of acquaintances," I said icily.

She laughed and waved a hand. "Oh, not like that. I meant that I heard about Barrett mistaking you for a member of the company and wanting to give my part away. Imagine!" She shook her head. "We've been teasing him about it. The fellow isn't nearly as clever as he believes himself to be."

Cassie turned her needles to start a new row. "Has Mr. Ward been a member of the Pierson Players very long?"

"Oh, yes, he was one of the originals, just starting out back then." She leaned close and added conspiratorially, "Greta took him under her wing, you know, and she has kept up with his career since. Despite their age difference, I think she's rather sweet on him."

"Really?" Cassie said. "She must be at least forty years older."

Mary put a finger to the side of her nose and whispered, "More like thirty years, I'd say. Barrett is older than he appears."

Miss Reid struck me as the quiet-observer type—one whose unremarkable features don't garner the attention of a beauty such as Miss Templeton. As such, it becomes easier to blend in at the periphery and watch people.

Rather than devolve into sordid gossip, however—at least the kind that's irrelevant to a case—I changed the subject. "What about you, Miss Reid—have you been with the acting company long? You seem to know a great deal about the people here."

She shrugged. "Only a few years, but we all spend a lot of time together. We don't have many secrets. And since we do the same performance circuit every year, I've gotten to know some the regulars at the places we stay."

The dinner bell chimed soon after, and Greta invited Cassie and me to join her group at the center banquet table. We had somehow gained favor with the lady. Perhaps stopping last night's intruder had done it—after the blood was cleaned up.

"Will Rose be joining us for dinner?" I asked Greta, as the footman helped seat us.

"Rose? I have no idea."

"No one has seen her since this morning," Cassie injected, "and she isn't in her room."

"That is hardly a concern of mine," the old lady said, with a careless flick of a braceleted wrist. "You simply do not understand those who live the theater life, my dear. They don't adhere to the stuffy protocols in which we were raised. Neither do I, frankly. My guests are welcome to come and go as they please. I don't keep track of their movements like some prudish chaperone. I only care that they pay their board and don't bring the police down upon our heads."

Cassie stiffened. "If Rose has suffered a misadventure, would it not be wise to inquire as to her whereabouts?"

Greta rolled her eyes. "If you feel that strongly about it, ask Mr. Chaffee. He mentioned he'll be down for dinner."

"Mr. Chaffee?" Cassie's frown cleared. "Ah yes, the theater manager."

As if on cue, the burly form of Al Chaffee, whom I'd seen from a distance in the theater but had yet to properly meet, crossed the threshold of the dining room. He was accompanied by a young lady, wearing a simple frock of sage taffeta. Neither the shade of green nor her obstinate expression flattered her pasty complexion.

"Who's that?" I murmured to Cassie.

"That must be Mr. Chaffee's daughter, Sally. Rose mentioned her, remember? The one who helps with sewing the costumes."

Greta offered her cheek to Chaffee as he approached. "Right on time, sir." She gave his companion a regal smile. "And good to see you as well, my dear. Please, have a seat. Anywhere you like."

He glanced around, as if weighing the best option for them both. His gaze flicked briefly over to us, then moved on. Understandable—he didn't know us in the least. Finally, he settled upon the chairs on either side of Miss Templeton and

Miss Reid—Greta didn't hold with alternating seats between men and women, apparently—and directly across from John Davis.

Davis was another fellow I was curious about. A valet, but a business partner in the Pierson Players? Seated at the head table, where Greta's special guests dined?

And a man who'd been at the hotel when our room was searched.

I watched him. After what was sure to have been a grueling afternoon of rehearsals, he was nonetheless engaged in an animated debate with another actor—Archie Jasper, to whom we'd been introduced earlier today.

Miss Templeton was observing Davis, too, though I wasn't sure what had sparked her notice. Poor Miss Reid, ignored, kept her attention on her soup.

There was no sign of the man Davis served as valet for. Perhaps Miss Finnerty's illness had dampened Ward's enthusiasm for dining at Marlowe House.

In that vein, I waited until Greta and Flora had ordered from the menu—the veal cassoulet—and opted for the same. Cassie did, too.

At a table of this size, discussion with anyone but those within arm's length was next to impossible, so questions for Chaffee about Rose would have to wait.

When Davis's vigorous hand gestures knocked over his water goblet and an attendant hurried to sop up the mess, Mr. Jasper shifted his attention to us. He was a dark-haired, clean-shaven young man, although whiskers would have better obscured his pockmarked cheeks.

"So, ladies. I understand you have been kind enough to keep Kay company in her illness." His voice was warm, solicitous, and altogether pleasant to listen to. One could imagine how well it conveyed onstage.

I inclined my head toward Cassie. "Actually, Miss Leigh has been doing so."

"Ah. Most commendable. I've wanted to pay a visit myself. How is she faring?"

Cassie drew breath to answer when Davis interrupted.

"Now then, my good fellow, you're not getting off so easily. You say it was Donckel, not Pepper and Dircks, who invented the ghost illusion? Preposterous. Explain yourself."

With an apologetic shrug in our direction, Jasper shifted his attention back to Davis, and I was left to my own thoughts —namely, Rose.

Was she deliberately avoiding us because of the man at the trolley stop? What was her connection to him? Had she known he was going to break into the hotel last night? The latter question was a disturbing one, as it suggested that her clumsy gaze out the window at dinner might not have been accidental, but rather a warning for the fellow to keep out of sight.

A name drifted across my thoughts, and I realized my table companions had shifted topics.

"I'm surprised Barrett is missing this," said Jasper, sitting back as his soup plate was removed. "Cassoulet is his favorite. From what I understand, the cook only prepares it once a week."

Pierson, sitting within earshot, gave a snort. "A lady friend, likely. No amount of veal can compete with that."

"A woman? This is only our second week in town," Jasper said. "No one moves that fast."

I focused my attention upon buttering the roll on my plate as I shamelessly listened. Cassie gave me a sideways smirk.

"Barrett is disappointed we have no billiard table here," Davis said. "He might have gone to the Southbrook Club in search of a game."

"My guess is poker," Jasper said. "He's an absolute fiend for cards—have you noticed? Quite good, too. Cleaned me out the other night. Last time I'll be playing the fellow for money."

At last, dinner was done and the guests began to disperse, most of them seeking out coffee and leisure in the music salon. Cassie and I made our way over to Chaffee, who was offering Greta his arm.

"Aunt Greta," I said, "would you introduce us?"

She frowned over the familiarity but made the necessary courtesies.

Chaffee bowed. "A pleasure, ladies. I would introduce you to my daughter, Sally, but she appears to have gone on to the salon."

"How do you like being a theater manager, Mr. Chaffee?" I asked, as the four of us stepped into the salon. "It must be challenging work."

"It is indeed." With a quick glance at his companion, he added, "but a privilege to work alongside a distinguished woman such as Greta Marlowe."

The old lady smiled.

"How long have you been running the theater together?" Cassie asked.

"Mr. Chaffee and I have known each other since my husband was alive," Greta answered, "but we've only been collaborating on the theater for the past three years. It was in disrepair after the bank had foreclosed upon the previous owner, and we took it over. Al has worked miracles with the place." Her expression brightened as strains of music from the piano drifted from the salon. "Ah—it sounds as if Mary is at the instrument tonight. Excellent."

I was about to pose my question regarding Rose when Barrett Ward—where did he come from?—came up behind us. "Ah, Mrs. Wynch! I'm so glad I've run into you. I have a favor to ask."

And without any apology whatsoever, he steered me by the elbow away from our group and out of the salon altogether. I helplessly locked eyes with Cassie. With a nod, she leaned toward Chaffee—to ask about Rose's whereabouts, I hoped.

Ward, with the self-important air of a man on a mission, led me over to a velvet-upholstered bench tucked into the crook of the main staircase.

We women have dealt with such high-handed interruptions by men for millennia. Best to get this over with. I folded my hands and waited.

After straightening his collar and tugging at his monogrammed cuffs, he launched into his speech.

"Madam, I have come to realize that my behavior last night was deeply distressing to you. I sincerely regret having said anything that might have offended. You see, I was under the impression that—"

I cut across the rest of the tedious explanation. "Please, give it no further consideration, sir. I barely recall the exchange."

A mixture of expressions crossed his features—relief, to be sure, but was that annoyance, too? How was it that I was not devastated by the unintended insults of the great Barrett Ward? I pressed my lips together to stifle a chuckle.

Relief appeared to win the day. His smile broadened as he reached for my gloved hand to press his lips upon it. "Well then! You are too good to me, my dear lady. Still, I must make it up to you. Would you and your friend Miss Leigh attend the performance on Friday evening? As my special guests, with front-row seats."

Upon my graciously accepting the invitation, we returned to the music salon.

Cassie joined me immediately and we found a quiet corner to ourselves. "Mr. Chaffee hasn't seen Rose since the early afternoon," she said, "but the costumes she was working on were finished and neatly hung up in the wardrobe room before he came to dinner."

"I'm relieved nothing untoward has happened to her, but I do suspect she's trying to avoid us."

Cassie frowned. "Avoid us...in order to protect that man we saw her with?"

"Exactly."

"But how would she know we're involved? Greta has kept the incident quiet." Cassie's expression cleared in understanding. "You mean—he recognized you as the one who shot him?"

"That must be it. He was waiting for Rose to come out of the greenhouse and then, when he saw me, realized the danger to himself."

"Who do you think he is to her?" Cassie asked. "A sweetheart? A relative? She obviously knows him."

I shrugged. "The important questions are—is she with him now? And how do we find them?"

"Do you think she recognized him last night when he was watching the hotel from the street?" Cassie asked.

"I've wondered about that." My gaze shifted to the far side of the salon, then stiffened at the sight of Miss Templeton, seated on the divan in a tête-à-tête with Sally Chaffee. Miss Templeton's complexion had turned ashen. Sally stood up in alarm and gestured to one of the maids. I was too far away to hear what was said, but a moment later a glass of amber liquid was thrust into her hands. Sally helped lift the glass to her lips.

"Poor Miss Templeton," Cassie murmured, following my gaze. "The evening has been too much for her, in her condition."

The piano music paused briefly, then resumed. Barrett Ward was being handed an envelope by the footman. Ward absently made his apologies, stepped away, and tore it open while Miss Reid took his place and launched into a bright tune.

I watched as he frowned over the slip of paper within and passed it to Davis, who had come up beside him. His frown bordered on a scowl.

My attention was diverted, however, by a footman heading my way, two more envelopes on his salver.

"Excuse me—Mrs. Wynch? Telegrams for you."

At last. But at such an hour... "These have only just arrived?" I reached for them, but unlike our impatient actor, I was not about to open them here.

The fellow shifted uncomfortably. "Er, they arrived a few hours ago—along with Mr. Ward's telegram—but the entire bundle had fallen behind the reception desk and had gone unnoticed until now. I do beg your pardon, ma'am." With an awkward bow, he left us.

It seemed safe enough to read them now. I noticed Davis had waylaid a maid, murmured something, and followed her out of the room.

"Well? Are you going to open it?" Cassie asked impatiently.

"Just a moment. I'll be right back."

I hurried out of the salon and took a quick peek down the main stairs. I could see the foyer and part of the front door from my vantage point, and the sight of Ward and Davis both putting on their coats and hats was enough to assure me they were heading out.

Good. I had something to take care of while they were gone. But first, I returned to the salon with the telegrams.

"Well? Is it from Frank?" Cassie asked, as I slipped my thumb under the flap. I'd forgotten to ask for a letter opener, but it was hardly necessary. Neither of the telegrams was sealed. *Hmm.*

I scanned the page.

F ALWAYS STUBBORN. SENDING SOMEONE TO TAKE OVER. BE OF ASSISTANCE TO HIM. DO NOT WARN HER SHE MAY BOLT.

~FRANK

I passed it to Cassie.

"How outrageous!" she exclaimed.

"A bit more quietly, if you please," I murmured. At her crestfallen expression, I added, "I don't like it, either, but we cannot discuss it here."

I pulled out the other telegram. Perhaps this was from the fellow being put in charge of the case.

"Who's that one from?" Cassie asked.

"My mother," I answered in a hollow voice. "Did you tell her where we were staying?"

"Um, well ..." She shifted uneasily. "She cornered me before we left and was quite insistent upon knowing what we were up to. You know how she can be," she added defensively.

Yes, indeed, I did know, but I was too busy reading the missive to answer.

LEONARD DISAPPOINTED YOU WERE NOT AT PARTY GIVEN IN YOUR HONOR. YOU SHOULD SETTLE DOWN WITH HIM INSTEAD OF PURSUING CHAOTIC LIFE WITH THAT OTHER MAN. CONTACT ME WHEN YOU COME TO YOUR SENSES.

~MOTHER

I could almost hear Mother's emphasis on *that other man*. Rarely did she call Frank by name.

At this point, I'd lowered the second telegram to my lap and Cassie had unabashedly crooked her neck to read it.

"Oh dear. I'm sorry, Pen."

"No matter." I slipped both telegrams back in their envelopes and stood. "I think it's time to retire."

Cassie promptly set aside her cup. "I'll go with you. I want to see how Miss Finnerty is faring."

We first went over to Greta, sitting alone in the window seat, to say our good nights. I leaned in close. "Are the arrangements complete for tonight?"

The old woman's eyes glittered briefly in annoyance, but she murmured, "We already have two fellows stationed at each of the staircases in the corridor outside our suite. There will be no trouble."

Once Cassie and I were out of earshot of the others on our way upstairs, I said, "I'm not really going to bed, but I do have to change first." My satin dinner dress was much too noisy and voluminous to creep about in. Besides, I needed my lockpicks.

"Oh? What are you up to?"

"With Ward and Davis out, this is my opportunity to search Davis's room. He was the only other guest here this morning, remember? I want to learn more about him if I can."

"I'm not sure what you can learn," Cassie said. "Nothing was taken from our room. Most likely a nosy servant is to blame."

I shrugged. "Perhaps. But something is going on with Ward and Davis. I'd like to learn more if I can."

"Isn't this taking us rather far afield from our primary mission of conducting Flora to New York?" she asked.

"Greta has precautions in place," I countered. "Besides, according to Frank, a man is coming tomorrow to take charge of Flora."

She searched my face for a good long minute. "All right, let me check on Miss Finnerty while you change."

I smiled. "Are you offering to be my lookout?"

She gave a snort. "It's obvious you need one. You won't have much time before the maids turn down the beds."

I can always count on Cassie, bless her.

I quickly changed into my reconnoitering dress, then reached for my pouch of lockpicks. I hesitated.

The pouch had been disturbed.

Everything was still in there. Then I checked the logbook. It had been riffled through—the ribbon was slightly askew. The loaded derringer—incompatible with my dinner frock and left behind—seemed to be in its place, but I didn't doubt that it had been examined, too.

I sat back on my heels, my mind turning over the possibilities. First the unsecured telegrams, and now a second search—successfully this time—of my hiding place. Someone was very interested in me.

Someone who now knew an uncomfortable amount about me.

I spent a few extra minutes devising a different hiding place for the pistol and logbook, although the point was probably moot, then slipped the lockpicks in my pocket and closed the door.

Cassie was coming out of Miss Finnerty's room.

"How is she?" I asked.

"Still regaining her strength. Flora will most certainly be playing the lead tomorrow."

I nodded. No surprise there.

Cassie frowned. "Are you all right, Pen? You're a bit pale."

I don't know why I decided not to tell her. Perhaps because it wasn't a discussion for the corridor. More likely, I didn't want to lose my nerve before breaking into Davis's room. "I'm fine. Let's go."

Barrett Ward had one of the larger private suites, located in the new wing of the second floor. Davis's room was a smaller one connected to it along a short, private corridor. Rather a break for me, as we were tucked out of sight of the casual observer passing by.

Cassie positioned herself just behind the corner to

monitor the hall. I pulled out my pouch and crouched at Davis's door.

After a few heart-pounding moments where the stiff lock bent one pick and I had to pull out another, I finally got it open. I gave Cassie a little wave and slipped inside.

It was dark as pitch. I groped to switch on a lamp, dislodging an array of knickknacks. At least now I could see.

Davis's room was nicer than ours, with flocked wallpaper and a deep-pile brown wool rug, though the room size was smaller since it was meant to be an attendant's quarters. There was barely space for the washstand, dresser, and narrow, iron-framed bed. Places of concealment were few. At least my search would be quick.

As I restored the knickknacks, I saw the dresser top was littered with framed photographs of Davis posing with different people. I recognized Ward and Pierson in one. The three men were standing stiffly together, Pierson in the middle, Davis and Ward in matching harlequin costumes.

Footsteps sounded along the corridor. I relaxed as they faded. Time to get to work.

After checking behind, beneath, and within the bureau drawers, I moved on to the bed frame. Apparently, room cleaning didn't extend to dusting the servants' quarters, and I'd already surmised that Davis wasn't exactly a tidy fellow. I put a finger under my nose to stifle a sneeze, then stretched flat along the floor to pull out a shallow trunk. Thankfully, it wasn't locked. I'd been in the room much too long as it was, and I was sure Cassie was nervously waiting for me to be done.

The trunk was stuffed to the brim with clothing and personal items. I sifted through it quickly, searching for evidence of how he might have gotten into our room—a lock-pick, a jointed key, a key maker?

A thorough search of the trunk turned up none of these.

He might be carrying something of the sort on his person, but it seemed doubtful.

One item I found of interest, however, was a gun—a top-break, double-action revolver that looked fairly new. The *SW* embossed on the wood grip told me it was a Smith and Wesson. It was unloaded.

Not a useful find, as there wasn't anything nefarious about Davis owning a gun—someone in his line of work who traveled a great deal might reasonably keep one as a precaution.

I put the revolver back where I found it, restored the trunk, and did my best to erase the marks where I'd disturbed the dust. One last survey of the room reminded me that I hadn't checked his dressing gown, on a hook by the washstand.

Inside one pocket I felt a crackle of paper and a small, oval lump. I pulled them out, smoothing the paper beneath the lamp and unwrapping the object. I very nearly dropped it in my surprise. It was a ruby pendant—a large gem, the size of a robin's egg—mounted in antique gold, encircled by tiny diamonds.

The note was written in a flowery, feminine hand, though its message was brusque and without salutation.

Here it is. I hope you choke on it.

~R.

A sharp knock upon the wall roused me from my thoughts. Cassie's warning signal. I extinguished the lamp, stuck the note and pendant back where it was, and flattened myself behind the door.

I heard male voices—Ward and Davis—coming from the adjoining room.

"What a night! I'm exhausted." It was Ward.

"It's regrettable that the cards didn't go your way tonight," Davis answered.

Ward muttered something I couldn't catch and then said,

"Go down to the study and fetch me some brandy, if you would. But stir up the fire first."

"Of course," came Davis's reply. Was there an edge of annoyance to the response?

I waited for the sound of the door, then kept a check on my patience until Davis's footsteps faded down the hall.

Now it was safe to move. Gratefully, I escaped to my room, where Cassie waited.

"Ugh, look at your skirts—they're filthy." She helped me brush off the dust. "Did you find anything?"

"Not what I was expecting. I don't think he's the one who searched our room either time."

"What do you mean 'either time'?"

Drat. Well, there's was no help for it now. "When I came up to change tonight, I noticed someone had disturbed my hiding place."

"Which means whoever it was has seen your lockpicks, logbook, and gun." Cassie sat on the bed with a sigh. "And you're sure it wasn't Davis?"

"Well, fairly sure. No sign of lockpicks or spare keys. But my search wasn't a complete waste of time." I described the note and jewel I'd found.

She brightened. "Then your instincts that he's up to something were correct."

"In a manner of speaking," I said dryly. "I hadn't considered him a blackmailer."

"'I hope you choke on it,'" Cassie quoted. "Yes, the sentiment would match the occasion. But who is he blackmailing? One of the women in the acting company?"

"Possible, though if the lady in question is being blackmailed because of an illicit affair, that implies a husband. Why else would one want to keep it quiet? None of the women in the company is married—except for Flora. After a fashion, that is. Perhaps it's a married woman that Davis knows through Ward."

"R," Cassie said thoughtfully. "The only woman with that initial is Rose, but she isn't married. Though a woman could be blackmailed for all sorts of indiscretions, I suppose."

"Indeed." I fell silent, mulling over the possibilities.

"None of this gets us any closer to keeping Flora safe," Cassie pointed out, "or to finding out where Rose is. Should you search her room next?"

"I already have," I admitted. "No help there."

"So, what now?"

"As far as Flora is concerned, there isn't any more to be done at the moment." I picked up Frank's telegram, glanced at it again, then threw it into the fire. Who knew how many eyes had seen it already, and I no longer had need of it. "Flora is protected tonight, and Frank's man is coming tomorrow to take over."

Cassie didn't answer right away, instead searching my face again—for what? The turmoil she suspected I felt at being replaced? I kept my expression neutral, hoping it didn't give away the tangle of thoughts and emotions that I needed to sort through in private.

"What about Rose?" she asked.

I grimaced. "I'll continue to inquire."

"And the other telegram?" she pointed to the one from my mother.

HOW MUCH BETTER YOUR LIFE WOULD BE IF YOU SETTLED DOWN WITH LEONARD.... The words were burned in my memory.

"It's of little consequence." I threw it into the fire as well.

We both retired after that. Even as Cassie's breathing settled into sleep, I lay awake for a long time, staring at the tin coffered ceiling, trying to sort through the people involved— Davis, demanding payment from the unknown lady who'd bitterly given up her jewel; the ambitious but close-mouthed Flora, and what secrets she might still be keeping; the two women she'd replaced, Miss Templeton and Miss Finnerty;

and Greta, the proud matron, barricaded at night behind doors now guarded by hired hands.

And amid these, I reflected upon the men who'd had a hand in shaping my life into what it was now. Frank, certainly —he is often in my thoughts, as is Phillip Kendall, the all-too-charming, supposedly reformed thief I've come to work with increasingly often. Though I tried not to think of him any more than I ought.

And now, thanks to my mother's telegram, a third man took up space in my thoughts—Leonard Frasier.

Long before Frank, there had been Leonard—the childhood friend and reliable companion. Our mothers had schemed about the match even as we toddled in our respective nurseries.

I'd been fond of Leonard during those early years, to be sure, and perhaps I still was. Agreeing to marry him had not arisen from breathless infatuation on my side, however. I had longed for a man who made my heart race and my mouth go dry, and that was not Leonard. However, he was kind, intelligent, and a man of means. Most importantly, both sets of parents expected it of us.

And the young Miss Hamilton generally did what was expected of her. Until, one day, she did not.

The brash, handsome Frank Wynch came into my life during my engagement to Leonard. Frank had been called in to investigate a safecracking ring that had struck a number of wealthy estates, including ours. Within weeks, I'd broken off my engagement and we'd eloped.

I didn't have the maturity at the time to understand that a man possessed of daring and passion can be unstable. I'd had no idea of the trouble we were headed for.

With the wisdom of hindsight, would I have traded the reckless whirlwind for placid security?

And now, Providence—in the form of my matchmaking mother—was asking me that question once again. Although

Leonard had eventually married another, she had died a few years ago, and he was free once again.

I turned my face into the cold pillow, aware that my dear female friend—instead of any of the men in my life, past or present—was snoring softly in a bed on the other side of the room. I felt, for the first time in a long while, the pang of loneliness.

I also wondered whether I had made an irrevocable mess of things.

CHAPTER 7

THURSDAY, MARCH 8

We awoke to a gray, overcast day that matched my mood in every way, although I had no right to be out of sorts—my arm was continuing to improve, and there'd been no disturbances during the night. One glance at the animated, clear-eyed Flora, chatting with her great-aunt as she passed the marmalade, indicated her restful night's sleep.

We were just finishing breakfast when Dr. Byrd made an appearance. His face brightened at the sight of the buffet—one had to wonder about his timing—and Greta graciously offered him a seat and waved to a footman to load a plate.

"Thank you, Mrs. Marlowe," he said, tucking in his napkin. "I haven't had breakfast yet—was up all night with a difficult lying-in. A happy ending, though. Baby boy and mother are doing well."

Cassie and I were about to excuse ourselves when the doctor made a motion for me to stay. "I'd like to see how your arm is healing, if you don't mind, Mrs. Wynch."

With a suppressed sigh, I refilled my teacup, sipped, and waited. Cassie flashed me a smile on her way out.

"It's kind of you to come without us sending for you," Greta said to the doctor.

He gave a nod. "You have three of my patients here, so it's an easy trip."

"Three?" I asked. "There's only Miss Finnerty and myself."

"And Miss Templeton," he said thickly, around a mouthful of scone, "although she is far less compliant than you and Miss Finnerty. Rather peevish about me checking her ankle. Seems to blame me because she couldn't return to the stage right away." He exhaled a martyred sigh. "You have no idea the abuse we physicians must endure."

After the doctor had finished his meal, he and I retired to the empty parlor. He unwrapped my arm and examined it beneath the bright light of the stained-glass floor lamp.

"The edges are still a bit raw," he murmured, half to himself.

"It feels better, though."

He looked up, startled, as if he'd forgotten the arm was attached to a conscious, thinking woman. "Ah, yes, yes. The rawness is to be expected, of course. It's undoubtedly healing. No sign of infection. Still, you must be careful with it." He let go of my arm and rummaged in his bag. "I'll apply a fresh bandage, then I must go and see how Miss Finnerty is faring."

"My friend checked on her last night and said she's better," I said.

The doctor merely grunted and focused on his task.

I heard the thunder of feet and the sound of voices gathering in the foyer. The cast must be heading to the theater. I was anxious to get there myself and see if Rose had returned.

Once the doctor had finished with me, I hurried to find Cassie.

But my friend had retired to our room and was lying down. "I'm sorry, Pen—my head aches dreadfully."

Poor girl. The strain of the past few days must be catching up with her.

"Don't worry, dear. Would you mind if I went to the theater without you? Will you be all right here?"

"Of course. I'll join you when I feel better."

Once at the Marlowe Theater, I went through one of the side doors that led directly to the workspaces behind the stage. Heaven forbid a creaking front door disrupt the rehearsal and earn me a black look from Greta or Pierson.

Clutter continued to accumulate against the walls between the dressing rooms, prop room, and manager's office. I sidestepped potted plants, rolled-up painted backdrops, and hand carts on my way to the wardrobe room.

Rose wasn't there, but the young lady I knew to be Sally was, her smooth brown hair gleaming in the light of a task lamp. She lifted her head. "Hello, can I help you?" Her mouth puckered. "You seem familiar."

"You may have seen me last night at dinner, although we weren't introduced then. I'm Mrs. Wynch. My friend and I are here in town to visit my husband's great-aunt Greta and his sister Flora."

"Ah, yes—someone pointed you out to me, I remember now. Nice to meet you, Mrs. Wynch. I'm Regina-Salvia Chaffee, but you can call me Sally." She grimaced. "It's easier to pronounce."

"Well then, Sally, you must call me Pen—it's short for Penelope, which is rather long-winded, as well. I was looking for Rose. Have you seen her?"

She shook her head. "Not yet, but I hope she comes in

soon. Mary's complaining something awful about how short her gown is." She gestured to the garment in her lap.

I could sympathize, having suffered more than my share of short gowns.

"I do see her point," Sally went on, "but there's just not enough material to let down the hem. I'll have to add some trim, I suppose."

"Where else might Rose be? It's rather urgent that I speak to her."

"But you're staying at Marlowe House—can't you talk to her there?"

"She hasn't returned since yesterday morning."

Sally bit her lip. "Now that you mention it, I didn't see her at dinner last night."

"Do you know where else she could be?" I asked again.

"Rose! Rose!" a male voice called from the corridor. It was Barrett Ward.

Sally clasped her needle more tightly. "What now," she muttered.

Ward strode in. His face was red with agitation, though the color quickly drained from his face when he caught sight of Sally. "Oh…it's you." He cleared his throat awkwardly. "Where's Rose?"

"That appears to be the question of the morning," I said.

Ward whipped around in surprise. "Oh—Mrs. Wynch, I didn't see you there. I beg your pardon for raising my voice." He stretched out his arms. "But you see the problem, do you not? I cannot wear this on stage."

The sleeves of his navy blazer were grievously mismatched, with one noticeably shorter than the other.

"Oh, dear," I said. "This is Rose's handiwork?"

Sally rubbed the back of her neck. "She wouldn't make mistakes like this. Something's wrong."

"I care little for whatever personal problems the woman might have," Ward retorted. "This is completely unacceptable." He shrugged off the jacket and thrust it at Sally. "Fix it."

Such rudeness seemed uncharacteristic for the courtly mannered actor who liked to charm the ladies.

Sally flashed him a sulky glare. "You may put it on that pile of garments, Mr. Ward." Her voice quavered. "I will get to it."

"What's going on in here?" It was Al Chaffee, who grasped the doorframe and leaned in. "I could hear you bellowing all the way from my office, Barrett." His gaze shifted to Sally, who was trembling now, and near tears. "What's wrong?"

She dabbed her eyes with the hem of Mary's dress. I passed her a handkerchief. When would these people leave? I was sure Sally knew more about Rose, but I couldn't continue with a crowd listening in.

Chaffee frowned. "I won't have you bullying my daughter, Ward. She's doing her best under difficult circumstances."

"I hold you responsible for our *difficult circumstances*," Ward shot back through gritted teeth. "Too many things are going wrong. Rose is doing shoddy work, and now she isn't even here when we need her. I'd say you aren't managing your people very well. The production is going to suffer for it."

Chaffee stiffened. "I'll get to the bottom of what's going on with Rose."

"You'd better."

"Barrett!" someone called. "Where are you? We're all waiting."

Ward scowled at Chaffee. "Let us hope the rest of my wardrobe isn't this wretched."

After Ward cleared the room, Chaffee bent close to Sally, gently brushing a strand of hair from her face. "Don't worry, dear, I'll handle it. I'll make sure he doesn't bother you again."

Sally sniffed into the handkerchief but didn't answer.

He didn't press and finally left us alone.

I closed the door, pulled up a stool, and sat beside the young lady. "Well, that was unpleasant."

She blew out a breath. "I'll be glad when the Pierson Players leave. They've been nothing but trouble."

"Mr. Ward in particular?"

"I don't know what you mean," she said, her voice toneless.

"Well, surely they're not all bad," I said.

"I guess not." She blew her nose noisily. "But I don't understand what's happened to Rose." She smoothed the folds of the dress in her lap. "I've known her for three years. She's ever so scrupulous about her work. And she wouldn't leave without a word to anyone."

"It is worrisome," I agreed. "Does she have family nearby she might be staying with? Or perhaps a sweetheart?"

Sally made a face. "She's sworn off suitors, and with good reason. Never mind that," she added, waving off my next question. "As far as family, her brother is all she has now. But she hasn't talked to him in months."

That you know of, I thought to myself. "Why is that? Are they estranged?"

She shrugged.

"What's his name?"

"Bobby Harper."

"He lives here in town?"

"Yes, but"—she seemed to pick her words carefully—"I don't think he has a fixed address."

"Oh? What does he do for a living?"

"He has no regular employment, which is a source of distress for her."

I grimaced. The fellow was going to be difficult to track down. "What places does he frequent?"

"I don't know him personally—I've never met him, in fact," she said. "What I know of him comes from Rose. But she mentioned that he was getting hot meals from the Church Street Mission when he's short on money."

Sally didn't know where the mission was, but I finally found a workman backstage who knew the place.

That done, I tried to make my way to the exit, a task made more complicated by the arrival of more workmen rolling in a large plywood set-piece. I opted to exit from the front of the theater instead, which meant skirting the stage perimeter so as not to disturb the players.

It was quite the rabbit warren. I had to follow the sounds of voices on stage to maintain my general sense of direction, careful to stay behind the back curtain all the while.

I had just reached stage left when something made me pause—a fluttering curtain at the edge of my vision. I stopped.

The curtain was just beyond the stage wing, near the set of counterweight pulleys that controlled the equipment overhead. Several winches, their pull-ropes wound around them, were visible from my vantage point. I took a few steps closer.

A dark-gloved hand came into view, quickly loosened a rope, and withdrew.

The catwalk, twenty feet above, tipped and slid downward at one end, over the spot where Flora and Barrett Ward stood.

"Look out!" I yelled, running toward them.

They gaped, frozen in place.

Miss Reid, standing a few yards away, shoved them and leapt out of the way herself as the lurching end of the catwalk crashed onto the stage floor.

The minutes that followed were a jumble of exclamations, hysterics, shouted instructions, and aimless milling around. In other words, the typical things people do when met with their own mortality.

Someone fetched Chaffee, and he took charge, ordering the workmen to check all the mechanisms—ropes, pulleys, latches.

Everyone was operating on the assumption that this was yet another accident. I was reluctant to disabuse them of the idea, as there were hysterics enough among the female players, save for Miss Reid.

But I had to alert Greta and Flora to what I'd witnessed. Flora was still a target. I doubted, however, that it was the same fellow who'd broken in with the knife. Another hired henchman must have taken his place. With the night-time precautions Greta had implemented to secure the hotel, they had resorted to sabotaging Flora on stage.

But why was Flora's death so important?

Pierson sent the actors back to the hotel for the rest of the morning so the workmen could check the equipment without a lot of people underfoot. "Be back and ready to work at one o'clock," he added. He gave Barrett Ward a pointed look.

That man grunted, shrugged on his coat, and left by the side door.

Davis, instead of following Ward, pulled Pierson aside. The angry set of Pierson's jaw made it clear the discussion was unwelcome.

I went in search of Greta and Flora. They hadn't left with the others—perhaps Greta was waiting to talk to Chaffee.

Flora was reclining upon the divan in the wardrobe room, eyes closed, with Sally applying a damp cloth to her forehead.

"Hello, Flora. Can we talk?"

She sat up. "Did you see how closely that missed me?"

"Would you mind leaving us to talk in private?" I asked Sally.

"Of course." She gathered up her needlework and closed the door behind her.

"What is it?" Flora asked peevishly. "I'm not feeling well enough for a chat. It's been a trying morning."

"Your morning would have been much worse, had it not been for Miss Reid's quick reflexes. You're in danger here, Flora. You must leave for New York immediately."

"Nonsense! The only danger here is from careless stage-hands who don't secure their ropes and latches properly. This theater has been plagued by all sorts of problems lately. Great-aunt Greta will not stand for it. She's going to speak with Mr. Chaffee."

I shook my head. "This was no accident. I saw someone loosen the rope."

She paled. "You...*saw* this? Who was it?"

I made a face. "All I could see was a gloved hand at the cleat. After that, my focus was on warning you and your fellows."

Flora absently plucked at the folds of her skirt.

She might as well have been plucking at my last nerve. "Flora," I said sharply, "look at me."

She raised her head.

"This is not a game. You cannot wish away the danger."

"How do you know I'm the target? The break-in was two days ago. This is the first incident since then."

I did wonder about that. What could have precipitated this attempt?

Perhaps the telegram from Frank had done it. Any number of people in the household could have read it before it reached me. If someone at the hotel was involved—a chilling thought—that person could have alerted their boss that additional reinforcements were on the way to keep Flora safe. Perhaps the decision was made to try once more, while the odds were in their favor.

Who could be the insider? One of the servants, or one of the players? Given the attempt that had just taken place, the latter made more sense. Who had been on or nearby the stage at the time? I could at least eliminate those.

Flora, Ward, Mary, Davis, and Pierson had been on or near the stage. That left Archie Jasper, Sally, and her father. And then there were the workmen, whom I knew nothing of.

All of them knew the stage area like the back of their hand. But how were any of them connected to Flora?

"You're not listening," Flora complained.

"Oh, sorry. What did you say?"

"Barrett was standing right beside me on stage, you know. Perhaps he's the target. And he was with Viola when the trap door gave way," she added.

I'd have to consider that. And it reminded me of something Ward had said to Chaffee just a while ago. *Too many things are going wrong.*

"Does Chaffee have any enemies? Could someone be trying to sabotage the production in general?"

She shrugged. "Not that I'm aware. But there is some bad feeling toward Pierson."

"From whom?"

"I have only rumors to go by, mind you," Flora said, "but there is talk that Archie Jasper resents Barrett playing the lead and that he's wanted better roles in Pierson's productions for months."

"Jasper could hardly achieve such a goal by undermining the production," I said dryly. "We need a better theory than that."

She shrugged. "You're the detective, not me."

CHAPTER 8

$\mathcal{A}$lthough it seemed unlikely that another attempt would be made today, I decided to delay my trip to the Church Street Mission and remain at the theater for the afternoon. There was also the possibility that Rose might return.

She had not made an appearance by the time the company was ready to stop for the day, however, and her prolonged absence had become painfully obvious. Chaffee strode in and out of the wardrobe room, ranting to no one in particular.

It was a weary, subdued group who returned to the hotel at tea-time. Flora and Greta went straight up to their rooms, but nearly everyone else settled in the parlor for tea. I wanted to check on Cassie first.

I found her out of bed and getting dressed.

"Feeling better, I see."

She smiled. "Yes, and ready to rejoin the world."

I tidied my hair in the mirror. "You missed a bit of excitement at the theater."

"Oh? Do tell."

Cassie blinked as I recounted what happened.

She looked askance, however, when I shared Flora's theory that it could be an attempt either to harm Ward or sabotage the production. "Maybe, but we shouldn't take any chances. We must get her to New York before she comes to harm."

"She refuses to budge on that," I said. "Perhaps the fellow Frank is sending will be able to accomplish what I cannot."

She shot me a look as we locked the door behind us. Well, perhaps my tone *did* have a bitter edge.

A strong cup of tea turned out to be just what I needed. The tensions among the other guests seem to have eased, and soon after, Kay Finnerty came down to join us. Her recent ordeal was evident in her pale cheeks and the thinning of her roundish face, but she seemed in good spirits.

"Miss Finnerty!" Cassie got up and crossed the room to greet her, clasping her hands warmly. She led her over to sit between us on the sofa.

"Do call me Kay," the young lady said, as Cassie rearranged a cushion for her comfort. "You've been so kind to me during my illness." She nodded in my direction. "And you as well, Mrs. Wynch."

I smiled. "Gladly, though you must call me Pen. It's good to see you up and about."

Cassie fetched a cup and was reaching for the pot when Kay stopped her.

"I'm afraid that's a bit too strong for me yet. The maid is bringing a tisane."

"Yes, of course," Cassie said.

Kay sat back and took in the room, watching Viola Templeton in particular, who was chatting with the attentive John Davis over by the bay window. Miss Templeton must have whispered something amusing in his ear, for he waved his arm with a laugh, dislodging the crutches propped against the table. He restored them to their place.

"I'm surprised Viola still needs crutches," Kay murmured.

"Surprised? Why?" I asked.

She shrugged. "Just an impression. It might turn out that I recover more quickly and play the lead when we move on to Philadelphia."

"She's determined to be healed by then," I said, recalling my earlier conversation with Miss Templeton.

"Either way," Cassie chimed in, "Flora will be out of a job, and just as well."

"Why is that?" Kay asked.

I frowned at Cassie. No one besides ourselves was supposed to know about Flora's legal trouble.

"Well, um," Cassie began, but was saved by the maid coming in with a tray.

"Miss Finnerty, here's your tisane," the girl chirped brightly. "Cook also added a few digestive biscuits, in case you're feeling up to it."

Kay's lips whitened at the sight of the innocuous snaps on the plate. "No, thank you." She reached for the cup and took a tentative sip. "This will be fine. If you could please take… the plate…away."

The maid gave a little bob, picked up the offending dish, and turned to me. "Mrs. Wynch, there's someone to see you. I've put him in the library."

Must be the man Frank had sent. I made my excuses and hurried out.

The gentleman was warming himself by the fire, his back to me as I entered. Before I announced my presence, I took a good look.

A typical rough-at-the-edges private detective this one was not. His dandyish cutaway of dark wool cassimere draped smoothly upon his wide-shouldered frame in a way that only custom tailoring can accomplish. His wavy brown hair was neatly trimmed at the top of a pristine-white collar. The hands clasped behind his back were free of ink or tobacco stains, and the nails were manicured. Strangely, in the first moment of seeing him, I was strongly reminded of Leonard Frasier—they shared similarities in hair color and build—but of course it wasn't him.

I shook myself. Mother's telegram had affected me more than I'd realized. Time to focus on the task at hand.

I stepped closer and cleared my throat delicately. The man whipped around. He was just as meticulously groomed from the front, with a smooth, lustrous brown mustache and long sideburns. A gold watchchain was visible from his pinstripe waistcoat.

"Ah! You must be Mrs. Wynch," he said in a booming voice. He gave a little bow. "Your husband Frank sent me to help with the, um…difficulty of Flora Richards."

"There's no need to shout," I retorted and went to the door. No one in the corridor, thank goodness. Nonetheless, I closed the door as much as propriety allowed—which wasn't as much as I would have liked—and took a seat.

"I beg your pardon, ma'am." He perched upon an antique rocker. "I'm accustomed to speaking before a court, which typically requires a different set of vocals entirely."

"Court? I thought Frank was sending another detective. Who are you, exactly…a lawyer? And you haven't told me your name yet," I added peevishly.

He spread his hands, as if expanding upon the apology. "It seems we've gotten off on the wrong foot. My name is Sanderson." He passed over a business card. "Daniel Sanderson, assistant district attorney for the City of New York. We're prosecuting Humphrey Richards for his role in the Morrow Gang's counterfeiting scheme."

"Ah, so you have ascertained who is behind the operation." At his blank expression, I quoted, "'The Morrow Gang.'"

"Yes, well"—he shifted in his chair—"let us call it a working theory. We have no proof, but would be very interested in interviewing him."

"I see. And what is your goal in coming here, rather than

waiting in the comfort of your office for Mrs. Richards to make her appearance on the appointed day?"

"Ah, Wynch mentioned your blunt manner of speaking."

Did he, now? One had to wonder what else Frank might have shared with the man. "How do you two know each other? I've never heard him speak of you."

"I don't know him personally—the district attorney does. Wynch did some work for our office years ago. When we learned Mrs. Richards was not, in fact, properly married to Humphrey Richards, and that her real name was Miss Flora Wynch, my boss thought it too much of a coincidence. We contacted Frank, and he told us where she was likely to be."

That made sense. "From what I understand, you deposed her shortly after that, via her written statement."

He gave a snort. "An account so evasive as to be practically meaningless. Perhaps you don't realize, and I do hate to point it out—as you are a family relation—but she is not an entirely trustworthy woman."

Hardly news to me, but I kept my expression neutral as he continued.

"She claims to know nothing about the business dealings of her—well, for the sake of simplicity and decorum, let us continue to refer to him as her *husband*. However, we find her claims of ignorance difficult to believe. He had a workshop at their home. We believe she can identify those who may lead us to Morrow. The ringleader has eluded us so far."

"How can you be so sure Flora can identify anyone?" *Besides Jimmy the Bagger*, I amended silently. She would have to be forthcoming with Sanderson about that.

"To begin with," he pronounced his words slowly and deliberately, as if addressing a dim-witted child, "her abrupt departure just before Richards' arrest implies guilty knowledge."

"Or the lady's desire to free herself from a brutish man," I said acidly. Sanderson's high-handed manner grated upon me.

I was being contrary, since the man's instincts were basically correct, though I doubted he'd have any luck catching the mastermind behind the scheme based on the bits and pieces Flora had recounted to me. But that wasn't my problem. Keeping my sister-in-law safe was. And the gloved hand grasping the catwalk rope was fresh in my mind.

"Let us return to your purpose in coming here," I said. "Do you intend to serve as protection for Flora until such time as she is interviewed by the district attorney?" Frank should have sent a bodyguard, not this pompous government official. "Are you armed?"

"What an impertinent question, and completely beside the point." He sniffed. "The woman should have returned to New York already. I don't understand why you would allow her to indulge in delusions of fame rather than compelling her to promptly carry out her civic duty. And now her life has been put in danger—evidenced by a second-story man breaking in. Clearly, a firm hand is needed. That's why I'm here."

"'A firm hand,'" I echoed faintly. The only *firm hand* here was my own, in controlling my temper.

His mustache quirked. "Don't feel badly, Mrs. Wynch— these are dangerous people." He gave a sigh worthy of one of the players in the theater company. "Wynch is getting sentimental in his advancing age, it seems. Sending his wife to do a man's job."

I ignored the gibe about Frank's age. This fellow wasn't much younger than he. And the *man's job* remark was a common bromide not worth wasting my breath upon. "You will compel her to leave by the morning train, then?" I should like to see how he'd accomplish that.

"Not exactly. A difficulty as arisen." He hesitated.

I folded my hands in my lap. "Yes?"

"One of the counterfeit plates Humphrey Richards made was never recovered. We believe she has it."

That changed things considerably. Visions of an extensive

police search of the entire hotel—and perhaps the theater, too —sprung to mind. And Greta looking on, mortified and seething. Not a pretty picture.

I didn't wish to believe it of Flora, and yet it better explained our intruder. The knife he'd carried was a poor assassin's tool but handy for self-defense, as I knew all too well.

What I didn't understand, however, was Flora's motive for taking the plate in the first place. A dangerous move, and what it gained for her in the end was unclear. She couldn't possibly use it herself.

"Mrs. Wynch?" his voice broke into my thoughts. "Are you attending me?"

"Oh, sorry. What were you saying?"

"I was saying that we must get the plate back, but discreetly."

I blinked. "Wouldn't it be better to confront Flora and, if she doesn't cooperate, bring in the authorities to conduct a search of the hotel?"

He grimaced. "That would be my first inclination, believe me. But it's more complicated than that. We don't want to risk eroding public confidence in the security of our currency. A search of this scope would be bound to draw the press."

An outraged Greta Marlowe would make sure of that. "The missing plate isn't general knowledge, I take it?"

"No, indeed. When the arrests first took place and the counterfeit scheme was reported by the press, our office announced that all the plates were recovered before any money had been printed."

I folded my arms. "And you knew this to be a false statement?"

"Not quite. We'd captured Richards and two others— likely couriers for the distributors. But no ringleader. And no one was talking."

"What made you suspect, then, that a plate was missing?"

"The first plate that counterfeiters typically make—and

oftentimes the only one—is the twenty-dollar bill. That's the biggest payoff for them—small enough to circulate without attracting notice, but profitable against their expenses." He took a breath. "And a few questionable twenties were confiscated recently at a local pawnshop."

"And you didn't find the twenty-dollar plate?"

"Only a fifty and a one-hundred. And there's no evidence of a destroyed plate."

"Flora may not have it," I pointed out. "Perhaps the ringleader had taken it into his keeping, particularly if he feared you were close to making arrests." Even as I said it, however, I didn't really believe it. Why, then, would someone break into Greta's suite?

"Let us hope she has it," he said. "And for her sake, that we find it."

"Is it that urgent? Surely, Flora doesn't have the means to use it for criminal purposes, and you have plenty of evidence already."

"This is a desperate group, Mrs. Wynch. I mentioned that we'd arrested three men. Last week"—he cleared his throat, his voice rough with emotion—"two of them were found dead in their cells. We don't know how it was done. Obviously, someone was bribed."

A feeling of dread plucked at my abdomen. "Was Humphrey Richards one of them?"

He shook his head. "Fortunately, we'd moved him to solitary confinement early on. He's safe for now."

"I wish I'd known this from the beginning," I said. "It would have changed my entire approach."

"Hardly information one can put in a telegram," Sanderson said dryly. "Your husband didn't know about the plate—only the district attorney and myself."

"And the Department of the Treasury, of course," I said.

The rocker creaked as he shifted. "We reported the plates we'd found, naturally, and yes, they are technically in charge of the investigation. However, my boss wants us to recover the missing plate ourselves, since it slipped through our fingers to begin with. We have our reputation to consider. Once we find it, we'll turn it over to the federal agents. That's why I'm here —to personally oversee matters."

"How do you propose going about this discreetly? You can hardly creep up the stairs and search Flora's belongings." He couldn't even register as a guest to monitor the lady, as the hotel was full.

"That's where you come in. Wynch says you have some talent in such matters."

Frank had communicated a great deal about me, it seemed.

"I know it will be difficult to accomplish," he went on, no doubt misinterpreting my silence for resistance, "but it's our best option. I want to return to New York with both Mrs. Richards and the plate and get this case wrapped up." He puffed out his chest. "Who knows, producing both may coerce Humphrey Richards to give up the whereabouts of the ringleader."

An ambitious fellow, riding his success on the backs of the women doing all the work.

"Aren't you concerned that a delay puts Flora at risk?" I asked. "The gang may strike again. There was an incident at the theater today, in fact. Someone—the culprit has not been found—loosened a rope that sent the catwalk crashing down on stage. It narrowly missed her."

Sanderson blinked in surprise. "Indeed? Are you sure she was the target?"

How odd, Flora had asked the same question. "I cannot account for it otherwise."

He waved a dismissive hand. "Between the two of us, we can keep her safe for the next day or so. The sooner you find the plate, the better. When can you search?"

"My best opportunity will be while everyone is the theater,

but someone needs to keep an eye on Flora there, given what happened today."

"I can do that."

I frowned. "The director will hardly allow you, a stranger, to be lurking about. You'll need a cover story."

"What would you suggest? Keep in mind, Mrs. Richards can't know what we're up to. If she catches on, she may destroy the plate or send it to someone."

"She may also bolt," I added. "Yes, I understand you perfectly."

"I think it would be best if I were an old acquaintance of yours," he said. "That way, our conversations won't attract notice. And we cannot use my real name. When she was first interviewed by the local authorities, my name was on the papers authorizing the deposition."

"She mentioned that, yes," I said slowly. I felt incredibly tired. Perhaps the day was catching up to me. I struggled to think of something even as banal as a name for him.

"Penelope?" a voice called from the doorway. It was Greta, who crossed the room in graceful strides. "Miss Leigh has been looking for you. And who is this?" she asked, as Sanderson stood.

He hesitated, mouth open.

The man was obviously ill-suited to improvisation. The task had fallen to me. "This is...Leonard Frasier," I blurted out.

Drat. Why did I say that? Well, there was no help for it now. "He's an old friend who's in town on business," I added.

"Ah." She held out a delicate hand, which Sanderson clasped and made a bow over. "And what is your business, Mr. Frasier?"

Again, Sanderson gaped.

Ugh, the fellow was trying my nerves. "He's a theater agent from New York. He's interested in seeing Flora perform," I improvised recklessly.

Greta's gaze lingered appreciatively over Sanderson's tailored suit, neat collar, and gold chain. At least he was dressed for the role.

"I hope you don't mind that I took the liberty of sending a telegram to Mr. Frasier," I went on. I was starting to get into the spirit of the story. "Since Flora won't have the chance to continue with the company when it heads to Philadelphia because of her...errand, I thought this opportunity might compensate her for her trouble." I was deep into it now. Greta would be furious when she discovered the pretense. With any luck, though, I'd never see these people again.

"That was most kind of you, dear." Greta was practically purring. She perched upon the settee, gesturing to a chair across from her. "Please, sir, make yourself comfortable. Tell me about your work. What qualities do you seek in the players? Flora has shown a natural talent for *soubrette* roles."

Sanderson cast a look of sheer helplessness over his shoulder as I sidled to the door.

I'd carried him as far as I intended to. *Time for a firm hand, Mr. Sanderson.*

I stifled the laugh that threatened to bubble up. "If you two will excuse me, I must find Miss Leigh."

I let myself out.

CHAPTER 9

FRIDAY, MARCH 9

The household was stirring early today, as tonight was the Pierson Players' first performance. Even before Cassie and I went down to breakfast, the anticipation was evident in the brisk steps along the corridor and the excited chatter of voices.

I'd told Cassie last night all about Daniel Sanderson and his mission, including my unfortunate slip in ascribing a pseudonym for him.

Her eyes twinkled in amusement.

"Don't say it," I said wearily. "I already know—I let Mother's telegram cloud my thinking. In my defense, Mr. Sanderson bears some similarity to him."

She chuckled. "You notice I didn't say a thing. But there's no harm done. Leonard is in Boston and will never know."

As we were tidying the room before heading to breakfast, she asked, "So, what's our plan for today? Are you going to search for the counterfeit plate?"

"Not during the day. Too many servants about. I wish I

could search during tonight's performance, but we've been invited to attend—as Barrett Ward's personal guests, no less. It would cause undo notice if we declined at the last minute."

"True," she conceded. "I suppose you'll have to wait until one of the Saturday performances, either the matinee or the evening."

"The latter, most likely, though it's hard to be patient."

"If Flora has it," Cassie said, "it isn't going anywhere. Not without her, that is."

"It's important that she not be alerted to my search. I'll have to be circumspect."

"You do that exceedingly well," she commented with a straight face. "What, then, are we doing today?"

"I think we should divide our tasks. Sanderson said he would stay at the theater in his guise of talent scout and monitor Flora. I would like you to go to the theater as well."

"You don't trust him?"

"Not exactly, but he doesn't think on his feet all that well. He froze when Greta came into the library yesterday. He may require your quick wits."

Cassie blushed charmingly at the compliment.

"Besides," I went on, "Rose might return to the theater. She must realize her job is at stake. If you see her, find out where she's been, and learn what you can about the man we saw talking to her—who he is and what she knows of his doings."

Her mouth quirked. "Is that all?"

I smiled.

"What will you be doing?" she asked.

"I'm going to try to find our wounded intruder. If he is indeed Rose's brother, I have a name, a general description, and a place to start my inquiry. Sally was helpful in that regard."

Cassie nodded. "She's a kind soul. It's unfortunate that she's saddled with all of Rose's work."

Breakfast was a quick affair, as Pierson was impatient to get everyone to the theater. He really was a funny little man, I reflected, watching him pace from table to table, thumbs hooked in the armholes of his russet-checked vest, standing over Flora and Greta as they lingered over their teacups.

Barrett Ward got out of his chair at Pierson's urging, tossing aside his napkin in good-natured exuberance. "Well then, let us get this show on the road, as they say."

Davis, who was helping Viola with her crutches, cast a quick glance at Ward, then Pierson.

I was missing something, but since it had nothing to do with Flora, Sanderson, or Rose, I decided it was best to focus on the task at hand.

I wrapped warmly against what I expected to be a windy, chilly March day, but I was pleasantly surprised to find it warmer than usual, even a trifle humid. I stuffed my scarf in my pocket—the one that held a handful of coins. My derringer was in the other pocket. Today I anticipated palm-pressing would be more likely than waving a gun around, but it was best to be prepared for both.

I took the streetcar to the corner of Church and Lafayette and walked down the block towards the Mission, set in an old storefront whose awning had come down long ago. Only the rusted bolts remained. But I knew I was in the right place, for painted upon the fly-specked, plate-glass window were the words: *Church Street Mission. Hours: Noon until two, four until six.*

I was an hour early. I circled the building, hoping for an open kitchen door and staff inside who might already be cooking, but the place was locked up tight.

"Ya gonna have ta wait, ma'am," a rough male voice called out.

In the alley across the street, three men stood around a wood barrel, playing cards.

I dodged a dairyman's dray as I crossed over to them.

They watched in curiosity as I approached. One fellow,

wearing a fraying houndstooth cap, said, "Don't look like yer in want o' a meal, lady."

The others chuckled, sending one man into a coughing fit. He politely turned away to spit downwind of me.

"Nah," another said, "she must be one of the sisters who works there. You're new, though," he added, raking me with a jaundiced gaze, "and much too pretty to be pouring coffee for the likes of us." He self-consciously smoothed his shaggy beard.

The third leaned towards the long-bearded fellow and said, in a more-than-audible whisper, "I bet she can reach the pots they got hanging up high, though!" He laughed at his own joke.

Chatty fellows. The best kind for what I wanted.

"I'm looking for someone," I said. "He comes here for a meal from time to time. Bobby Harper. About so tall"—I held a hand up to my chin—"slight build, blond hair, good at climbing."

The long-bearded fellow narrowed his watery eyes. "What do you be wanting with *him*?"

I fingered the money in my pocket, unobtrusively singled out three coins, and clasped them in my palm. "I don't want to cause him trouble, if that's what you mean."

I meant it—Bobby was a minor player. I was after the man who'd hired him. And I wanted to find Rose and be sure she was safe.

"His sister is quite worried about him," I added.

"Well, ah—if we see him, we'll let 'im know," the man in the cap said.

"I would prefer to talk to him myself." I held up a coin.

The bearded fellow eyed it with interest. "Haven't seen 'im in a week."

The third man snorted. "That usually means he's on a job and can feed his-self. But he'll be back."

I handed the coin to the third man, who deftly tucked it away.

I held up another. "Where else does he go?"

The second coin was irresistible to the fellow in the cap. "There's 'nother place across town—in the basement of the Masonic Lodge, on 30th Street. The coffee's not bad, but ya have to sit through a sermon on how to improve yourself."

The shaggy-bearded man gave a snort of derision. "Nothin's ever free these days."

True enough. I passed over the coin. "Thank you."

The Masonic Lodge was equally disappointing in terms of results. No one had seen Harper in the past week. I sighed. Either he was hunkered down somewhere or long gone, and Rose with him.

There was nothing more to be done today about finding them. I returned to the theater.

Cassie and Sanderson were standing just off the left wing, chatting in low murmurs while Pierson and Greta spoke with a tearful Flora.

I touched Cassie's arm. "What's happened?"

She grimaced. "Nothing nefarious, just opening night nerves, I expect. She's forgetting her lines."

"Then nothing untoward has happened?"

Sanderson shrugged. "All is as it should be."

"Any sign of Rose?" I asked Cassie.

"None." She grimaced. "Chaffee is furious. Sally's trying to do the work of two. I've offered to help—she's going to bring some pieces back to the hotel for me to hem. Did you make any progress in your inquiry?"

I shook my head.

Sanderson perked up at that. "May I have a word, Mrs. Wynch?"

Cassie remained where she was, watching the progress upon the stage. Flora had dried her tears and was giving it another go.

Sanderson drew me deeper into the curtained recess of the wing. "What did Miss Leigh mean by 'inquiry'? I thought you would use this opportunity to search for the plate."

"It wasn't my intention to mislead you in that regard. Searching Greta's apartment is nearly impossible during the daytime. There are too many servants underfoot. I've been trying to locate our intruder."

"Intruder?" His frown cleared. "Ah, you mean the fellow you allowed to get away?"

"I wounded him first," I replied tartly. "Sufficient to deter him from making a return."

"Then why search for him now? A needle in a haystack. You must know he's long gone."

"Possibly," I admitted. "On the other hand, he may be too injured to travel." I recounted seeing him with Rose, followed by her disappearance, and what I'd subsequently learned about the man. "If I can find him, I may be able to learn who hired him," I finished.

His expression sobered, and he was quiet for a long while. I seemed to have plucked a nerve. A competent lady detective? How to reconcile such an aberration.

"I must concede," he said at last, "you have made impressive progress. Though it will hardly matter once we have Mrs. Richards and the plate in my keeping and safely on their way to New York. We must maintain our focus upon that, madam, not chase side alleys for former principals who no longer have a role to play." He grinned, seeming to recover his good humor. "The air of the stage is making its mark upon me, *ha ha*."

I gritted my teeth and reminded myself that Frank asked me to assist this fellow.

"Former principal or not," I said, "where there's one crook for hire, there are sure to be others to take his place. I don't believe the counterfeiters have given up. They must know, as we do, that Flora has the plate hidden away somewhere."

He nodded his agreement. "You will conduct your search tonight?"

I grimaced. "I'm already committed to attending the opening night performance. Tomorrow will suffice."

His face creased in a scowl. "You're going to gad about in your female finery and watch a play instead of doing your job?"

A few heads on stage swiveled toward the sharp tone. Pierson frowned in our direction.

I clenched my fists in the folds of my skirt and dropped my voice by sheer effort of will. "Barrett Ward invited us to attend the opening as his special guests. To decline at this point would draw far more attention than we could wish. The plans were in place before your arrival and certainly before I was aware there was an object for me to locate. If Flora does have the plate, it will still be wherever she's secreted it. After all, she has no idea of who you really are and what you're after."

"You'd better be right—"

I put a quick hand on his arm to silence him. I tipped my head, listening.

"What is it?" he whispered.

I shifted the curtain. Several workmen were winding rope and stowing tools, but none was close enough to have heard us. I shook my head. "Never mind."

"How do I look?" Cassie swished the skirt of her evening gown in delight.

We were in borrowed finery this evening, as neither of us had brought the sort of attire one wears for theatergoing. Kay had lent Cassie a charming chartreuse lace confection, with close-fitting sleeves, a full taffeta skirt, and a froth of organdy at the throat.

I was attired in a high-necked gown of myrtle satin, courtesy of Miss Templeton's prodigious wardrobe. As it had been loose in the bodice and short at the hem, Sally had tacked in the waist and basted in a ribbon of forest-green lace at the bottom edge. She had also borrowed a few pieces from the theater's vast collection of female fripperies—a faux-pearl necklace and white-feathered fascinator for me, and a delicate tiara of paste emeralds and diamonds for Cassie. The effect against my friend's dark hair was striking, and quite sophisticated.

"Positively regal," I said.

Her pale complexion pinked. "And you as well. Let me just fix this." She reached up to adjust my fascinator. "It tends to lean."

We descended the stairs. All was quiet, as everyone in the company had gone ahead to the theater immediately after an early dinner. I glanced back up the steps ruefully. It would have indeed been the ideal time to search for the plate.

"Forget something?" Cassie asked.

I shook my head.

We deemed our evening pumps unwalkable and took a hansom. It was slow going, however, as the line of carriages approaching the theater meant we were inching our way towards the middle of the block.

"Sorry about the traffic, ladies," the cabbie called down. "It's going to be a good opening, though! Look at all the people!"

Indeed, a veritable throng was making its way up the stone steps into the theater by the time we pulled up to the curb and were handed down. The pair of grand, rosewood doors had been thrown open wide, and we easily followed the crowd into a capacious vestibule.

Glittering lights from the crystal chandeliers illuminated

the festive couples and families in their best attire. Staircases at our right and our left, ornamented to resemble Venetian balconies, led to the galleries above.

I didn't know what to rest my eyes upon first—the gleaming brass handrails, the plush burgundy carpet, the oak-panel scrollwork—as we made our way in.

"Tickets, ladies?" a man dressed in an usher's uniform inquired.

I handed them over.

"Ah, first row! You must be Mr. Ward's special guests," he said eagerly. "He told us to look out for you." He waved to another fellow in similar attire, standing beside the orchestra pit, who hurried up to us. "Freddie here will escort you to your seats and take care of anything you may require. Enjoy the show."

As we followed the second usher to our seats, Cassie whispered, "Barrett Ward is quite esteemed, isn't he?"

"I suppose," I said absently as we passed beneath the balcony. I'd never understood why the first row was considered a privileged spot. In my mind, it feels as if one is staring up at the players' ankles. I would have preferred an elevated position.

As we approached the family section, I saw Sanderson, smartly attired in black evening tails and white waistcoat, step into the aisle to allow an elderly woman and her husband to pass.

He caught sight of me and gave a bow. "Mrs. Wynch... Miss Leigh...how charming to see you again. Such excitement in the air tonight!"

"Yes, indeed," I answered.

"Why are you all the way back here?" Cassie asked. "I would have thought Greta would insist upon a front row seat for you to observe Flora."

He grimaced. "Never cared for the front row. Told her I

wanted to get a sense of how well her protégé could project back here."

Smart. Perhaps there was hope for him as a dissembler, after all.

We were blocking the aisle, so we said our goodbyes and moved along.

Cassie pulled out a pair of opera glasses once we'd settled in our seats.

"Where did you get those?"

"Kay lent them to me."

I chuckled. "You'll hardly need them here, short of inspecting any spots on Ward's cravat."

She shrugged as she applied it to her eyes. "It keeps me occupied." Suddenly, she stiffened.

"What is it?"

"Chaffee, Pierson, and Sally—in what appears to be a distressing conversation." She passed me the glasses. "There, off to the right. It's a little hard to see. They're standing in the shadow between the stage apron and the emergency exit."

I squinted through the lenses, trying to see where—ah, yes.

Sally was hiding her face in her father's chest and obviously crying. Chaffee absently patted her back, but his scowl in Pierson's direction was unmistakable. Pierson, for his part, wore a rueful expression, but otherwise appeared unperturbed.

"What's happening?" Cassie whispered.

"Chaffee's pushing his daughter aside…. Oh dear, I think he's going to strike the fellow—"

I saw no more, as the house lights dimmed and the audience applauded the rising curtain.

Comedies were not generally my favorite form of entertainment, but this one was diverting enough and received several hearty laughs from the audience—most importantly, at the points where one *should* laugh.

With all the rehearsals I'd witnessed this week, I was able

to identify some of the corrections they'd made, and a few of the less successful changes. Ward, for example, kept forgetting that he was now supposed to stand to Flora's left instead of to her right, with the result being that he would remember mid-line and take a few dancing side-steps to correct himself. Poor Flora was forced to swivel her head to keep up with him.

Mary played her unsubtle role as the hapless-in-love "Amazonian" to great comedic effect. Two women I didn't recognize—recruited from the local drama society last-minute to cover the remaining secondary female roles, Cassie whispered—did passably well. Davis and Jasper pronounced their lines with professional ease, though Davis nearly backed into a potted plant at one point.

Flora was the surprising success of the night. It's a truism that one cannot predict how a live performance will turn out based upon rehearsals, and tonight certainly proved it. Her movements on stage were fluid, assured; her voice projected clearly and carried nuances of emotion that I had not expected.

Cassie noticed, too. "She's actually quite good," she murmured. "It's a shame she doesn't have a genuine theatrical agent to observe her."

"Who knows?" I whispered back. "Perhaps one is in attendance tonight."

When the curtain finally dropped to enthusiastic applause, Cassie and I decided to skip the numerous curtain calls that were sure to follow and exit ahead of the crush. An attendant was running up the side of the stage with a floral bouquet. Perhaps we could get a head start on the line of carriages waiting outside.

Despite our best efforts, it was quite late when we returned to the hotel. Of course, we were still well ahead of the cast.

Kay Finnerty came down the stairs as the maid was helping us out of our wraps. "Cassie, my goodness—the gown looks stunning on you."

Cassie smiled. "Thank you for the loan—I'll go up and change out of it right now."

Kay waved a hand. "Nonsense. There's plenty of time to return it. Besides, there's a buffet laid in the salon for everyone's return. Won't you come?"

"You seem to be feeling better," I observed.

The young lady grinned. "Oh yes. In fact, I plan to attend the matinee performance tomorrow, so don't tell me how everyone fared—I want to see for myself."

"I can imagine," I said, as we followed her up the stairs to the salon, "but wouldn't you like to know whether there will even be a matinee tomorrow?"

Kay's face fell. "No—it was that bad?"

Cassie chuckled. "Pen's just teasing you. On the contrary, it was a rousing success."

Kay clutched her chest in a mock-dramatic gesture. "Thank goodness for that."

Miss Templeton was already ensconced upon the sofa in the music salon, sipping tentatively from her cup. She grimaced. "Would one of you mind bringing over the cream?"

Cassie went to fetch it. Kay and I sat down across from her.

Miss Templeton looked me up and down. "I wouldn't have thought my gown would fit. You seemed to have made it work."

I inclined my head, recognizing the remark as the closest I would come to a compliment from the woman. "Thank you for allowing me to borrow it. Sally has promised to restore the dress to its original condition tomorrow and have it promptly returned."

Miss Templeton shrugged and gestured to her ankle. "I won't be attending any formal affairs in the near future."

"It is no better after all this time?" I asked. "You may want the doctor to look at it again."

Miss Templeton stiffened. "The man is a quack. I want

him nowhere near me unless I'm bleeding to death." She must have caught the dubious glance Kay and I exchanged, for she added defensively, "If you must know, my ankle *had* started feeling better yesterday, but I tried walking on it in my room and reinjured myself."

"How unfortunate," I said.

"Yes, of course," Kay soothed. "No one's doubting you, dear."

"I do not like being hobbled, believe me," she said plaintively. "Being waited upon lost its appeal long ago. And sleeping in the housekeeper's quarters is not my idea of comfort."

Cassie returned with the cream pitcher.

"Being stuck in the hotel, however, has not been without its excitement," Miss Templeton continued. "There was a disturbance a little while ago."

"Oh? Of what sort?" I asked.

"I was reading downstairs in the parlor when I heard shouting. I had just reached the corridor to see what was happening when a man hurried by—nearly knocked me down —and then one of the footmen ran past soon after."

"Oh my," Cassie said. "Who was it? A thief?"

"If so, he was a very well-dressed one," Miss Templeton said with a laugh. "He was wearing an evening jacket and white-silk waistcoat."

Every instinct told me it must have been Sanderson, slipping away from the play early to take matters into his own hands.

"Why was he being chased?" Cassie asked.

I had a bad feeling about this.

"I was told that the footman found him lurking in the stairwell on the fourth floor," Miss Templeton said. "When the fellow fled, the servant pursued him."

"Did he catch him?" Kay asked.

I held my breath for the answer, but the lady shook her head.

"Does anyone know who he is?" Cassie asked.

Before Miss Templeton could answer, we were interrupted by the arrival of the Pierson Players.

Viola plucked at my arm amid the hubbub. I leaned close.

"I was the only one who got a good look at him." She flashed me a mischievous grin. "I could have sworn it was your friend, Mr. Frasier. But that makes no sense, does it, Mrs. Wynch?"

CHAPTER 10

SATURDAY, MARCH 10

The buoyant mood continued over the breakfast table, as Greta read aloud from the reviews of the play.

"Last night marked the debut of Miss Flora Wynch, a previous unknown in the acting sphere. The lady's depth of feeling as the aggrieved-but-scheming Maggie Chillingham is striking in one so young, and her strongest scenes were met with wild applause." Greta smiled at her great-niece and resumed reading, "This reviewer will be watching her budding career with great interest."

Mary Reid leaned forward eagerly. "Any mention of the supporting players?"

"You're in this one." Flora obligingly passed over one of the news sheets. "Keep it. We bought several copies."

Barrett Ward, usually absent at an early breakfast, had made an exception this time. He took a seat beside Mary, read over her shoulder, then looked up with a horrified expression. "'Mincing steps'…what in thunder does that mean?"

Greta and Flora exchanged an amused glance.

Pierson, who was reading from his own stack of papers at a table apart from the others, lowered his sheet and called over, "It means, Barrett, that for today's matinee, you'll need to keep your stage left and stage right directions straight. You were practically dancing around poor Flora last night."

Barrett opened his mouth to retort, but Pierson waved a placating hand. "Now, now—a minor detail, not worth getting worked up over. Read the review in the *Morning Journal*, where they refer to you as the 'dark-haired Corinthian'—that'll cheer you up."

Archie Jasper hurried into the dining room at that moment, still shrugging on his morning coat, his usual clean-shaven face shadowed with bits of stubble. "So—how are the reviews?"

"Wonderful," Miss Reid breathed.

Pierson gestured to Jasper to join him. "You're mentioned in this one." He passed him a paper. The fellow read it avidly.

I got up to add some toast to my plate and passed their table. Pierson was leaning close to Jasper, and I just caught what he whispered as I helped myself to the chafing dishes.

"We'll be making a change in Philadelphia, Archie. I want you to assume the part of Maxwell."

Jasper's eyes widened. "What about Barrett?" he murmured.

"I'll tell him tomorrow—when we're finished with the Southbrook performances. Keep it to yourself for now."

"Naturally."

Oh ho, Ward wouldn't like that at all. Not my concern, of course. I had business of my own to settle, including giving Sanderson a piece of my mind for nearly blowing his cover, not to mention undermining our chances of retrieving the counterfeit plate. I'd rather not risk him coming here to discuss it, though. If Miss Templeton saw him, she might decide to tell Greta on the spot. I'd send a note to his lodging and arrange a time to meet.

Another question troubled me. How did Miss Templeton know Sanderson—that is Mr. Frasier—in the first place? I would have to ask Sanderson about that.

I was just about to excuse myself when a maid came in with an envelope for me—securely sealed this time.

Sanderson had anticipated me, it seemed.

You have no doubt heard about last night and surmised it was me. Please meet me at the Mercer Gardens in an hour so we can talk.

Yours, DS

"Is everything all right?" Cassie asked, as I tucked the paper away.

I made a face. "Let us hope so."

The public garden near the town square, though chilly this time of year, was as good a venue as any for such a meeting. The space was replete with benches and an open-air gazebo where couples could sit and converse without raising eyebrows.

I spotted him—he was wearing a gray sack coat and dark bowler today, but the lustrous mustache and side-whiskers made him unmistakable—over by the benches encircling the drained fountain.

He gave a bow at my approach. "Good morning, Mrs. Wynch. Surprisingly mild weather we're having today, is it not?"

"I'm not interested in small talk, Mr. Sanderson. I want to know why you were so foolish as to sneak into the hotel and attempt to break into Greta's suite."

He ducked his head sheepishly. "I had no plans to *break in*. I merely wanted to see where their quarters were situated." At the sight of my skeptical expression, he added, "Well, perhaps

I intended to try the door handle, just in case someone had neglected to lock it."

I blew out an exasperated breath. "You didn't get that far, from what I heard."

"Dratted footman saw me peeking through the door of the stairwell to check the hall. Those carpets are so thick I couldn't hear the fellow moving about. I had no idea anyone was up there." He spread his hands in apology. "I am not accustomed to skulking and prying."

"That's why you need to leave the skulking and prying to professionals," I said tartly. "Like it or not, Mr. Sanderson, I am such a person. I have both the tools and the experience to proceed in this matter, whereas you do not. I would appreciate you leaving such tasks to me in the future."

"Yes, ma'am," he said meekly.

"We have the additional problem of Viola Templeton recognizing you as you ran out."

"So that's who I nearly bumped into," he murmured. "She came out so suddenly, I barely had time to dodge out of the way. Who else did she tell?"

"No one that I know of—yet. Greta and Flora are unaware. They've been absorbed in the theater columns. What I don't understand is how Miss Templeton knows you— by your alias, that is."

"Mrs. Marlowe and I encountered her on our way out of the library the day I arrived. It was a good while after you left. Mrs. Marlowe made the introductions." He grimaced. "Nosy sort. Was lingering near the door."

"Was she, now?" I hoped that was the only time the woman had been hovering nearby.

Sanderson broke into my thoughts. "Do you think she'll say anything?"

I had no illusions about Miss Templeton's discretion. "When it suits her, she will. You'll need an excuse prepared for that eventuality."

"What sort of excuse?"

Must I think of everything? I stifled a sigh.

When I didn't answer, he went on, "Do you still insist upon waiting until this evening's performance to search Mrs. Marlowe's suite? The matinee would suit better. If you can recover it then, I'll at least have time to telegraph the office with word that it has been secured. Tonight would be too late for that, and the telegraph offices are closed on Sunday."

Ah, so that was why he was so anxious. "Have your superiors been giving you difficulties about the missing plate?"

"Not exactly." He shrugged. "But it never hurts to make a favorable impression. So, what do you think? Will you give it a try?"

I had to admit, I was curious about the plate, too, and waiting was not one of my strengths. "I'll watch for an opportunity, but I cannot promise. I'll send a note if I'm successful."

"Excellent," he said enthusiastically. "Perhaps we should work out a code, in case your note is read by another."

I rolled my eyes. "Hardly necessary."

"No, no, I think it's a good precaution." His brows drew together as he thought. "What about—'child found in good health.' That would be for when you find the plate," he clarified, as if I were as obtuse as the aforementioned child. "And 'child still missing' if you come up empty. What do you think?"

"I have no words," I said dryly. "All right, we'll do it your way."

I returned just as the cast was leaving for their matinee performance. Kay went with them. Although she was not going to perform, her excitement at the outing was conveyed by her pink cheeks, shining eyes, and brisk step as she climbed into the carriage with Greta, Flora, and Mary to ride to the theater.

As things quieted down in the hotel—not even Miss Templeton was underfoot today, having retired to her room with a headache—I began to wonder if I might be able to get into Greta's apartment after all.

Cassie was in the library, knitting. I poked my head in. "Do you have some free time?"

She tucked away her work. "What do you need?"

"I require your services as a lookout once again," I murmured, then froze as we passed the first-floor window of the foyer.

"What is it?"

I gestured to the window. Sanderson was across the street, idling by a lamp post. To give him credit, he carried a newspaper that he glanced at on occasion, but when he caught sight of me, he tucked the paper under his arm, waved, and gave me a thumbs-up sign.

"Mercy," I muttered.

"Oh dear," Cassie said, following my gaze.

Sanderson gave her a wave as well.

My best option was to ignore him and hope none of the staff noticed him.

I retrieved my lockpicks on our way to the fourth floor. At the top of the stairwell—the one that extended to the roof—we waited, listening. I heard the voices of maids in Greta's apartment, chattering as they finished up their work. Then, finally, the sounds of retreating footsteps, heading toward the far stairwell. I didn't know what Sanderson was complaining about—I could hear the footfalls without difficulty.

Once we were alone, Cassie whispered, "What if someone comes? There's no wall to tap on. You'll be too far away."

"Keep out of sight up on the landing near the roof exit," I said. "If you hear someone on these stairs, come down to meet them and create a diversion that's loud enough for me to hear."

She grinned. "Is the choice of diversion entirely at my discretion?"

I smiled back. "Absolutely."

"What about the other stairwell?" she asked.

"I'll wedge that door shut. One would assume it's sticking."

"Good luck," Cassie said.

I was going to need it.

It's a little unnerving to proceed by stealth in daylight. I felt as exposed as a hunted rabbit as I moved past the bright windows along the hall. I blew out a breath for courage, pulled out my picks, and set to work.

A newer lock such as this took me longer, but I eventually had it open. Before going in, I hesitated, listening. Not a peep from the stairwell or from within. I slipped inside and shut the door quietly behind me.

Flora's bedroom door was to my left, the door unlocked. I went in there first.

The room was well appointed, with space for a small divan and occasional table, a vanity table swathed in lace curtains, a dresser, an enormous armoire, and a tall poster bed. After searching behind every door, under the bed, and in all the drawers, I had to concede there wasn't anything even resembling a plate to be found.

Next, I headed to Greta's bedroom, pausing in the apartment's foyer to listen for Cassie's voice. Silence. Satisfied, I moved on.

Greta's room was more spacious than Flora's and contained an impressively sized dressing closet. The results were the same, however. No plate.

I returned to the large living room between the two bedrooms. This was the only area left.

Where could the plate be hidden in such an open space as this, where the risk of discovery was greater?

Perhaps Greta had a safe. That would make sense, since the woman possessed a number of expensive jewels, and I had only seen a handful—none of them terribly valuable—in a case on her dressing table.

I began my search for it, examining framed artwork, shifting lighter furniture pieces, and running my fingers along the decorative paneling near the fireplace.

It was the latter spot where I finally found it. One of the panels, when pushed, released an inner spring that popped it open and revealed a metal door with a combination lock.

Now what? I was no safe-cracker. We'd need help.

With a sigh, I pushed the panel back into position, restored the chair I'd shoved out of place, and left.

"A safe-cracker?" Sanderson exclaimed in surprise.

"That's why I came myself to tell you the news. We hadn't worked out a code for that one," I added wryly.

"Yes, that is a setback," he murmured.

An understatement, to say the least. I had no criminal contacts in Southbrook.

We were sitting in the drawing room of his lodging. It wasn't as large as the one at Marlowe House, but at least we had it to ourselves.

"Perhaps your husband knows someone in the area," he said.

"There's no time to contact Frank, wait for an answer, and then act on the information. Your best course now is to demand the safe be opened and searched, bringing in the police if Greta refuses." All too likely, I reflected.

"If we go to the police, we'll have to specify exactly what we seek," he protested. "Remember what I said about publicity?"

"You have little choice."

"Mrs. Marlowe may have the combination written down somewhere. You could search for that."

"It would be the height of foolishness to write down a safe combination," I retorted. "She's too shrewd."

He flashed me a smug smile. "Women are often foolish. Even the shrewd ones."

I would dearly love to wipe that smirk from his face, but the statement was true enough. "She may have written it down for Flora's benefit," I conceded reluctantly, "in case she wanted to use the safe for just such a purpose."

"Exactly."

A search of that sort would add time to an already risky endeavor, but we were out of options. One could hardly roam the streets in search of a safe-cracker.

"All right," I said finally. "We'll proceed as you say, on one condition."

"What's that?"

"That you give the hotel a wide berth tonight. The last thing I need is you lurking across the street and drawing attention to yourself. You increase the risk of my being caught."

He scowled briefly. "Very well."

"And you must be patient," I said. "I doubt I'll be able to send word before tomorrow. Agreed?"

"Of course."

Why did I have difficulty believing he would keep his word?

CHAPTER 11

*C*assie was pacing the foyer upon my arrival back at Marlowe House. "Oh, Pen! It took you forever to get back."

I barely had time to unpin my hat and hand my coat to the maid before Cassie dragged me by the elbow down the corridor.

"What on earth is going on?" I asked.

She came to an abrupt stop just as we reached the library door. "Leonard Frasier is here," she hissed.

"You mean Sanderson? That's impossible—I've just left him." I wished she wouldn't refer to the man by his alias. I was having a difficult enough time keeping track of all the moving parts of this case. It seemed to change on an hourly basis.

She shook her head vigorously. "No—*your* Leonard. The real Leonard Frasier."

I sat down abruptly on a bench. "My Leonard," I echoed.

Cassie sat down beside me. "Apparently your mother sent him to check on you."

Oh, Lord. "Where is he now?"

She nodded toward the door. "In there."

"Please tell me he didn't give his *name* to anyone when he arrived?" Of all the ridiculous predicaments to be in.

"I don't think so," she said. "He was approaching the check-in desk when I saw him. You could have knocked me over with a feather."

I could imagine. "When was this? I haven't been gone that long."

"Twenty minutes ago. I sort of scooped him up and deposited him in the empty library."

Bless the girl's quick-wittedness.

"I didn't provide him with any sort of explanation," she added. "I left that for you to handle."

I grimaced. It was a predicament of my own creation. I may as well be responsible for the cleaning up.

I stood and smoothed my skirts. "Well then, let's go greet the man."

Leonard was standing before the bookshelves that housed Greta's impressive collection of Shakespeare's plays, running a finger over the spines. At the sound of the door opening, he whipped around.

He was just as I'd remembered, and I wondered at ever seeing Sanderson's resemblance to him. Though both had wavy brown hair, Leonard's was touched by gray at the temples. Both were wide-shouldered, Leonard was leaner around the middle. Most of all, the difference was in the eyes —Sanderson's were a soft brown, and Leonard's were a shade of gray that changed according to his mood.

I extended a hand in greeting as Cassie took a seat at a discreet distance. "Leonard. It's a...surprise to see you here."

His warm, firm grip brought back long-forgotten times. Ballroom dances, open-air drives, lingering looks...as well as uneasy restlessness, childish excuses, and angry recriminations. It was a chest-constricting tidal wave of sensations that left me trying to catch my breath.

He observed me closely. It felt as if those steady gray eyes weren't missing much.

"Cassie expressed a similar sentiment," he said finally. "I thought your mother was going to send you a telegram to expect my arrival."

I shook my head. "She sent a telegram, but there was no mention of a visit."

"Strange."

Not so strange, I reflected wryly. Mother didn't want to afford me the chance to run off again.

"I regret the imposition, but I was hoping we could talk." He stepped back, smiling at me appreciatively. "You're looking well, Pen. Despite your mother's worries, it seems your profession suits you."

Cassie let out a chortle—poorly disguised as a hiccough—and kept her gaze on her needles.

"Let's sit down," I said. "We have a lot to cover before we're interrupted by other guests wishing to use the room."

Leonard frowned in Cassie's direction. "Yes, I do have some...questions."

As did I, but mine could wait. The sooner he understood our situation, the better. I settled upon the sofa, Leonard on the ottoman across from me.

"I assume your first question," I said, "is regarding Cassie's anxiety about you giving your name to the desk clerk."

"Exactly." He sat back and folded his arms. "Care to explain?"

His expression shifted from grave to annoyed to amused as I detailed the arrival of the assistant district attorney from New York who was taking over my case, followed by my spur-of-the-moment invention of one Leonard Frasier, theatrical agent.

Even Cassie, familiar as she was with the ignominious details, had to bite her lip to keep from laughing.

"That's, um, quite a story," he said, clearing his throat.

At least he wasn't angry.

I pressed on. "Your sudden presence complicates matters. Can we count upon your discretion? It's essential that Flora remain unaware of who Sanderson really is until he's ready to take her in charge." I'd omitted mention of the counterfeit plate. The story was complicated enough.

He shrugged. "I suppose, though what name I'm going to go by eludes me at the moment."

"We'll think of something," Cassie said.

"Nothing far-fetched or fanciful, ladies," he warned. "I wouldn't be able to keep up such a pretense."

"I doubt it will be necessary. The hotel has no rooms available. The place is full up because of the Pierson Players."

"How unfortunate." His face creased in disappointment. "I'd hoped to spend more time with you, Pen. I'll check with the clerk, just to be sure. Once you have an appropriate name for me," he added.

"That brings me to my questions," I said. "How long do you intend to stay, and why are you here?"

He glanced at Cassie. "It's rather private."

Cassie started to get up, but I waved her back.

"Whatever you want to say, you can say it in front of Cassie. I have no secrets from her. Besides, you've known her for as long as I have."

He flushed, then blew out a breath. "Yes, we've all been friends since we were children. I value that."

I smiled. "As do I. And I've appreciated your correspondence. I regret I haven't been as regular at my end."

Silence.

"It's unfortunate I had to leave Boston so abruptly before seeing you," I added politely.

He raised an eyebrow. "You mother is of the opinion that you deliberately ran out on the dinner she had planned."

Cassie shifted in her seat and yanked at her yarn ball.

I gritted my teeth. It didn't matter that the assessment was correct—Mother should never have said as much to Leonard. "I take it she has sent you as a proxy, to voice her grievance at my defection?"

He blinked at the ferocity of my tone. "Not at all. She's worried about you, as am I. Why did you leave?"

"I told her why," I answered. "I had a case."

He raised a skeptical brow. "That seems awfully convenient."

"Perhaps, but surely you can see what she is up to. My mother is the most meddlesome matchmaker, which is totally inappropriate in my case. She cannot accept the reality that I'm not a free woman."

"According to your father, whether you're free or not is entirely your choice."

If only my parents would refrain from airing my personal affairs. "Even if I were free, you and I tried this before, remember? Before I met Frank. It was obvious we didn't suit."

"Was it obvious?" he asked. "Not to me. Besides, that was a decade ago. People change. And the fact that we have remained friends—good friends—shows we're compatible." He reached over and clasped my hand. "Seeing you again— here—brings that home to me. Don't you know how I feel about you, Pen? I love you."

Cassie stood. "I'll be in the hall."

I barely registered her departure. I gently pulled my hand away, though I missed his warmth as soon as I did so. "Love me? I don't understand how that can be."

"You don't remember the last time we saw each other— when you worked at the Comstock mansion?"

"Yes, of course I remember."

How could I forget? It had been November of '85, and the first time I'd worked with Frank since our separation. The successful completion of the case had launched my solo work for William Pinkerton. I smiled to myself.

But Leonard misinterpreted my smile. "Ah, you do remember. The time we kissed on the balcony. You cannot tell me you didn't feel anything then."

Lord, I didn't remember that at all. What sort of hard-hearted woman was I, to overlook a tender moment? Shouldn't it have been a noteworthy occasion? It wasn't as if I went around kissing men at every turn.

Well, there had been *some* kisses since then. I felt a flush rise to my cheeks. And more than a little noteworthy. "So much has happened since then," I said softly. "All you and I have left are reminiscences. We barely know each other now."

He moved to sit beside me on the sofa. "I want to change that. If you would free yourself from Frank Wynch and open your heart to other possibilities, we could see what develops."

There were more romantic possibilities in my life already than I knew how to handle, without adding Leonard to the mix.

"That's not a step I'm prepared to take."

"I see." The disappointment in his voice was unmistakable.

We were quiet for a while, each lost in our own thoughts.

He leaned forward. "Can we at least spend some time together before you head back to Chicago?"

"We don't have much time to spare," I said apologetically. "Cassie and I leave tomorrow with Sanderson to escort Flora to New York. The plan is to head home to Chicago directly from there."

He scanned my expression, perhaps trying to assess the veracity of my statement. Not that I could blame him.

"At least allow me to take you to dinner," he said finally.

I wasn't sure how to answer that. Would dining with him convey the wrong impression?

The uncertainty must have shown on my face, for he added, "I have no expectations of convincing you to give up your life and follow me to the altar." His eyes took on a mischievous glint. "Although perhaps if I were the glamorous theater agent my namesake pretends to be…?" He winked.

I couldn't help but chuckle at that.

Cassie burst in the door. "Come quick! They're moving Rose's belongings out of her room."

I hurried to follow, with Leonard right behind.

Greta stood in the foyer—the cast had obviously returned from their matinee performance—directing two footmen laden with boxes. "Put those in the storeroom for now." Her jaw clenched. "If I don't hear from that woman soon, they're all going out to the curb for rubbish collection."

"What's going on?" I asked.

"Rose is far behind in her rent," Greta said. "I'd given her extra time as it was. And now for her to drop out of sight… I'm convinced she's skipped out on us. Al already fired her for abandoning him in the middle of a production."

"Would she leave all of her things behind?" Cassie asked skeptically, gesturing to the satchel and boxes.

"The more reasonable explanation," I said, "is that some mishap has befallen her. We need to go to the police and report her missing."

"Who's Rose?" Leonard murmured in my ear.

"Rose Harper," I whispered back. "You may remember her. She was a classmate with Cassie and me—you recall that dreadful ladies' academy I complained about having to attend? Now she works as a seamstress for the Marlowe Theater—or did—and boards here. But she's disappeared. I've been trying to find her."

"Ah yes, I remember Rose," Leonard murmured, half to himself.

Greta hadn't heard our quiet exchange, but she was vigorously shaking her head at Cassie. "The hotel is full, and we are turning away potential guests! Just this afternoon, I was told a gentleman came to inquire about lodging. I'm tired of losing money to keep a room empty for someone who isn't using it."

"I was the gentleman in question." Leonard stepped forward and bowed gallantly over Greta's hand. "Allow me to introduce myself. Mr. ...um...Montague. A friend of Mrs. Wynch and Miss Leigh."

One had to admire his quick thinking. We'd had a sad paucity of it lately.

"Yes, well—I'm Mrs. Marlowe," the lady said, grudgingly stopping in mid-tirade to remember her manners. "I run this establishment."

"*No*—not Greta Marlowe, nee Wynch?" He gestured to me. "You didn't tell me you were staying in the company of such talent, Pen."

"You know me?" Greta gave a suspicious frown. "You seem too young to remember my time in the theater."

"Ah, but my father told me about you. He raved about the gifted dancer who lit up the boards in New York. He was a particular fan of your performance in *The Merry Dutch Girls*."

The old woman thawed considerably. "That was my favorite musical as well. How kind of you to share the story."

"I can certainly sympathize with your current predicament, ma'am," he said smoothly, removing his pocketbook from an inner jacket pocket. "Tell me, what does Rose owe you? I should like to pay it."

"Really?" Greta self-consciously straightened her cuffs and smoothed her skirt. "That's most generous."

"Not at all. I was stopping in town to visit several friends— including these ladies," he said, sweeping a hand in our direction, "but now that I hear of Rose—another old acquaintance —I am most concerned."

"As are we all," Cassie said. "Isn't that right, Mrs. Marlowe?"

Greta grunted. "Yes, of course."

"Then if I may prevail upon you, ma'am," he said, "I should like to stay in her room these next two nights while I inquire in town about her. I'm prepared to pay extra for your trouble. Just freshen the room, change the linens, and I'll be fine. And you can put her belongings back in there. They won't bother me."

Greta smiled. "I'll have it seen to, Mr. Montague."

Cassie's gaping expression no doubt matched my own. I'd had no idea Leonard had it in him.

We gave him time to get settled into Rose's room—conveniently down the hall from ours—before tapping on his partly open door.

He waved us in. "Shall we search through Rose's belongings? Perhaps we can find a clue as to her present whereabouts."

"Good idea," Cassie said, closing the door behind us, "though I'm surprised to hear you propose it."

He made a face. "It's true that I'm reluctant to violate the young lady's privacy. I don't see an alternative, however."

I viewed the stack of boxes with a skeptical eye. "I'm not sure how fruitful it will be. I searched the room when she first went missing. There is no personal correspondence."

Cassie reached for Rose's satchel. "Maybe you missed something."

I shrugged and set to work.

The boxes that Greta's servants had packed were a hodge-podge of books, sewing supplies, a couple of framed photographs, a modest jewelry box, and toiletries.

"All too much of this week has involved searching people's belongings," I grumbled, shifting aside a tin of buttons.

Cassie held out a hand. "Let me see the button box. Ladies like to hide things in the strangest places."

I passed it over and continued my survey. Shoes, a scarf, and a couple of shawls. No help there.

"Nothing but buttons," Cassie muttered, handing it back.

"I'm not having any luck, either." Leonard picked up a photograph in an oval, gilt frame. "This must be a picture of Rose, taken in her youth."

"Let me see." I held the faded tintype up to the light. Yes, I recognized Rose, who appeared to be in her teen years. A much younger boy, towheaded, stood beside her, the two of them attired in their summertime Sunday best. He must be her brother. I thought I saw a resemblance between the boy and our intruder, but perhaps I was trying too hard to make the connection.

The pair was posed in front of a store with a striped awning and a freshly painted sign. *Harper's Grocery.*

I felt a prickle of excitement. Rose's family was native to Southbrook, and I remembered that her father had been a grocer. Back when we were in school together—nearly two decades ago—everyone knew what everyone else's father did for a living, paying particular attention to which girls were there on a charity scholarship. Those students were often snubbed by the petty girls from prominent families, but Cassie had formed a warm friendship with Rose from the very beginning and—when Rose wasn't actively annoying me—I sort of followed along.

Perhaps the store was in town. Could it possibly be in business after all this time?

"What are you doing?" Leonard asked, as I pried off the back of the frame.

"Checking for a notation. Most people write the year and the location—ah." I squinted to better read the faded inscription on the back.

Rose and Robert, Harper's store opening. Mackay Street, 1869.

Cassie craned her neck to see. "Mackay Street—is that here in town?"

"One of the staff can tell us," I said. "There's no street number visible, though, and we don't know if the property is still in the family. The photograph is nearly two decades old."

"It's a place to start, nonetheless," she said. "Even if the family has moved on, the people they sold it to might know something."

I bit my lip as I checked my watch. The Pierson Players would be leaving soon for their evening performance. Finding the safe combination—if it was in Greta's apartment to begin with—would take a while. There wasn't time for me to chase down this lead.

Leonard was observing me quietly. "What do you need us to do?"

≈

"It's settled, then," I said, moving aside as a maid came in with fresh towels for Leonard's room.

He murmured his thanks as the girl deposited them and left, flicking us a glance of curiosity on her way out.

"What is it you'll be doing in the meantime?" he asked.

"I can't say. It's connected to the case."

He frowned. "That makes me distinctly uneasy."

Cassie gave a bark of laughter. "Welcome to my day-to-day life. I worry about her all the time. But I've learned that she has to go her own way." She clasped my hand. "Promise you'll be careful?"

I smiled. "Of course."

Cassie and Leonard had been gone an hour before I

headed to the fourth floor to search for the safe combination. Circumstances were in my favor tonight, as Greta had put the housekeeper in charge of organizing an elaborate buffet in the music salon when the cast returned, to celebrate the success of the Pierson Players' Southbrook run. This meant the entire staff was being pressed into service to move furniture, decorate the room, and prepare the food. No one would be turning down beds anytime soon.

I unlocked the door to Greta's suite with the ease of practice, shut it without locking it in case I needed a quick escape, and waited until I reached Flora's room to turn on a lamp. It was the likeliest place for the combination to be secreted. If it existed.

Finally, I found it—a tiny, rolled-up strip of paper with the writing I sought, hidden in Flora's sewing basket.

I hurried to the safe and turned on the nearest light.

It took me a few tries—there were no lefts and rights indicated—but finally I got it open.

I didn't have enough illumination to see into the recess, so I pulled out everything—mostly jewel cases and ribbon-tied envelopes—and brought them over to the lamp on the credenza. My pulse beat faster when I curled my fingers around a cloth-wrapped bundle. It was heavy, hard, and flat. This had to be it. I unwrapped it with trembling fingers.

The dark felt fabric fell away, and there it was—a quarter-inch-thick steel plate, roughly six inches long by two inches across. It was etched. I didn't take the time to make out the writing, however. It had to be what Sanderson and his office were after.

Even as I felt a sense of exultation at the find, my heart was heavy with the proof that Flora—and Greta, who had to have known—were not the innocents they'd pretended to be. I had to wonder, now, whether Flora had been complicit in her husband's scheme all along. Had she only managed to escape arrest because of her helpless air and her husband's refusal to cooperate with the authorities?

I was so lost in my thoughts as I considered the repercussions that I had ceased to pay attention to my surroundings.

To my great misfortune.

Before I could react to the faint rustle of fabric behind me, I felt a burst of pain in the back of my head. Then blackness.

CHAPTER 12

J had an odd dream, and Leonard was in it. Cassie, too, but she was standing farther away, pacing a cold room and wringing her hands. Leonard crouched beside me, stroking my hair and murmuring something. I struggled to catch it.

Pen...Pen....

"Pen."

It wasn't a dream. I opened my eyes.

Leonard was bending over me as I lay sprawled on Greta's foyer floor. Cassie was nowhere in sight. I must have dreamt that part.

As I propped myself up on my elbows, I was engulfed in a wave of nausea and the room swam in my vision. I took a slow breath, in and out. Better. "Help me stand, would you?"

He frowned. "Are you sure? All right—easy, now."

Once I was vertical and the room had stopped tilting, I went over to the table where I'd been inspecting the plate.

"It's gone."

"What's gone?"

"Never mind."

"Who attacked you?" he asked.

"I didn't see him."

"Is it the counterfeit plate that's missing?"

I made a face. "Cassie told you?"

He gave a sheepish shrug.

I surveyed the room. "Oh dear, there's blood on Greta's floor again."

"Again?" he asked.

"Long story. How did you know where I was?"

"When we couldn't find you upon our return, I wormed it out of Cassie. Don't blame her," he added quickly. "I rather insisted."

Cassie didn't seem particularly difficult to worm confidences from lately, but I let that go for now. "Did you pass anyone on the stairs?"

"Not in this stairwell, though I thought I heard the click of a door closing at the end of the hall."

"Probably the other stairwell door." I should have wedged it shut again.

Leonard's mouth set in a grim line. "When I get my hands on the miscreant, I'll make him answer for this. Do you have any idea who might be responsible?"

I shook my head, which I immediately regretted. I touched the back of my head gingerly, feeling a lump under the stickiness of matted blood.

"That will need tending to," he said. "Should I get a doctor? I noticed a sign in front of a building just down the street."

"No need. Cassie can tend to it." I didn't think I could explain another injury to the sharp-eyed Dr. Byrd. No one is that accident prone.

Leonard passed me his handkerchief to wipe my hands. "Now what? It's nearly midnight. The cast will return to the hotel soon."

"Heavens, it's that late? Well, then, I may as well stay here.

I need to talk with Greta and Flora." I should send for Sanderson as well, late as it was.

"Surely it can wait. We should at least get your wound dressed. Besides, there's someone who's anxious to talk to you."

"You mean Cassie? You can tell her what happened."

His smile grew wide, almost triumphant. "Not Cassie. Rose."

"You found her," I breathed.

"Indeed we did, and she has a story to tell. She's in my—I mean, her—room."

I was anxious to talk to Rose, so we left the scene as it was, with Greta's safe still open and its contents—minus the plate —strewn upon the table. No need now to conceal the fact that I'd been there.

Amid the exchange of exclamations and embraces in Rose's sitting room, I related the attack upon me, though I omitted mention of the plate in front of Rose. I first wanted to see what she knew.

Leonard rang for hot tea, and Cassie fetched bandages and a water basin.

As Cassie began cleaning my head wound, Rose perched on a rocking chair and watched me apprehensively. The pale lips and shadows above her cheekbones spoke of exhaustion.

I had little sympathy to spare, however. My head was already throbbing, and we had a long night ahead. I got right to the point. "Your brother was the second-story man who broke into Greta's quarters a few nights ago?"

She gave a sniff. "Unfortunately, yes, that was him. I've tried for years to get him to work a respectable job, but he invariably gets into trouble."

"Where is he now?" I asked.

"Out of reach." Her tone was brusque.

Leonard nodded. "There was no sign of him when we found her."

"Where was that?" I asked.

"In the apartment over the grocery store on Mackay Street." He crossed his legs as he settled into a chair.

"A family friend owns the store now," Rose said. "He bought it after my father died. I went to him for help. I didn't tell him exactly what happened, just that Bobby was injured. He let us stay in the rooms upstairs. Then I found a man who would tend to his wound without asking questions."

"Wound?" Leonard asked. "What happened to him?"

"I shot him," I said simply.

In the silence that followed, Rose resumed the thread of her story. "Bobby is now safely away. I was trying to figure out what to do about my own situation when Cassie and Leonard showed up. I have to say, it was a surprise to see Leonard, another old friend from my school days. But I half expected you'd be the one to find me, Pen, since you're the detective."

I raised an eyebrow at Cassie.

She shook her head. "I didn't tell her, and neither did Leonard."

I supposed it wasn't difficult for Rose to guess at my identity, given that I'd shot and chased her brother, but she seemed to know for a certainty...then I realized. "You were the one who searched our room." The missing hour that morning.

"Yes," she said. "After Bobby intercepted me at the streetcar stop and he said you were the woman he'd grappled with—the one who'd nearly kept him from getting away—I figured you were more than you appeared to be. I hurried back to search your room. I didn't find the gun—were you carrying it?"

I inclined my head in acknowledgment.

"But I found your logbook and lockpick tools."

"How did you get in?" I asked. "Do you have lockpicks of your own?"

She shook her head. "The bolt wasn't fully engaged—a lot

of them at the hotel stick or don't completely latch. I was able to work it open."

It had been my own fault, after all. I made a mental apology to the housekeeper and maids. "My hiding place didn't appear to be tampered with."

"I know that old trick, with the hairs." She shrugged. "I merely took note of their positioning and restored them."

"It appears you need a different method, Pen," Cassie said.

That was a problem for later. "But other things were disturbed," I pointed out, "which alerted us to the intrusion."

Rose grimaced. "That was after I'd found your cache. I panicked when I heard someone coming. I wasn't as careful restoring everything." She squinted at me over her spectacles. "So, why are you here? Not for a visit, obviously. Is it to protect Flora?"

"What makes you think she needs protection?" I asked sharply. Who was asking the questions here?

"Not from my brother," Rose amended hastily. "He's never harmed a woman."

"Well, he stabbed Pen," Cassie retorted. "I'd say his streak of not harming women has come to an end."

The seamstress flinched.

Leonard's brow furrowed in my direction. "The fellow stabbed you?"

I motioned to my forearm. "Frankly, I'd forgotten about it."

"Being hit over the head might have diverted your attention," Cassie said caustically, rinsing a bloodied towel in the basin.

"Bobby was only trying to escape," Rose bristled. "He wouldn't take a job where he was supposed to hurt anybody."

"What exactly was he hired to do?" I asked. "And who hired him?"

"He refused to say. He didn't want to put me in danger. All

I know is he was supposed to recover something Flora had taken."

We already knew as much. Then I had a thought. "Are you sure, positively, that he's out of town? Any possibility he could have returned tonight to finish the job?"

"I saw him board the train an hour before Leonard and Cassie showed up at the door. He was long gone. Besides, he's still in rough shape. He can barely stand upright."

The room grew quiet.

"I'm sorry," Rose said finally. "I wish I could be more helpful." She flexed her hands in her lap. "I've made a mess of things, haven't I? Now I have no job, and Greta is likely to kick me out."

"Perhaps not," Leonard said. "Your account has been settled here."

She flashed him a grateful look. "I promise to pay you back as soon as I can."

He waved a hand. "Think nothing of it."

"You see," Cassie said, "Greta has no reason force you out now."

"Of course she does." Rose gave a bitter laugh. "My brother is a criminal whom I aided in escaping. Hardly respectable behavior. She is within her rights to refuse me lodging."

"She doesn't have to know the intruder is your brother," Cassie said. "We can keep that to ourselves."

"Besides," I said, "Greta is in no position to take the moral high ground. Her own relation, to whom she has provided aid, has engaged in a number of criminal—"

Shrieks of female outrage sounded overhead.

"Oh dear," Cassie said, reflexively glancing at the ceiling, "Greta and Flora must be back."

I stood. "I'd better get up there. But first—" I reached for the pad and pencil on Rose's desk, scribbled Sanderson's hotel address, and handed it to Leonard. "Would you please bring

Mr. Sanderson here?" I gave a rueful smile. "I seem to be asking you to fetch a number of people this evening."

He reached for his jacket. "My visit has certainly been more, ahem, eventful than I'd anticipated." He flashed Cassie a glance of amusement, which was returned in kind.

Obviously, the two had decided to humor the irregularities of the case, bless them. Nothing Cassie wasn't accustomed to, but new territory for Leonard.

"I'd normally wait until a more respectable hour," I explained, "but circumstances warrant an official reckoning with Flora as soon as possible. That's why we need Sanderson. I'll go upstairs in the meantime and tell them what happened."

Leonard reached for my hand. "Must you go up there now —and alone?"

His concern was so palpable—evident in the narrowed gray eyes, his warm hand enveloping mine—that it nearly undid my composure.

"I've already been hit on the head once tonight." I affected a nonchalance I didn't quite feel. "I doubt lightning will strike twice."

With a shake of his head, he left the room. I got up to follow.

"What do I do now?" Rose asked.

Must I have an answer for everything? "I'm sure you and Cassie can put your heads together. I have to go."

"Good luck," Cassie said.

I paused with my hand on the door. "Whatever you decide, keep in mind that Greta is clearly in a high temper. Best that you stay out of her way until she settles down." And when would that be? I had no idea.

~

Flora was reclined on the divan as an anxious maid fanned her with a scented handkerchief. The servant kept glancing over her shoulder, as if expecting marauders to burst through the door any minute.

Greta, still wearing a fox-fur stole, stood by the safe in close conversation with the housekeeper. She started toward me as I walked in, her frame rigid with anger. Flora turned her face aside and continued succumbing to the vapors.

"It's best that we talk in private," I said quickly, with a nod toward the housekeeper.

Greta waved an impatient hand toward the housekeeper and maid. "Go, both of you—I'll ring when I want you."

Once we were alone, Greta pointed toward the open safe. "You had something to do with this, didn't you?"

"I'll get to that in a moment. First, let us talk about what's missing from your safe." I inclined my head towards toward the scattering of items on the table.

The color quickly drained from her cheeks. I don't think she'd realized until this moment that the plate was gone. I was sure that Flora had, however.

Greta tossed her stole on the sofa and nudged Flora's foot. "Sit up. We have no time or leisure for histrionics. I can no longer protect you."

With a final sniff into her handkerchief, the young lady swung her feet off the cushion and assumed a more decorous posture. Her tear-streaked face was red and puffy. I could see the remnants of stage makeup at the edges of her hairline as she tipped her face up.

"Did you take it?" she asked bluntly.

"I *saw* it. Briefly." I grimaced and touched my head. "But someone attacked me and got away with the plate. I didn't see who it was."

"How did you know it was here to—to begin with?" Flora asked, her voice breaking. Greta sat beside her and patted her hand.

Neither woman seemed particularly concerned with my injury. Not that I was surprised.

"We'll get back to that later." I would gladly leave the explanations to Sanderson, along with the revelations of his identity and mission. "The most important question now is—who knew you had it?" Seeing Flora hesitate, I added sternly, "I have a pounding headache and little patience for further prevarication."

She blew out a breath. "No one, I swear."

I didn't believe her. "Let's start with who knew the plate existed. Your husband, of course—he's the one who made it. What about Jimmy the Bagger? Would he have been aware of the specifics of your husband's work?"

"Perhaps."

"Who else?"

"Humphrey and Jimmy the Bagger talked about someone named Morrow," Flora said grudgingly. "It sounded as if he was running the scheme and fronting the money for it."

Flora did, indeed, know more than she'd let on. "So—Morrow, your husband, and Jimmy the Bagger. That makes three." Then I remembered something. "You mentioned earlier that your husband had been complaining to someone when Jimmy was putting pressure on him. Do you know who he was talking to?"

She shook her head.

"What did the man say when your husband complained?"

"They were whispering, so it was difficult for me to make out everything." She closed her eyes, concentrating. "But he did promise—" She stopped.

"Promise what?" I asked impatiently.

"That Humphrey would be warned if the police were getting close, so he'd have time to get away."

"It appears that promise wasn't kept," Greta said, "as he's sitting in jail right now."

Flora bit her lip.

I sat up straighter. "There *was* a warning, wasn't there?"

Flora twisted the handkerchief she was clutching. "A note was delivered a couple of days later, when Humphrey was out."

"What did it say?"

"That the authorities were closing in. It told him to go into hiding for a while."

"He never saw it, did he?" I asked.

Silence.

"You kept it from him?" Greta's tone was incredulous.

Flora held out a pleading hand to her great-aunt. "You must realize—he's a horrible man. He settles quarrels with the back of his hand. You said it yourself, Aunt Greta—I was miserable. So why would I help him? If he was arrested, what was that to me?"

"What did you do after that?" I asked.

"I'd been working up the nerve to leave him, and when I saw the note…it seemed my best chance. Maybe he wouldn't be able to come after me. I packed a few things and searched his workshop before I left."

"Is that when you found the plate?" I asked.

"Three of them, actually."

That was in line with what Sanderson had said. "What made you decide to take one?"

"If the police couldn't hold him long, I knew he'd show up here looking for me. I figured I could use it to bribe him into leaving me alone."

I stifled a sigh. Taking it had only encouraged desperate people to try to recover it. Instead of protecting her, it had put her at further risk.

Greta shifted impatiently. "We're still no closer to answering the question of who struck Penelope and took the plate."

"Perhaps it was the man who broke in a few days ago," Flora said.

I shook my head gingerly. "Our second-story man has left town. It's possible someone else was hired to take his place, but I wonder if the ringleader—Morrow—had a spy already staying here at the hotel." My opened telegrams pointed to that, and if the same person who'd opened them had also been directed to monitor my movements, I would have led them right to the plate.

I bit back a sigh. It would then have been handed off to someone outside the hotel. We'd never see it again. "Have you made any recent hires?" I asked Greta.

"Our clerk, Barnaby, started work here the day after Flora arrived. But his references were excellent." She pursed her lips as she thought. "No, wait—this happened around eleven this evening, correct? He would have closed the office and gone home before then."

"He certainly isn't here now," Flora said. "The clerk's office and reception area are shuttered for the night."

"Anyone else?"

"Two of the three stable boys we employ are new, but none of them ventures beyond the kitchen for their meals."

That left only the Pierson Players. "How well do you know the actors?"

Greta's eyes blazed briefly, but then her expression grew thoughtful. "I see your point. I don't know of any who've had shady dealings."

"One hardly advertises such." I resisted the urge to roll my eyes. "Is anyone new to the company for the Southbrock performances?"

Greta shook her head.

"How could it be any of the players?" Flora asked. "We were all together on stage tonight."

"Well...Jasper was only needed for the first act," Greta said.

"He was at the curtain call, though," Flora said.

"Yes, but there was more than an hour in between," Greta said. "We're only two blocks from the theater."

"Then it's possible he slipped out," I said. "Who else would have had a sufficient gap of time during tonight's performance?"

Flora gave a helpless shrug. "I wasn't keeping track of everyone on stage. It was hard enough remembering my lines, where to stand...and Barrett kept throwing me off-kilter."

"I was busy helping Pierson." Greta tapped her chin thoughtfully. "John Davis might have had enough time."

I bit my lip. There were a lot of people to sift through.

"Miss Templeton and Miss Finnerty were here during that time," I mused aloud. "What do you know of them?"

Greta clucked her tongue. "The notion of a woman is far-fetched. Whoever it was lifted my heavy Ming vase to strike you with." She gestured ruefully to the shards still on the floor. "And Viola is still getting around on crutches."

I wasn't ready to eliminate anyone yet, but even if Miss Templeton or Miss Finnerty was responsible, I was stumped as to the motive.

A tap upon the door was followed by the maid opening it. "Ma'am? Two men to see you."

At last, Mr. Sanderson. And, of course, the ever-diligent Leonard would be sure to have escorted him personally.

"At this hour?" Greta asked.

"It was at my request," I said.

Her brow creased in a puzzled frown. "Well, show them in."

As Sanderson crossed the foyer—Leonard just behind him —Greta gasped in surprise. "Mr. Frasier! What are you doing here?"

Leonard, no doubt bewildered by Greta's use of his actual name and forgetting momentarily that I'd appropriated it on Sanderson's behalf, stepped forward, mouth open, to explain himself.

I interrupted, "If I may have a moment alone with this gentleman?" and linked my arm through Leonard's to lead him out of the room.

Sanderson put up a hand. "Mrs. Wynch. Take Mrs. Marlowe with you, if you would. I wish to speak with her niece alone."

Deprived of witnessing the denouement, I scowled at him.

I could see Greta wasn't thrilled, either. "What do you mean? I insist upon staying with Flora."

Flora said nothing, blinking in confusion.

Sanderson passed Greta a business card from his pocket. "Here is my real name and the nature of my authority in this matter. I would advise you not to embroil yourself further, madam. Otherwise, our office may have to bring charges against you as well."

Greta read the card, then eyed her great-niece.

But Flora remained still, watching Sanderson intently.

"I'll send for you when I need you, Mrs. Marlowe," Sanderson went on. "Why don't you join the party downstairs? When we arrived, people were beginning to wonder where you and Mrs. Richards had gotten to. Now, if you'll excuse us?"

He closed the door part of the way, leaving a gap for the sake of propriety.

The three of us stood in the hall, flummoxed as to what to do next.

CHAPTER 13

*I*t was Greta who recovered first. She leaned close to me, eyes snapping in anger. "You lied to us! You set a—a *trap* for Flora!"

Leonard stepped forward protectively.

I ignored him and scowled at Greta. "If you had been forthcoming with me from the beginning and told me about the plate," I said icily, "it would not have been necessary."

She had the grace, at least, to look abashed at that.

"You and Flora have been lying to me the entire time," I went on, "even after a man broke into your suite and I risked my life to protect you." I shook my head. "I realized neither of you could be trusted, so I agreed to help Sanderson find where you'd hidden the plate."

Leonard frowned in confusion. "Why didn't he simply bring in the police and conduct an official search of the premises?"

"He was under orders from his boss to recover it as discreetly as possible."

"I suppose it could be problematic," Leonard conceded, "if word got out about the possibility of counterfeit currency circulating."

Greta distractedly played with the long strand of pearls at her neck, her fingers twisting the rope into knots until I thought it might break.

At last, she lifted her head. "I regret my role."

I waited for more, but that was apparently all I was going to get.

She gestured helplessly toward the partly open door. "What do we do now?"

"I'd say we do just as Sanderson suggests," I said, "and join the others in the salon. Word of the disturbance may have spread."

She bit her lip. "Explanations would be awkward in the extreme."

"You don't have to stray far from the truth," I said. "You can tell everyone there was a burglary while you were all at the play."

"And that it perturbed the young lady greatly and she needed to lie down," Leonard chimed in.

"Exactly," I said. "In fact, I should like to come with you. It would be interesting to see how the others react to the news."

"You really believe one of them is responsible?" Greta asked. "I thought our discussion was sheer speculation."

I shrugged. "It's as good a starting point as any." I glanced at Leonard. "Would you like to join us?"

His mouth quirked in distaste. "I'll leave the inquiries in your capable hands. I'm going to check on Miss Leigh and see how she is faring with R—her task."

Thank goodness he'd caught himself before mentioning Rose's name in front of Greta.

"Good idea." I pursed my lips in a rueful smile. "I know this wasn't the evening you expected, but I'm grateful for your help."

He bowed over my hand. "My pleasure."

Greta paused before the hall mirror and tucked a few silver strands into place. "All right. I'm ready."

Once we reached the third floor, she opted to descend via the main staircase. It would take a dire circumstance indeed to keep Greta Marlowe from making as grand an entrance as possible.

As much as I disliked the woman, I could not help but admire her iron composure.

The doors of the music salon had been opened wide, with buffet tables lining both sides of the corridor beyond.

People hurried over to greet us, Barrett Ward the first among them. "Greta!" he cried, clasping her hand. "Oh, we just heard about the burglary, my dear! How horrible for you." He tucked her arm through his proprietarily and led her into the room. "We must absolutely pamper you while you tell us all about it." He snapped his fingers at one of the footmen. "Get Mrs. Marlowe some champagne." He leaned close to add, "That will fix you right up."

Ward seemed inclined to keep Greta to himself for a tête-à-tête, but as soon as Pierson spotted her across the room, he waved them over to join their group. I trailed behind. Not only was I curious to hear how she would recount the incident, but the coffee table they were seated around was laid with tiered plates of sandwiches and pastries. My stomach rumbled.

Miss Templeton shifted to make room on the settee for Greta. "Another break-in—oh, dear." She gave a cluck of sympathy. "How upsetting it must be."

Greta grimaced. "My staff is not as discreet as I would wish." She scowled at the liveried servers circulating the room.

"I'm afraid that was my fault." John Davis gave an apologetic bow. "I heard a shriek, saw servants rushing up the stairs, and took a peek at what was going on."

Greta blinked. "That seems rather an invasion of privacy, sir."

"My intent was to lend assistance," he said, "but the housekeeper saw me and shooed me off."

I wasn't sure whether Davis's admission or the behavior itself surprised me most. Probably the former. I wondered how much he'd overheard. I hadn't seen him at all.

"Was anything taken?" he asked.

Greta looked a little queasy in the face of that question. "That is still being, um, determined," she said faintly.

Kay handed Greta a flute of champagne. The palm of her hand was bandaged.

"What happened to you, Kay?" I asked.

She started, nearly spilling the liquid. "Oh! I was merely careless with a sharp pair of scissors while ripping out a hem. Quite silly of me. It's nothing, really."

But the vase shards on Greta's floor were too recent of a memory for me to take her account at face value. Could she have been my attacker? She'd been here the entire evening. Now that she'd recovered from her illness, she could have hefted the vase.

The bigger question, however, was why.

Archie Jasper came over with a plate of canapes, which he presented to Greta with a flourish. "You must be famished after your ordeal."

"Thank you," Greta said. She politely took a nibble of one, then set it aside.

"How is Flora faring?" he inquired.

"As well as can be expected," Greta said. "She's lying down."

"Oh, I do hope she will be joining us," Ward said eagerly. "She should be here to celebrate her triumph on the stage! An ingenue of her caliber hasn't been seen in our little group in quite some time."

Kay, Miss Templeton, and Miss Reid each stiffened, but Ward was ignorant of the fact that he'd managed to insult the entire female cast within earshot.

Pierson picked up his glass. "I, for one, anticipate effusive reviews on the morrow. I haven't seen such a promising start to a new play in years. We're grateful that Mrs. Richards could stand in so admirably while Miss Templeton and Miss Finnerty were recuperating, are we not?" He smiled at the two ladies in question.

The man was ever the diplomat.

Each nodded her agreement, though enthusiasm was distinctly lacking.

"As I told you before, Mr. Pierson," Miss Templeton said, "I'll be ready to resume *my* role when we reach Philadelphia."

"Indeed?" Barrett Ward murmured.

"Well, then." Pierson said, "here's to success at our next stop. To Philadelphia!" He raised his glass.

Al Chaffee and Sally approached the group as the others followed in the toast.

"Sorry we're late," Chaffee said. "I wanted to make sure everything was put away and the theater locked up."

Greta smiled. "I appreciate such attention to detail in my theater manager." She turned to Sally. "And your hard work, young lady, has not gone unnoticed. You have dealt with particularly difficult circumstances these past few days. Thank you for pitching in."

The young lady blushed. "I appreciate the sentiment, Mrs. Marlowe. But I still don't understand what happened to Rose."

Greta scowled. "I'd rather we not discuss the subject. It has been a difficult enough evening."

Sally perched upon the stool at her feet. "Of course, ma'am. It must be an exhausting endeavor for someone of your age, to be so active in a play production."

Oh Lord.

"Sally!" Chaffee chided.

Kay and Miss Templeton hid smiles behind their teacups. Miss Reid's snort became a coughing fit. She excused herself.

"It's not my age that is a trial to me, young lady," Greta snapped. "My suite was broken into tonight while we were at the theater."

Sally put a hand to her mouth, turning to the others. Jasper nodded in confirmation.

Most of the group drifted off to other spots after that—Miss Reid, Kay, and Sally to the pianoforte, Davis to fetch buffet items for Miss Templeton, and Greta to chat with Chaffee.

Pierson and Ward were likewise in close conversation. Judging from Ward's somber expression, I wondered if he was learning of his demotion for the Philadelphia leg of their tour.

Soon after, Flora came down, Sanderson at her elbow. The music stopped, and the group turned to face her, bursting into warm applause.

It was too much for Flora. She reached for Greta, put her face in her shoulder, and wept.

During the tumult of embraces and well-wishes from the cast to Flora, I pulled Sanderson aside. "What happens now? You have the witness but not the plate."

"Yes—about that," he began, stepping back farther from the others. "Mrs. Richards has admitted taking it, but I want to be sure that's what you saw. Can you describe it?"

"I didn't have the chance to examine it closely. I can tell you it was a solid, flat, metal plate—about this wide and this long." I held my hands apart. "It was etched, but the light was too dim to make out what was on it."

"It does sound like what we're after." He shook his head. "How unfortunate you allowed it to get away from you. That seems to happen to you quite often, doesn't it?"

"Were you the one who took it?" I shot back. I don't even know what made me pose the question, but it had been a difficult evening and my head was throbbing.

His forehead creased in surprise. "My dear lady, you are not making sense. I'm the one who asked you to get it for me in the first place. And I did exactly what you required of me—I stayed away from the hotel and waited for you to send word." He scowled. "If I had been here, the outcome might have been different. Our chances now of tracking it down are rather remote."

"Not necessarily." I discreetly inclined my head toward Kay. "Note that Miss Finnerty has a fresh cut on her hand."

He raised an eyebrow.

"Whoever took the plate struck me with a vase that shattered into sharp pieces," I explained. "He—or she—could have been cut by it. Further, Kay was here at the hotel at the time."

"Indeed." He flicked her speculative glance. "What do you know about her?"

"Precious little, I'm afraid. I have no idea what her motive would be. The same holds true for the others. Miss Templeton was here the entire evening, too. Further, I learned from Greta that both Davis and Jasper could have slipped away during the performance and still have been back for the final curtain. So there are four possibilities, but no motive for any of them."

He shifted uneasily as he eyed the room. "I don't like that Davis fellow. Seems rather secretive."

I had to agree, though there was nothing secretive about the way he was attending to Miss Templeton these past few days. A budding romance? Hardly relevant to Flora and her troubles, of course.

"My point," I said, "is that if someone here is responsible, it may be hidden away at the hotel. You could question them in your official capacity and search their rooms."

He made a face. "You are already aware of the difficulty in doing that. And we're nearly out of time."

"Are we taking Flora to New York tomorrow, then?"

"We? There's no need for you to accompany us. Your job is done. That doesn't mean I don't appreciate your efforts,

Mrs. Wynch," he added hastily. "You tried your best, I'm sure. But I will handle the matter from here on."

How typical of the man. "Aren't you worried about Flora slipping away from you if you have sole custody of her?"

"I'm more concerned with her 'slipping away,' as you put it, before we reach the train station in the morning. In fact, I've decided to stay here tonight. That way, I can be sure she doesn't flee. The maid is setting up a cot for me in the living room of Mrs. Marlowe's suite."

"Is that why you accompanied Flora down to the party, to monitor her movements? It's a bit of a risk. The cast knows you as Mr. Frasier, the theatrical agent."

"Yes, and we're maintaining the pretense. That's for Mrs. Richards' benefit, to avoid embarrassment. Only we few know my real capacity. She's telling her great-aunt of our arrangements even now, see?"

Flora was indeed murmuring something in Greta's ear. Judging from the old lady's frown, she was none too happy about it.

"Speaking of embarrassment," I said, "you'll want to give Miss Templeton a wide berth." I inclined my head discreetly in that lady's direction. "She might ask you why the footman was chasing you last night."

"Duly noted," he said curtly.

"With the people in question occupied down here, I could ask Greta for the keys to their rooms and do a quick search before the party breaks up," I suggested.

"Interesting idea," he said thoughtfully. "But I believe *I* will take charge of the search this time. Should I find the plate, I want to make sure it doesn't disappear once again." A mocking smile tugged at his lips.

"Fine by me," I retorted, "but that will mean leaving Flora unmonitored."

He glanced uneasily at the young lady, who had taken a seat with her great-aunt beside the fire.

As entertaining as it might be to witness Sanderson struggle with his predicament, I was more than ready to put this day behind me. "If you'll excuse me, I believe I'll retire. Good night."

He made a formal bow over my hand. "I doubt I'll be seeing you again, Mrs. Wynch. Let us say our goodbyes now. Thank you for—"

He was interrupted as Barrett Ward approached us.

"Mr. Frasier!" he called heartily. "Tell me more about your work as a talent scout. Is it only young actresses you seek, or do you recruit veteran players such as myself?"

I took the opportunity to slip away upstairs and head back to Rose's room.

Cassie opened it at my knock.

"Come in, Pen," she murmured. "Maybe you can talk some sense into her. Leonard and I are getting nowhere."

Leonard, who had stood at my arrival, flashed me a tired grimace and resumed his seat upon the rocking chair.

"What's the problem?" I asked.

Rose dabbed at her eyes. "I want to go downstairs *now* and apologize to everyone—Greta and Mr. Chaffee in particular. I'm tired of hiding. I spent nearly a week doing that already."

"I can understand that. Sally's been worried about you, too."

"Exactly. I need to explain."

A soft sound reached my ears. Leonard, still seated, had his chin tucked into his chest and was snoring softly. I motioned to Cassie and Rose. "Let's discuss this in our room."

We tiptoed out and softly closed the door behind us.

CHAPTER 14

*J*n the end, Cassie and I convinced Rose that everyone involved would fare better with a good night's rest.

"You can talk to Greta and the others at breakfast tomorrow," I said.

"But they're leaving for Philadelphia then," Rose objected.

"Not quite so early." Cassie went over to the dresser and opened a timetable. "The train doesn't leave until noon on Sundays." She looked over at me. "We could catch that one as well and make the connection to the Chicago line from New York City."

I was more than ready to return home. "Agreed." I wondered mischievously if Sanderson would be traveling with Flora on the same train. We'd end up accompanying him, after all.

Rose sat down abruptly on the vanity stool. "I may have to leave town, too, depending upon how I'm received."

Cassie crouched down and put an arm around her shoulders. "Give them a chance. These aren't strangers—they're people who've known you for a while."

That reminded me. "The Pierson Players come here every year, correct?"

Rose nodded.

"Have you known Kay and Miss Templeton very long?"

"Oh, three years, at least. Viola, I mean," she amended. "This is Kay's second season."

"Do you know anything about their families or who they associate with outside of the acting company?"

"Why? What do you suspect them of?" Rose asked.

"The attack on me tonight and theft of what your brother was after," I said bluntly.

Rose's brow arched.

"I wouldn't call it a full-blown suspicion," I clarified. "But both were here this evening during the performance. It seems prudent to learn more about their backgrounds. And I saw that Kay's right hand was bandaged. She said she accidentally cut herself with sewing scissors."

Cassie leaned forward in interest. "You believe her injury might be from the vase you were struck with?"

I shrugged.

Rose spread her hands in a helpless gesture. "I'm not sure what I can tell you about either lady. Whenever they're here, their time is almost entirely taken up with performances or preparations. No outside visitors, family or otherwise. That's true of most of the players. They socialize with each other, of course." She made a face. "Sometimes that's problematic."

"How so?"

"Barrett is rather a magnet for the ladies in the company. I don't see the appeal, frankly, but at one point or other he's been involved with nearly every one of them."

"Really?" Cassie asked. "All of them?"

"Well, not Mary Reid. Viola was the first that I was aware of, a couple of years ago."

"That's surprising," I said. "She doesn't hold him in high regard now."

"I heard a rumor that Greta went straight to Pierson when she saw him courting Viola—and then again last season, when it was Kay. The woman has strong opinions about the actors becoming involved under her roof."

Or perhaps, if Greta was "sweet on him," as Miss Reid had postulated, she would be jealous of perceived rivals.

"I suppose it's never a good policy," Rose went on. "But no matter Viola's current feelings for Barrett, she has never forgiven Greta for interfering."

"She does seem to hold a grudge easily," Cassie murmured.

I'd seen that for myself. "Has Ward behaved himself since his involvement with Miss Templeton and Kay?"

Rose bit her lip. "Well...."

"Yes?" Cassie prompted.

"I loathe telling tales." She blew out a breath. "I saw Sally sneaking out of Barrett's room early one morning, though she didn't notice me, thank goodness. That would have made it awkward for us working together."

"Oh dear," Cassie said. "Does anyone else know?"

"Not that I'm aware."

"When was this?" I asked.

"The week before you arrived."

I bit back a sigh. None of this was getting me any closer to figuring out who took the plate and where it might be. Of course, if Sanderson's search proved successful, the point would be moot. I hoped he was finished by now. Footfalls and voices in the hall suggested the party was breaking up.

I reached for the doorknob.

"Where are you going?" Cassie asked.

"To collect a spare pillow and blanket. We'll give Leonard the room for tonight. Rose can stay here with us."

There were no pillows to be found in the third-floor hall closet. I called to Meg, who was hurrying past.

"Could I have an extra pillow, please?"

The girl reluctantly stopped, her teeth nervously tugging at her bottom lip. "I'm sorry, ma'am, I can't help you now—Mrs. Young's fit to be tied, and if we don't find—" She stopped herself abruptly. "Would you mind fetching it yourself? There's a whole shelf o' them downstairs in the linens room."

"Of course," I murmured, but she was already rushing off.

The linens room turned out to be on the ground floor, adjacent to the housekeeper's suite. The rumbling sounds from the boiler in the cellar below could be felt as well as heard from here. I glanced at the partly open door of the housekeeper's quarters. Poor Miss Templeton, stuck down here this whole week. At least the inconvenience would end tomorrow when she left with the rest of us.

With the door of the linens room—more of a large closet, really—open at my back, I reached for the stack of pillows wedged on an upper shelf. They all came down upon me, of course. Splendid.

The sound of Barrett Ward's deep baritone beyond my shoulder made me jump. "Well, well, if it isn't the injured damsel."

It took me a moment to realize he wasn't talking to me. I was hidden from view.

"Leave me alone, Barrett," a lady's voice snapped. Miss Templeton.

I clutched the pillow to my chest and shamelessly listened.

"Why've you been pretending your ankle is hobbling you?"

"Who says I'm pretending?" Her tone was belligerent.

He chuckled. "That won't work, my dear. I saw you cross the room with perfect ease in your hurry to close the door just now. You're as spry as the rest of us."

"Well, aren't you clever. Why don't we call it the resilience of youth. Something you cannot claim, unfortunately," she said tartly.

"I'll ignore that." His voice hardened. "Why the pretense?"

"You know why." Her tone had grown sulky.

"How could I?"

"You want me to say it out loud? All right then. I did it to protect myself—from you."

"Excuse me?"

"Sally came to talk to me after my so-called accident," she hissed. "She'd seen you adjust the latch beneath the trap door. And I remember that you steered me over to that very spot during rehearsal. You were oh-so-careful to stand away from it yourself, of course."

"That's ridiculous." His voice was hoarse. "She's lying. Besides, I saved your life."

"Too many people were watching, I expect. Or you lost your nerve."

"Why would I hurt you? I cared about you once."

"But now I'm a liability, aren't I? Because I know all about your misspent youth. Hardly exemplary background material for reviewers to publish."

"You didn't tell—?"

"No. But I can't be the only one who knows."

Ward murmured something I couldn't catch. I inched closer to the end of the door.

"I'm not so sure I should stay quiet now," Miss Templeton said in reply.

"Did you have anything to do with Pierson replacing me with Archie?" Ward's voice held a wounded edge.

Silence.

"You'd better not be meddling in my affairs, Viola," Ward growled. "I will not allow you to ruin my career."

"Career? Ha!" came the response, followed by the sounds of a ringing slap, a gasp, and the door slamming shut.

I waited for Ward's footsteps to recede down the hall. I

expelled a breath I didn't realize I'd been holding. What an ugly encounter.

I shoved the remaining pillows back into place, closed the closet door, then promptly backed into Sanderson standing in the corridor.

I stifled an exclamation. "What are you doing here?" I hissed. I headed for the stairs, Sanderson following.

"Quite a heated exchange," he murmured.

"You heard?"

"I was just coming out of the library. Difficult not to."

I dropped my voice, even though no one else was around. "How did your search go?"

He shook his head. "By the time I could speak privately with Mrs. Marlowe to get the keys, some of the guests were already heading up to their rooms."

"Everyone leaves tomorrow," I said.

He scowled. "Don't you think I know that?"

"Your only option is to begin a formal search, public as it may be."

He stopped abruptly on the steps. "I'd hoped it wouldn't come to this," he muttered, half under his breath.

"If you call the local police station first thing tomorrow," I said, "it shouldn't be too disruptive. On a Sunday morning, such a search may not even be noticed by the public at large." I kept my tone reassuring. He seemed quite stricken at the notion of defying his boss and risking public attention.

He gave me a sharp glance. "I will see to it. Good night, Mrs. Wynch."

CHAPTER 15

SUNDAY, MARCH 11

I woke early—not surprising, since I'd given Rose my bed and opted to pile blankets and pillow on the floor. I sat up and tentatively felt the lump at the back of my head. Better. I had only a dull headache now.

I flexed my injured arm. Thankfully, it didn't bother me much. I suppose Cassie was right—one can only keep track of a single ailment at a time.

Murky light sifted through the gaps of the window blinds. I squinted at my watch. Seven o'clock. Had Sanderson sent for the police yet? What time was considered decorous on a Sunday morning to subject an entire establishment to the ignominy of a search?

I got up and dressed in the gloom so as not to disturb Cassie and Rose, then quietly let myself out of the room.

I wasn't the first guest up. As I crossed into the dining room, Kay was loading a tray with tea, toast, and a small pot of marmalade.

"Hello, Kay." Eyeing the tray, I asked, "Taking breakfast up to your room?"

She shook her head. "I thought I'd bring some to Viola and retrieve a dress of mine that she borrowed. I want to make sure I get it back before our trunks are loaded."

"You're leaving on the noon express? Cassie and I are taking that one as well."

"Excellent! I'll be glad of the company. Mary and Viola are agreeable enough traveling companions, but we're together all the time. If you'll excuse me."

I had just poured my own tea when I heard a shriek from below.

I ran toward the source. Kay stood at the threshold of Viola's bedroom, a scattering of broken crockery at her feet.

"Kay! What is it?"

She pointed, and I squinted in the gloom of the drawn shades. Miss Templeton was sprawled motionless upon the bed, face contorted. The upper torso of her nightdress and the surrounding sheets were stained with a dark substance that could only be blood.

I caught Kay as she crumpled.

The disturbance soon reached the upper floors. A tousled-haired Leonard joined us minutes later, dressing gown hastily tied over his nightshirt. He pushed his way through the group of kitchen staff who had hurried to the scene.

"Are you all right? Was it you who screamed?" He distract-edly ran his fingers through his hair.

"That was Kay. Would you check on her?" I pointed to the chaise, then continued to survey the room. Several items littered the floor— a pair of reading glasses, an overturned brass lamp, and a feather pillow, its casing bloodstained and torn. Dresser drawers had been pulled out, the hanging clothes in the armoire were disarranged, and a nearly empty jewel case stood open upon the bureau.

Kay groaned.

Leonard helped her sit up. "Are you all right, Miss Finnerty?"

"I—I suppose."

Leonard frowned as he watched me survey the area around the bed. "Examining a dead body is hardly a task for a woman. You and Miss Finnerty should return to your rooms and leave this for the police."

I suppressed an undignified snort. "I promise not to succumb to the vapors. Besides, I've already checked the body." Out of sheer reflex—the victim's chest wound appeared un-survivable—I had felt for a pulse with no result. The skin was already cool, though the limbs had not yet stiffened. And the fingernails—they were interesting. "I do hope the coroner can tell us more."

"It's obviously a—" He stopped abruptly as the sounds of the boiler hissing and clanking reverberated in the room. "What on earth is that racket?"

"Greta needs to repair her boiler. It's situated just below us —what were you saying?"

"That it's obviously a burglary." He waved a hand toward the jewel box.

"Perhaps. There was a struggle, certainly. If you look at her fingernails, several are torn."

He showed no inclination to approach the bed. Kay, face hidden by her handkerchief, huddled in the chair and ignored us both.

"I found this slip of paper under the bed skirt," I went on. "It's difficult to say how long it has been there, or if it's important at all." I held it out.

"'Please forgive me,'" he read aloud. "I don't know what to make of it, either."

I'd returned the paper where I'd found it when a disturbance at the doorway caught my eye. Davis was pushing through the growing crowd. I glimpsed Cassie and Rose behind him. Soon everyone would be tramping in here.

Leonard turned back to Kay. "Can you stand now, Miss Finnerty? Here we go—easy, now." He supported her by the elbow as she stood on wobbly legs.

Davis came charging into the room, face distorted in distress. "Viola! Oh my God."

I stepped in his way. "I'm sorry. There's nothing you can do for her. We must call the police. Do you know if Greta has been informed?"

He swallowed but didn't answer. All of his attention was upon the still figure on the bed.

The situation was devolving quickly. I needed to get the room cleared.

"Cassie," I called, finally spotting her dark head in the crowd, "would you and Rose make sure Kay gets to her room to lie down?"

"*Rose?*" a voice exclaimed. It sounded like Chaffee, though I couldn't see him. "When did you arrive? Where have you *been?*"

Oh dear. Well, she'd wanted a chance to clear the air and reconcile with the players. Not exactly the best timing. Few things are in life.

Leonard remained behind as Cassie and Rose led Kay— also coaxing Davis, thankfully—out of the room.

"Could you find Greta and make sure she has called the police?" I asked, keeping my voice low. "And ask Sanderson to join me here."

He scowled. "Why Sanderson? I can help with whatever needs to be done."

"I appreciate that. However, he's the closest to a law enforcement official we have—at least until the police take charge." I also wanted to talk to him about what this might mean to his case.

At least Leonard didn't argue about it, though his lined brow made obvious that leaving me alone with a corpse troubled his masculine sensibilities.

Once he was out of the room, I closed the door to everyone else with a muttered excuse, then started my search for the plate in earnest. I had a feeling I wouldn't find it.

Within minutes a neatly attired Sanderson—a sharp contrast to Leonard's previous disheveled state—let himself in. He sucked in a sharp breath at the sight of Miss Templeton on the bed.

"You don't feel faint, do you?" I asked in alarm, as he groped for a chair.

His expression was sheepish. "My apologies. Mr. Frasier told me, of course, but that hardly prepares one for the reality of it."

I didn't imagine dead bodies fell into his lap all that often. His dealings with the criminal element were relegated to bland documentation.

Suddenly fatigued—it had been a long morning already, and there was more to come—I sat upon the chaise across from him. "Has Greta sent for the police?"

He nodded.

"I see two possible motives," I began, "but neither is without its complications."

"What's so complicated about a simple burglary?" he interrupted.

I would have expected more imagination from the fellow. "Simple? Hardly." My tone was perhaps more caustic than I'd intended. "We're missing a counterfeit plate, if you'll recall."

"I find it hard to believe Miss Templeton could have taken the plate from you," he said. "More likely a man. Though it wouldn't hurt to search the room, I suppose."

"I already have. It isn't here."

"Then we're back to the simple solution." He gestured to the open jewel case. "It's all here, plain as day—missing valuables, a ground-floor bedroom.... Was her door locked?"

"It was not," I conceded. "Kay brought her a breakfast tray and apparently walked right in after knocking."

"Is there evidence that any of the street-level windows or doors had been forced?"

"I haven't had time to examine them."

"I'll go check." He stood and hurried out the door, obviously eager to leave the room.

I blew out an exasperated breath. So much for reviewing the possible motives for Miss Templeton's murder. Perhaps the police would be more receptive, although experience had taught me otherwise.

When the police came, the first thing they did was send away the carriage that had come to load the trunks and other belongings headed for the train station. We were instructed to remain on hand to be interviewed.

I settled in the dining room with Cassie and Leonard, though no one had much of an appetite. Guests drifted over to the buffet table, idly picking up the teapot to help themselves, and just as distractedly setting it back down.

"Everyone is at sixes and sevens," Cassie murmured.

"Rose is the only one busy at the moment." I nodded toward the table beneath the windows in the dining room. There she sat, talking earnestly to Sally, who listened with arms folded and a mulish expression.

Leonard shifted irritably. "It's tedious to simply sit here and not be able to help." He stood. "I'm going to see what's happening."

Just then, a uniformed patrolman entered the room, cast his glance around, then lit upon me.

"I'm next," I said. "See you later."

I followed him to the study, where a man in his late fifties stood, politely waiting. His thinning salt-and-pepper hair was meticulously slicked back, his spotless gray tunic uniform fastened up to the collar in a double row of shiny brass buttons.

"Mrs. Wynch?" His voice was already hoarse with fatigue. "I'm Lieutenant Malvern. Please, have a seat."

As he gestured to the chair, I noticed Daniel Sanderson sitting in the window seat beyond, giving me a casual nod as he pulled out his watch.

"What is he doing here?" I asked, sitting in the chair indicated.

"Mr. Sanderson has informed me of his purpose here at the hotel," Malvern answered. "He's been quite helpful in sharing details of the principals in the case. Including you, ma'am."

"I see. Most commendable, but you still haven't answered my question, Lieutenant. Why is he here *now*?"

"He is of use to me," the lieutenant said curtly. "Now, then, let us proceed to our first order of business. I've been informed that you are a—what is it you do, exactly? Are you a helper of some sort? Not an actual detective, obviously."

"I am, indeed, employed by the Pinkerton Agency as a detective," I said. "Difficult as that may be for you to conceive."

He lifted a shoulder. "As you say. And I understand from Mr. Sanderson that you are armed?"

"True." I realized the import of his question. "You believe *I* shot Miss Templeton?"

Malvern didn't bother to answer. "Would you go up to your room and fetch your weapon, please?"

"No need." I pulled my derringer out of my skirt pocket and handed it over.

He blinked. "Do you typically carry a gun to the breakfast table?"

"These are not typical circumstances."

"Quite right," Sanderson murmured.

The lieutenant examined it closely. "*Hmph.* Hasn't been fired recently." He handed it back, and I tucked it away.

"I take it you haven't found the weapon yet?" I asked.

He grimaced. "We're searching, believe me."

"Did anyone hear the shot?" I asked.

The question was met with silence at first. I've been told I have an annoying habit of asking policemen as many—or more—questions as they put to me. I waited.

He decided to humor me, apparently. "No one heard anything untoward."

"I suppose that isn't surprising, since the housekeeper's quarters are just above a very noisy boiler."

Malvern gave me a probing look. "You're a sharp one. That's the likely explanation. Though it appears as if the killer tried to further muffle the noise by firing through a pillow."

I agreed such a maneuver wouldn't accomplish much, but there might be a different explanation. "Perhaps he—or she, I suppose—used the pillow to try to subdue her, or even asphyxiate her. But she put up a fight—you noted the broken fingernails, Lieutenant? You must have—so then, the killer was forced to shoot."

Sanderson's face took on a grayish pallor at my candid account. Even the lieutenant shifted uncomfortably. I've also been told I can be rather blunt.

Malvern cleared his throat. "The doctor will be better able to determine all that. Now, if you are finished dominating my inquiry, ma'am, I would appreciate you answering *my* questions." He sat down at the desk and consulted a small, brown, cardboard-backed notepad. "I understand the hotel suffered a break-in several nights ago and then there was an assault upon you last night. Why do you think that would be?"

I looked at Sanderson. "You haven't told him?"

"Oh, he has," the lieutenant said. "I want to hear it from you. From the beginning." He turned to a fresh page.

Sanderson gave a slight nod in my direction.

I took that to mean that I could be forthcoming about the counterfeit plate, along with the rest of it. Thankfully, I detest having to amend accounts and keep track of falsehoods. Particularly where law enforcement is concerned.

I launched into the story, and it took a while before I was finished.

The policeman got up and began to pace. "I thought we were dealing with a simple thief, surprised in the process of stealing valuables from a lady's room." His gaze flicked to Sanderson. "Do you believe that whoever is directing the counterfeiters' gang sent the killer to get it from her?"

"I had not wished to believe it when Mrs. Wynch first raised the notion," Sanderson answered, grimacing in my direction by way of apology, "as that would mean the plate is irrecoverable. But now...." He shrugged.

"I did posit such a theory," I said, "but I must point out there are certain difficulties in that regard. If Miss Templeton was the one who hit me and made off with the plate, why would she do so? And how would the counterfeiters learn she had possession of it?"

The men exchanged blank stares.

"I have another idea," I said. "What if Miss Templeton's death was personal?"

"Oh?" Malvern folded his arms. "Go on."

"Have you spoken with Barrett Ward? He's the lead actor of the Pierson Players. Or was," I amended.

"Not yet. We'll get to everyone eventually. Are you suggesting this man held ill will towards the lady?"

Sanderson, obviously seeing where I was going, straightened in his seat. "That's right, I'd forgotten—last night's argument between Ward and Miss Templeton. You could be right."

"An argument? Regarding what?" Malvern asked.

I recounted Miss Templeton's belief that Ward had staged the accident that injured her. "She said she feared for her safety at his hands," I finished.

Malvern was scribbling in his notebook at a furious pace. "How did he answer the accusation?"

"He denied it, but she alluded to knowing uncomfortable truths about his past. She wondered if that was why he wanted her out of the way."

"Anything else?"

"He accused her of being responsible for the loss of his lead role for the next stop of their tour. 'Meddling in his affairs,' he called it. He warned her about ruining his career. I heard a slap as well." I grimaced, remembering. "I didn't see who struck whom."

"Most disturbing." Malvern went to the door and murmured something to the policeman standing in the hall. Summoning Ward next, most likely.

He resumed his seat. "Exactly when did this argument take place?"

"Quite late…one o'clock this morning?" I glanced at Sanderson for confirmation.

He nodded. "Maybe even past that. It was after the cast party had dispersed."

"Mere hours before she died." Malvern sighed and closed his notebook. "Now there are at least two motives to consider."

I didn't envy him his task. "I assume we must remain at the hotel until you finish your search?"

"That is correct," he said stiffly.

"Does that apply to Mr. Sanderson and Mrs. Richards as well?" Sanderson may not have the plate, but at least he had Flora.

"I'm afraid so." Malvern flashed the man a rueful look. "If

all goes smoothly, we may finish our inquiry in time for you and your witness to catch the late-afternoon train."

"As long as we leave no later than tomorrow, we should be fine," Sanderson said. "But if I might ask a favor, Lieutenant —may I accompany your men in their hunt for the weapon? I can keep an eye out for the plate."

Malvern frowned. "It's rather irregular."

"We have been at the whim of irregularities," Sanderson protested. "First, in the instance of Mrs. Wynch having recovered the plate only to have it taken from her by force, and now, the death of the unfortunate actress."

We did seem to be stymied at every turn, I reflected. "It had been Mr. Sanderson's intent to call your station this morning, Lieutenant, to request a formal search of everyone's belongings before they left town. Unfortunately, we had to call you for another reason entirely."

"I see," Malvern said slowly. "Very well, Mr. Sanderson, you may go along, but only as an observer, do you understand? I want no interference in their task."

"Where are they now?" Sanderson asked.

"Currently, they're going through the packed trunks that were to be loaded onto the stagecoach. Tell Sergeant Carver I gave you permission."

Sanderson inclined his head in acknowledgment as he got up to leave. "Thank you." With a slight bow to me, he added, "If you'll excuse me."

"I believe that will be all, Mrs. Wynch." Malvern stood, as did I. "The patrolman will escort you back to the dining room."

"Is there anything more I can do?"

"No, ma'am. I would advise you, however, to refrain from sharing the content of our interview. My job is difficult enough without the complication of gossiping women."

I gave a non-committal shrug. I had no intention of following his advice. Gossip can be a useful tool.

As I was about to follow the patrolman out, the lieutenant added, "Make sure you know where your weapon is at all times. We still have a killer unaccounted for."

I hardly needed to be reminded of that.

A policeman burst in. "Sir!" he cried. "Mr. Ward is gone."

"What do you mean *gone?*" Malvern thundered.

"He's not in his room. No one has seen him."

"Did he leave a note?" I asked.

The patrolman glanced uncertainly at me before turning to the officer.

The lieutenant grimaced. "Answer the question."

"No note. His belongings are there."

"John Davis didn't go with him?" I asked. "That's his valet," I added, noting his furrowed brow.

"No. Mr. Davis is in the salon," the policeman said.

"We should check Ward's room," I said to Malvern, "to see if he left any sort of clue as to where he might have gone. If you ask Davis to join us, he can help with that."

"Us?" Malvern said sarcastically. He hesitated for a long moment, then sighed. "All right, we'll both go. Patrolman, have Davis brought to Ward's room. And send men out to check the cab stands and train station."

The space was a disheveled mess of heaped-up bedclothes, half-open drawers, and clothing draped over bedposts and chairs. The disorder was different from that of Miss Templeton's room, however. It had more of the feel of a slovenly occupant than a frantic search by an intruder.

Malvern wrinkled his nose in distaste. "You say he has a valet? Fellow's not doing his job."

"On the contrary," came a soft retort. Davis had walked in so quietly that Malvern, facing the window, whipped around in surprise.

John Davis looked like a different man today. Gone was his energetic air and brisk movements, replaced with a heaviness evidenced by the dull-eyed expression, the slumped shoulders that creased his jacket, the hands held limply at his sides.

"Before Barrett retired last night," he went on, "everything was in order."

"You're John Davis?" Malvern asked. "Ward's valet?"

He gave a nod, then jerked his thumb in my direction. "Why is she here?"

I suppressed a smile. That sounded familiar.

"Never mind that. I'm asking the questions," Malvern said sternly. "Why do you call your master by his first name?"

Davis's pencil mustache twitched. "Ours is not the traditional master-servant relationship. We're friends. He needed a valet and asked Pierson for one. As I have only an auxiliary role in our current production, I was available."

"Fine, fine," Malvern said impatiently. "We can't locate Ward. Do you know where he would be?"

"You've checked everywhere?" Davis asked.

"Of *course* we've checked everywhere," the policeman snapped. "I wouldn't be asking you otherwise."

"I'm afraid I can't help you. He and I intended to leave with the rest of the group today. I was not aware of any other plans."

"Take a survey of Ward's belongings," Malvern said to Davis, "and tell me if anything's missing."

Davis started sifting through the drawers and the armoire. He was thorough, especially with the top dresser drawer, moving items aside to look in the back.

"Well?" Malvern said.

Davis pushed the drawer closed. "It appears his toiletry kit, a change of linen, and an extra shirt are gone."

"When did you see him last?" I asked, which earned me a scowl from Malvern.

Davis puckered his brow as he thought. "Late last night. I

was one of the first to leave the party—he was still downstairs then—but later, I heard him enter his room. From the sounds of slamming drawers and heavy footsteps, I could tell he was angry, so I let him be."

"Do you know where he would go to elude capture?" Malvern asked.

Davis blinked at that. "Capture?"

"It's safe to say he killed Miss Templeton and has now fled," Malvern said.

Davis folded his arms. "Barrett can be many disagreeable things, but he's no murderer. There must be another explanation."

The policeman glared. "We'll decide that when we find him. What places does he frequent here in town?"

"Besides here and the theater? Our production schedule doesn't afford much time for leisure." He bit his lip as he considered. "There is one place—a gentleman's club recommended by one of the staff. Barrett likes to play cards." He reached for a sheet of paper and pencil on the nightstand, scribbled something, and handed it to the policeman. "Here's the address."

I hung back to talk to Davis as Malvern hurried out of the room, barking orders to a patrolman.

Davis frowned as I closed the door. "What is it?"

"The lieutenant didn't notice what you were doing." I inclined my head toward the drawer. "I saw you move something to better conceal it. Did you plan to take the gun away with you to cover for Ward?"

CHAPTER 16

*H*e gaped at me for a good long minute. "You really are a detective," he said finally.

I had yet to convince Malvern of that, but Davis's comment made one thing clear. "You were the one who searched my room and found my lockpicks and journal."

That would have been the second time—Rose had already admitted to the first break-in. Greta should really attend to the door locks of the guests' rooms. They were child's play, even for amateurs.

"Not me—Viola," he said. "She'd heard gossip about a night-time intruder. When she noticed your injury the next day, she got suspicious."

Miss Templeton had been more ambulatory than I'd thought, even back then. "Was she suspicious enough to monitor my telegrams as well?"

He cleared his throat awkwardly. "Let us say she took advantage of opportunities."

"And you were in her confidence."

He ran a weary hand through his hair. "There were no secrets between us. I loved her."

I felt a twinge of pity for the fellow, but we didn't have

much time before Malvern realized he hadn't yet searched Ward's room for the weapon.

I reached deep into the drawer Davis had been fussing with and pulled out a heavy, cloth-wrapped bundle. I nudged aside the covering—one of Ward's distinctive monogrammed handkerchiefs—to reveal a Colt pocket revolver, a common sidearm during the war. "Pocket" was certainly a misnomer, as this one sported a six-inch barrel. A few tiny pin feathers clung to the trigger ring. I leaned in and caught the faint scent of gun powder residue.

His frown cleared as I held it out for him to see.

"I imagine you're relieved it isn't yours—a Smith and Wesson double-action revolver, isn't that right?"

He nodded. "When I felt it in there, I wondered if somehow…. Wait—how do you know I even have a gun, much less what kind it is?"

I let him figure it out.

"You searched my room," he said finally.

There seemed to be a lot of that going around. "Where is it now?"

"Locked in Chaffee's office at the theater, last I knew. He'd asked to borrow it after someone broke into the ticket office last week and stole a drawerful of cash. He's often in his office alone late at night. I'd forgotten to get it back from him." He eyed the weapon in my hand. "But after Viola was shot, I couldn't help but wonder what might have happened to it."

"For the sake of full disclosure, you'll want to tell Malvern." I gestured to the Colt. "How long has Ward had this?" Things weren't looking good for the aging actor.

Davis sat down abruptly on the vanity bench. "I have no idea. I've never seen it before."

"In these weeks of spying on him, you've never seen this weapon?"

He bristled at that. "*Spy* is a strong word."

"But an accurate one," I said dryly. "Pierson asked you to

do it, didn't he?" That would explain why the director finally acquiesced to Ward's demands for a valet. Who better positioned to monitor someone than a valet?

I took his silence for affirmation. "Why spy on Ward?"

"Well, um…Barrett can get himself into predicaments."

"Of what sort?"

Davis swallowed, as if wishing to take back the word, then plowed ahead. "He'd skipped out on a couple of gambling debts last month…and then a hotel manager at our last stop complained about missing jewelry."

"I see." Welching was one thing, but thievery would be another matter entirely, and ignored at one's peril.

"Pierson didn't want to do anything drastic, though," Davis said, "until he had proof. Barrett may not be an extraordinary talent, but he's been a reliable, versatile actor for the Pierson Players."

"You uncovered that proof," I said. "A jewel."

He bit his lip. "You found that, too?"

I still felt a chill, recalling the bitter note. *I hope you choke on it.* At first, I had thought Davis to be the blackmailer, but Ward—the avid card-player ever in need of funds—made more sense.

"Tell me—who is *R*?" I asked.

He shook his head stubbornly.

I let it go for now. "Ward must have realized it was missing and that you were the one to have taken it. What did he do?"

He shrugged. "What could he do? He knew he'd been caught. I told him straight out that I was going to Pierson with it, and he'd better have an explanation ready."

"What did Pierson do? Did he return the gem?"

As I asked the question, I realized I'd seen part of it for myself. Just before the opening curtain Friday evening—the interchange between Pierson, Chaffee, and Chaffee's daughter Sally. Chaffee had been poised to strike Pierson, as Sally sobbed on his shoulder.

Sally. *Regina Salvia.*

The young woman who, by Rose's account, had been involved with Ward. Given the angry interaction between them at the theater, however, the relationship had not ended well. Did Ward's blackmail end the dalliance, or did that come later? What had he threatened to tell?

The notion of Sally as Ward's blackmail victim also explained the stage accidents. The seamstress could have managed them easily, as she was ever-present and intimately familiar with the stage workings. Naturally, she saw Ward as a threat. I recalled Flora's words. *Barrett was standing right beside me on stage.... Perhaps he's the target. And he was with Viola when the trap door gave way.* Flora had been right.

I resolved to have a talk with Sally once this business was resolved.

I was too preoccupied to know whether Davis answered my question, but the sound of rapid footsteps outside brought our conversation to a halt.

Malvern flung open the door. "What are you two still doing in here?" His gaze dropped to the gun in my hand. "Don't tell me," he said faintly.

"This appears to be what you're looking for," I said, passing him the bundle. "It was in the top dresser drawer."

He gave a grunt. "If you would go about your business and *leave me to mine,* I'd be grateful." He turned to Davis with a scowl. "You, stay here. I have additional questions for you."

I half expected Sanderson to be dogging Malvern's heels, but there was no sign of him when I left the room. I had to admit to a sense of relief. His involvement in the lieutenant's investigation had given him a smug air that I didn't care for. In a way, I rather preferred the fellow I'd initially met, who didn't think so well on his feet and liked to come up with ludicrous code phrases to communicate.

He must still be occupied in the search—which would end

now that the gun had been recovered. I went in search of
Cassie.

I hadn't gotten very far before Greta intercepted me on
the stairs.

"May I speak to you?" she asked, her voice subdued.

I followed her into the music salon. It was hardly the
welcoming space of last evening. Instead of basking in the
warmth of candlelight and congeniality, we shivered in the
gloom of the watery, late-winter light coming through the
windows. The padded chairs were lined up against the sides
of the room like regimental soldiers, and the pianoforte was
closed tight.

"I wanted to speak with you about Flora," Greta said,
breaking into my thoughts. "I'm uneasy about her going back
to New York."

And no wonder. "Are you concerned about her husband's
cronies coming after her during the trip?" I asked. "Or the
possibility of the authorities deciding to prosecute you both
when you get there?"

She glared. "Has anyone ever told you that you're exasper-
atingly blunt?"

I shrugged.

"Both concern me, of course," Greta acknowledged, "but
it is Flora's reaction to all this that worries me most. She acts
like hunted prey. I believe she's fearful of Sanderson. She
won't talk to me."

"But you are accompanying her to New York, yes? That at
least will put her mind at ease."

"He refuses to allow it."

I blinked. "Really? Did he say why?"

"He claimed I would aid Flora in slipping away from him
during the trip."

"That's absurd." The mental image of Greta in her
advanced years trying to keep up with Flora as they dashed
for a hansom was enough to make my lips twitch.

She grimaced. "Exactly."

"I can talk with him, though I cannot guarantee my words will carry any weight."

"I would appreciate that," she said.

"I have one condition, however."

"Oh?"

"You must find a way to compensate Kay Finnerty for what you have done to her." I didn't trouble to keep the brittleness from my voice.

She opened her mouth as if to deny it, then slumped in her seat. "How did you know?"

"Gossip reached my ears. Your visits to the kitchen are rare, and yet you did so during dinner preparations that day. Whenever someone deviates from their usual way of doing things, it's inevitably noticed."

"They all know?" She gripped the chair with a pale-knuckled hand.

"Not exactly. The prevailing opinion is that you inadvertently used a spoiled ingredient because of your lack of experience. Which is more grace than you deserve," I added severely. "What did you put in her food?"

She swallowed. "Tinned chicken. Yes, it had, *um*, spoiled. I wanted to only incapacitate her. Just for a few days. I wasn't trying to kill her."

"But that could have been the result."

She spread her hands in a helpless gesture. "What would you have me do? I dare not admit anything to Miss Finnerty. I would be ruined."

"You would. But a confession isn't what I have in mind. I'm giving you a chance to find a way to make amends to the young lady." Greta would be evading proper punishment, which did not sit well with me, but we had more dire matters to settle. "We still have time before Malvern releases everyone. Do not squander the opportunity."

She gave a stiff nod. "What's this I hear about Barrett—is he really gone?"

"It's true. The police are on the hunt for him now. A gun —likely the murder weapon—was found in his room, and Davis says he's taken some personal items."

She shook her head. "I don't understand it."

"You heard nothing untoward last night?"

"How could we?" Greta retorted. "Sanderson had us confined to our bedrooms after the party."

"He locked you in?" I asked incredulously.

"Not quite, though we certainly felt like prisoners. He moved the cot into the foyer of the apartment, right across the doorway, and slept there all night. Can you believe it? I took a sleeping draught and went to bed. Flora did the same."

We were both quiet for a while.

"I don't know how the hotel is ever going to recover from —" Greta broke off at the sound of frantic tapping on the windowpane.

We turned our heads toward the sound. Flora, wearing a maid's hooded market cloak, stood outside. She pointed toward one of the latched side doors. Greta hurried over to open it.

"Thank goodness." Flora gasped, quickly pushing the door shut and leaning against it to get her breath. "I thought the policeman out front was going to catch me for sure."

"What were you doing out there?" Greta asked reprovingly.

"Don't worry, Aunt Greta, everything is going to be—" Flora stopped abruptly, noticing me in the gloom.

But it wasn't me she was looking at, apparently, for a male voice behind me said, "No one is supposed to leave the building while it's being searched."

Daniel Sanderson stepped into the room. He flashed me a scowl. "Mrs. Wynch, I would have thought you, of all people, would know better." He fixed his attention on Flora next. "Where did you go?"

"Out for some air," she answered, sticking out a mulish chin. "I am tired of being locked up and treated like a criminal."

"I wouldn't throw that word around, if I were you," he warned. "You're dancing close enough to that line as it is."

I didn't believe Flora's story, either, but I wouldn't get anything meaningful out of her in front of Sanderson. I had to get rid of him if I could.

"Did you hear about the gun's discovery?" I asked him.

He nodded. "I'm more concerned about the plate. It's nowhere to be found."

Greta cleared her throat. I knew she wanted me to keep my promise.

I tipped my head in her direction before turning back to Sanderson. "I understand that you refuse to allow Mrs. Marlowe to accompany her great-niece when you take her to New York."

His eyes flicked over to Greta, then back to me. "That is correct."

"You must realize the impropriety of traveling alone with a woman who is not a relation. Mrs. Marlowe accompanying you will lend the necessary respectability."

He gave a snort. "'Respectability.' Mrs. Richards has hardly behaved in a respectable manner."

"Mr. Sanderson," Greta said, her voice thin with fatigue, "I understand your concern that she might run away. What if I promise to make sure she does not? You have no quarrel with me, I assume?"

He had no time to respond before Flora interrupted.

"Aunt Greta." Her voice held a steely edge. "Do not beg this man for anything." She took a step toward Sanderson, hands on her hips. "Do as you please, sir. It makes no matter. I will not allow myself to be cowed by you anymore."

He blinked in surprise.

I had to admit to surprise as well. Flora was hardly behaving like the "hunted prey" Greta had described. What had changed?

Sanderson broke the silence. "If you'll excuse me, I have other things to attend to."

"Yes, of course you do," Flora murmured, watching him leave. She squared her shoulders. "I'm heading to the kitchen," she said to Greta. "Would you care for a cup of tea?"

"I—I suppose, dear." Greta followed her out, glancing back at me in confusion.

I understood how she felt.

It wasn't until late afternoon that Lieutenant Malvern stepped into the parlor—most of us were gathered there, in anticipation of dinner—to finally take his leave of us.

Pierson leaned forward eagerly. "Have you caught Ward yet?"

John Davis shifted in his chair. "You treat him as a fugitive, Nat. Barrett's our friend."

Pierson shook his head. "Between the gun in his room and his abrupt departure, it's clear he's guilty. And then there's— never mind."

Malvern frowned at Pierson. "What do *you* know about a gun in his room?"

The director waved a dismissive hand. "One hears things."

Malvern lifted a questioning eyebrow in my direction. I shrugged. It hardly mattered now.

"Besides, Lieutenant," Kay chimed in, "you've interviewed us twice now, and the second time it was all about Barrett. It hardly takes a genius to figure out why."

"Lord save me from precocious females," the policeman muttered.

"Well?" Greta asked impatiently. "What happens now? Are the guests free to leave?"

He nodded. "I've finally received confirmation that the gun found is the murder weapon. Based on everyone's account, we have a good idea of how events transpired. There's no reason to keep you people here any longer."

A collective sigh of relief could be heard throughout the room, but Pierson shifted irritably in his seat. "I wish you could have finished sooner, sir. We might have made the 4:15 train. Now we must wait until morning. We've lost the day."

"A young woman has lost her life," Malvern retorted. He gestured to a uniformed man who held a pad and pencil at the ready. "The sergeant here will verify your addresses in case we have further questions. I already have the itinerary for the rest of your tour. Should you decide upon any deviation, or in the unlikely event you hear from Ward"—he handed Pierson a card—"you must contact me immediately."

"Of course," the director said.

"Let us know when you catch him," Al Chaffee said, his tone fierce. And no wonder, considering the distress Ward had caused his daughter.

"*If* they catch him," Miss Reid chimed in.

"Don't worry—we'll get him," Malvern said.

CHAPTER 17

MONDAY, MARCH 12

"Well, this is a surprise," Cassie said, drawing open the curtains of our bedroom.

Rose and I came over for a look. At least a foot of snow blanketed the ground, streets, and buildings. And it was still coming down, thick and fast.

"Quite unusual for the middle of March," Rose said. "Especially since the temperatures have been mild lately. Early spring is so unpredictable."

"The wind is picking up, too," I said. "We'd better retrieve our heavy coats from the luggage before we head to the station."

Cassie let the curtain drop. "I hope it won't delay the trains."

That sentiment was the central concern among the acting company and the sole topic of discussion in the breakfast room when we joined the others. It was as if the murder had never happened.

Several guests congregated at the windows, where the

blinds were raised for whatever weak light could be had, to augment the illumination from the chandelier and wall sconces.

Mary Reid stepped back from the window with a sigh. "I wish we'd gone yesterday. Travel today is going to be a mess."

"We'll want to make an earlier start," Pierson said. "Better to wait at the station than not get there at all. I'll arrange it with the desk clerk."

On his way out, he stopped by the table where Flora and Sanderson were seated. He said something to her I couldn't catch, gave a formal bow over her hand, and continued out of the room.

Flora was at her ease this morning, drinking her tea and chatting with Rose. Remarkable—here she was about to be escorted to New York to testify against her husband, a prospect that had had her in a panic only two days ago.

Sanderson, on the other hand, appeared quite harried. His glance shifted to Flora, then to the windows, then to Greta. At one point he noticed me watching him and looked away.

I supposed it was natural to feel the weight of responsibility when one was transporting a witness, and a reluctant one at that.

Kay drifted over to their table, a plate of toast in her still-bandaged hand.

As my own stomach was rumbling, I made my way over to the buffet, where Greta, attired in a traveling outfit, was in close conversation with the housekeeper. Both surveyed the table with deep frowns. Finally, the housekeeper shook her head and left.

"Is everything all right?" I asked.

"The weather is affecting our larder." Greta gestured at the meager spread—sliced bread beside the toasting rack, a jar of marmalade, two teapots, a creamer pitcher, and the sugar bowl. "The milkman couldn't get us a complete delivery this morning—his own supplies are delayed by the snow. We

barely have enough milk and butter to get us through breakfast. And with yesterday being a Sunday and the stores closed,
we're completely out of other essentials we were counting on
getting today."

"I expect the grocer's boy would have difficulty delivering
supplies in this weather," I said.

"I've sent a couple of men out," Greta said, "but I wonder
whether anything is open." She made a face.

"Perhaps the snow will stop soon."

"Let us hope so," Greta said. "We're low on coal, too.
We're expecting a delivery this afternoon. I'm not sure they'll
be coming." She surveyed the room. "I hate to leave town
when things are in this state."

"Your housekeeper is quite capable," I said reassuringly.
"Does this mean Sanderson is allowing you to accompany
Flora to New York?"

"He said nothing on the subject. I'm taking that as
assent." Her jaw clenched as she glanced over at him, sitting
beside Flora. "I dare him to try and stop me."

I glanced back out the window, where the snow was
swirling against the buildings, all but obliterating the view
across the street. "The weather may have more to say on the
matter than he does."

"Doubtful." She gave a grunt. "No snowstorm has stopped
the trains during my lifetime."

I changed the subject, inclining my head toward Kay, who
had finished all but the crusts of her toast. "She's in good
spirits this morning. Did you have anything to do with that?"

"Brilliant deduction," she said acidly, then softened her
tone as she watched Kay from across the room. "Now that
Viola is no longer, *um*, with us"—she paused, but elaborated
no further—"and Flora will be unavailable for the Philadelphia tour, I urged Pierson to abandon his original plan to
contract an outside actress he knows and to instead promote
Kay. It would also involve an increase in salary."

"And that salary, I assume, is being augmented by you?" I asked.

"Naturally, in addition to a sizeable costume allowance." She smiled. "Pierson was happy to accept the additional funds. I encouraged him to see it as a sponsorship of sorts, since Kay is an untested quantity."

"That was more generous than I anticipated," I murmured.

She shrugged. "It never sat well with me that the men earn more than the women, anyway."

While I was happy for Kay, the sight of her bandaged hand reminded me that I had yet to determine her possible involvement.

There wasn't much time before everyone scattered. The time to talk to her was now.

Muttering excuses to Greta, I hurried to intercept Kay as she left the dining room.

"May we talk?" I asked.

She froze. "What about?" she asked warily.

Now I knew she was concealing something. She'd never been reluctant to converse before.

I drew her into the empty music salon. Our heels echoed hollowly on the parquet floor. "I need your help."

"Me?"

I gestured to a chair. "Please, have a seat."

She perched upon the chair's edge.

"This isn't generally known," I began, "but I was attacked in Greta's suite while the play was going on Saturday evening. You and Miss Templeton were the only two—besides the servants—here at the time."

She bristled. "Are you accusing *me*?"

"I didn't say that." My gaze dropped to her bandaged hand, which she covered reflexively. "I was hoping you might have seen or heard something that could help me identify who is responsible." I gave a shrug. "Obviously, I cannot ask Miss Templeton."

She stood. "I'm sorry, I can't tell you anything. If you'll excuse me, I have some tasks to take care of before we leave."

As I watched her hurry away, I couldn't help but wonder if Sanderson's plate was leaving with her.

I returned to the breakfast room, nearly empty now, the guests having dispersed to finish travel preparations.

Cassie stood by the double window. I joined her there to survey the scene.

The sweepers along the main thoroughfare were working industriously to make a path for vehicles and pedestrians, but the snowfall was filling in the gaps as quickly as they could be cleared.

"This doesn't look promising," I said.

She sighed. "I overheard the housekeeper saying the telephone is out now. At least Pierson got his call in to the coach service before it happened." She pulled her shawl closer against the draft. "The sooner we're home, the better I'll feel."

I heartily agreed with her. "You're all packed?"

She nodded. "I'll be in the parlor with my needlework. Let me know when the coach arrives."

I was feeling too restless to sit. As the kitchen seemed to be the hub for the latest information, I volunteered to help bring down dishes from the dining room. Normally such efforts from a guest would be rebuffed, but the staff who didn't live on the premises hadn't made it here yet.

I was bringing in the last tray of crockery when a man came through the kitchen door, snow crusted to the knees of his trousers. "A fellow named Pierson requested a coach to the station? I'm the driver."

The cook frowned. "Why didn't you ring at the front?"

"I'm not here to get them. The coach is stuck at the bottom of the hill. I had to leave it. Mine isn't the only one, either. I got the horses unhitched, at least. They're keeping warm in your stables for now." His teeth chattered as he tucked his hands under his arms.

"You poor man." The cook's assistant clucked her tongue. "Have a sit by the fire. I'll get you some hot tea. There's only tinned milk to go in it, though."

"No matter." He blew out a breath, shrugged off his coat, and draped it over the drying rack used for linens.

"I'll get the sugar," I offered. As I put the bowl on the tray, I asked the man, "Have you heard any news?"

"Telegraph is out. We're completely cut off from everyone." He shook his head in disbelief. "Never thought I'd see the day."

"What about the trains?"

"An eastbound one was leaving the station when I left to come here, but I doubt any more'll make it out today. The Hartford Express got stuck just north of us. They're scrounging up men to go dig the locomotive out. Passengers have been walking along the tracks to get back to the station." He took a long sip and sat back. "Don't envy them that. The snow's fillin' in fast, and the wind is whipping up drifts somethin' fierce."

Greta came into the kitchen on the heels of that remark. "The men aren't making any progress in keeping the walks clear. I told them to focus their efforts on the hatch to the coal chute—if we're lucky enough to get a delivery—and on clearing the roof. With this much snow and no end in sight, we can't risk it collapsing." She nodded toward the cook. "Keep the stove going just hot enough for the kettle. If the lads are lucky enough to return with coffee, make a large pot of it."

The kitchen door opened again, letting in a swirl of cold air and snow along with two fellows I recognized as Greta's footmen.

"Get that door closed!" the cook barked.

They fought the wind that kept it ajar and finally got it

shut. Dazed, they stood beside the door, covered head to toe in snow.

Greta eyed the nearly empty sacks they clutched. "It appears you were not successful."

"We walked to three grocers before we found one open," one said.

"And his shelves were practically bare," the other chimed in. "But we got some more tinned milk, a can of coffee, and jam. But no eggs or butter, and the butcher was closed, so no fresh meat. Sorry, ma'am."

"Well, that's something," the cook's assistant said briskly, reaching for the goods. "Better change into dry clothes before you catch your deaths. I'll make you something hot when you come back."

"Not yet." Greta held up a hand. "First go up and help the stable lads clear off the roof." She grimaced at the glum-faced fellows. "It shouldn't take too long."

With a chorus of weary sighs, the two men buttoned up their coats once more and trudged back out.

It is an odd thing, how people react when plans change unexpectedly and when what is to follow is unknown. I'd seen it in myself in times past—the restlessness, the need for activity, the indecision as to precisely how to occupy oneself. Such a phenomenon was at work in our guests today. Folks perused bookshelves, took turns at the piano, and played lackluster rounds of card games. Invariably the activity would conclude with pacing to the window to gaze upon the growing snow drifts and exclaim at the ferocity of the wind.

The servants, of course, had no such dilemma as idle time. One sad task left to the housekeeper and the only two maids who lived in was cleaning the bedrooms once occupied by Miss Templeton and Barrett Ward. Linens were changed, trunks were packed and moved out of the way, and blood was scrubbed from the floor of the housekeeper's quarters so Mrs. Young could move back in. I shook my head in wonder at the iron will of the housekeeper, not at all fazed by the prospect of sleeping in the bed of a murdered woman. Leonard planned to occupy Ward's former room once that was done, which meant that Rose could move back to her room so that Cassie and I weren't cramped for space.

No travel didn't mean no visitors, however. Shortly after dinner—a meager affair, consisting of cold ham, jellied tongue, yesterday's biscuits, and canned peas—a group of four women and six children arrived at our doorstep, escorted by a pair of sturdy fellows from the train station.

The new arrivals stepped inside with their sacks, baskets, and other belongings, blinking at the sudden brightness. And no wonder, as the wind had knocked down the electrical lines supplying the streetlamps outside. It must have been a challenge to navigate the dark, snowy streets, even with lanterns. At least the gas lights in the hotel were still working, though the occasional sputtering of the sconces did not bode well for our continued good fortune.

The commotion brought Greta to the foyer. "What is this?"

One of the men—obviously in charge—tipped his soggy cap. "Sorry to bring you extra company without any notice, ma'am, but with the phones out, I figured we should just show up. I'm the station master." He gestured to the group. "These are some of the stranded passengers from the Hartford Express. The men are bunking down in the station, but we hoped you could accommodate the ladies and their young ones."

"Yes, of course," Greta said, with a gracious nod. "We don't have any spare rooms, but we'll do our best to make you all comfortable in the salon."

The harried expression of one young woman smoothed as

she bent down to unbutton her daughter's jacket. "Much obliged, ma'am."

"You poor things," Cassie clucked, reaching to divest another child of his coat, "you must be perishing cold." She first had to pry a covered basket out of the boy's stiff grip. I heard soft mews come from within.

The station master handed Greta a rucksack. "Some extra provisions, with our compliments."

Before he turned away, Greta asked, "Our coal delivery never came. We're almost out. Can you help us?"

"I'll send some fellows over with sacks. Won't be until the morning, though."

Greta bit her lip. "I suppose we can manage until then."

Leonard, Rose, Cassie, and I pitched in to assist Greta's staff in settling the new arrivals in the music salon, where a wood fire was stoked for their comfort. Extra chairs, ottomans, cushions, and blankets were set out, along with a buffet table of comestibles and hot beverages. The wall sconces finally expired by the time we were done—undoubtedly the gas lines were affected now, too—so the staff pulled out candelabras and placed them throughout the room. Dim illumination, to be sure, but it made for a cozy atmosphere.

The bustle of activity drew the attention of those upstairs who'd been moping in their rooms. As guests joined the travelers in the salon, the gathering took on a picnic-like atmosphere. The kitten was released from its basket, given a bowl of tinned milk, and permitted to wander around. Children sat cross-legged on the floor. Miss Reid went over to the piano and played a lively tune. Harmonicas materialized out of the pockets of two boys—brothers, as it turned out. Soon most in the company were singing along to familiar songs.

Cassie and I made room on the divan for Rose.

"How are you faring, Rose?" I inclined my head towards Chaffee, who was turning sheet music for Mary—and Sally, too, who sat beside her on the piano bench. "Have you been forgiven? Do you have your job back?"

"I'm not sure about 'forgiven.'" Her lips pressed together in a grimace. "But, yes, I've been reinstated as the theater's seamstress. I think he did it more for Sally's sake than anything else."

I bit back a sigh. My talk with Sally was long overdue. Although her role in the theater's "accidents" could not be proved and Miss Templeton—the only person directly harmed by her actions—was now dead, I wanted to rattle the young lady sufficiently so she would not resort to similar tactics in the future. Many men would come and go and inevitably break one's heart. Attempted murder was hardly the remedy, even in the face of blackmail.

Leonard, who'd finished bringing over chairs from the library, perched on the ottoman at Cassie's feet. "Thank goodness that's done."

"You've been put to work a great deal lately." Cassie clucked her tongue in sympathy.

The corners of his eyes crinkled in a warm smile. "Happy to help, my dear lady."

She blushed. At the sight of the children running out of the room to chase the kitten, who had apparently decided to explore the hallway, she changed the subject. "Crowded though we are, the infusion of new people is the very thing we need to lift us out of our bleak mood."

I was inclined to agree. And now, for the first time since recent events had unfolded, I could catch my breath and attend to the friends who had stayed by my side through it all —Cassie and Leonard.

Leonard had made no further romantic overtures toward me since the day of his arrival. In the intervening days, I had to admit, I'd barely noticed. Who could blame me, after all? He was acceding to my wishes, was he not? But as I glanced at my two friends, I realized another explanation was worth considering.

Mary, her harmonica accompanists having deserted her, struck up a sweet, nostalgic ballad. The room quieted as we listened.

My own thoughts drifted, to a longing for home, to the prospect of spending time with the two very different men in my life who made things so complicated…and unquestionably interesting.

Out of the corner of my vision, I saw Cassie slowly, tentatively, stretch out her hand and brush Leonard's where it rested on the cushion between them. His fingers flexed, then clasped hers.

I smiled to myself. It made all the sense in the world.

With Rose back in her own room, I had my proper bed again. I was anticipating my first comfortable night's rest in a while.

Ironically, sleep eluded me. I was warm enough under my pile of quilts, and the only sounds intruding upon my consciousness were the rattle of the windowpanes and Cassie's soft snore.

I watched the flicker of the hurricane lamp reflected upon the painted tin ceiling as the minutes ticked by.

Enough of this. I threw off the bedcovers, retrieved my slippers and robe, lit a candle in its holder, and crept down the stairs. I should be able to find something in Greta's library to quiet my mind.

Except for the wind, which continued to whistle through every crevice, all was quiet. Even the boiler—having run out of coal and non-functional now—was silent.

A soft clink of glass caught my attention, coming from the kitchen. Who else was up at this hour? I changed direction.

Sally Chaffee stood at the sink, washing out her glass. She

was in her nightgown, hair in a long, brown braid down her back. She obviously couldn't sleep, either.

I cleared my throat, and she sprung back with a soft yelp.

"Sorry to startle you." I kept my voice low so as not to disturb anyone in the servants' quarters nearby. Or, heaven forbid, the housekeeper.

"I was just getting some milk to help me sleep. The tinned stuff is awful, though." She grimaced.

I motioned for her to join me at the scuffed worktable and pulled out a stool. "Why are you having trouble sleeping? Something on your mind?"

She shot me a wary look.

I allowed the silence to stretch, giving her time.

She rested her elbows on the table, propping her chin in her hands as if too tired to hold up her head a moment longer. "I've made a sad mess of things. Viola's dead and Barrett is gone, all because of me."

I folded my arms. Youth's predilection for assuming the world revolves around them—for good or ill—never ceases to surprise me. Sally had certainly created chaos and put people at risk, but others had made their own disastrous choices.

She eyed me expectantly, no doubt assuming I would cluck over her in motherly fashion.

I had no intention of soft peddling my response. "You come to that conclusion because you staged the theater accidents meant to harm Barrett Ward? And then frightened Miss Templeton by placing the blame on him when your plan went awry?"

Sally sat up straight.

I went on, "The day Ward complained about Rose's poor alterations and directed his anger at you, you lashed out again, did you not? You uncoiled the catwalk rope. Did you want to kill him then, or merely frighten him?"

"I—I don't know." Her voice quavered. "He—he betrayed me. You wouldn't understand."

"On the contrary—I know what he did. I assume you got the ruby back?"

She blinked. "How did you find out?"

"It hardly matters now. What he did was unconscionable, but that doesn't justify your actions. And yet, even after you saw what happened to Miss Templeton, you did it again. On either occasion you could have killed someone."

The color drained from her cheeks. "I—I know," she stammered. "I'm horrified that I just snapped like that. I'm truly sorry."

She didn't meet my gaze, instead fixing her gaze upon the braid that she nervously wrapped around her fingers. Her misery was all too evident.

Despite my anger, I softened my tone. "However, you are not responsible for Miss Templeton's demise or Mr. Ward's flight. There had been other factors at work, things that happened between them long before your, um, association with Mr. Ward."

The braid dropped from her fingers. "You know about that, too?"

I shrugged.

"It was only once." She blew out a breath. "I broke it off with him after. He didn't like being rejected and turned to blackmail—to get back at me, I suppose." She gave a shaky laugh.

"That seems to have been a familiar theme between you two—revenge." What Sally couldn't understand at her age—though perhaps this sad experience would help—was that the urge for retribution kept one emotionally tied to the person one was trying to separate from.

I grimaced. It had taken a while for me to learn that myself.

"What did he threaten you with?" I asked. "Not the affair, surely—that would get him into equal trouble."

She plucked at her sleeve, taking a while to answer. "I'd

told Barrett a secret about my father, which would have ruined him if it got out."

I could take a guess at what that might be, recalling the circumstances under which Greta had assumed joint ownership of the theater, but I asked a different question. "What are you going to do next time?"

She blinked in confusion. "Next time?"

"Betrayals are bound to happen in life. Sabotaging stage sets cannot be your favored method going forward. I doubt your father's business will survive it."

Her lips quirked at that. "Don't worry. I've learned my—"

She broke off as we both heard it—the creak of door hinges at the end of the hall, and the shuffle of stockinged feet.

I reached for my candle and hurried toward the sound, Sally right behind me. The cellar door at the end of the hall stood open.

Splendid. Just the place I wanted to explore on a night like this.

"Who do you think it is?" Sally whispered.

"Only one way to find out," I murmured back.

Taking a breath for courage, I held my candle high and started down the narrow steps.

My light couldn't penetrate past the bottom of the stairs, however. Off to my left came more sounds—a crate being shifted, perhaps.

"Hello?" I called. "Who's here?"

"Ma'am!" a boy's voice exclaimed. He stepped into the light as I advanced. It was the older of the two brothers who had arrived this evening. His thin face was pale and his eyes wide and luminous against his dark, tousled hair. He expelled a breath. "You scared the tar outta me." His gaze swept past me to Sally. "Hullo, miss."

"What are you doing down here?" I chided. "You're old

enough to know better than to wander strange places at such an hour."

"Please," he chimed plaintively, "you hav'ta help me. She's stuck. I can't get her out."

"Stuck? Who?"

"Cleo. My kitty. Over here."

We followed him to the back corner beside the coal chute. Crates had been shoved into the space between the chute and a tall, rusted barrel that reached nearly to my chin. I heard faint mewing, but it was difficult to pinpoint where exactly.

"How did you come to search for her here?" Sally asked.

"I caught her exploring the cellar earlier tonight," he said. "Something has her attention down here—mice, I 'xpect."

I suppressed a shudder at the thought, though it was all too likely. Even had there been no mice before, the storm would have driven them inside for shelter.

"When I woke up and she was gone," the boy went on, "I figured she'd come back."

"Very clever." Though shutting her in her basket for the night would have been cleverer still.

The mews grew more strident. I set the candle on a low shelf to free my hands. "All right, let's get her out."

After several minutes of Sally, me, and the boy shifting crates—my night robe was bound to be filthy by now—a gray-and-white ball of fur shot out from a crevice in the wall, dashed between our legs, and ran up the stairs.

The boy mumbled his thanks and ran after her.

"I'll make sure he gets back to where he's supposed to be," Sally said. She hesitated, then pressed my hand briefly. "Thank you, Mrs. Wynch."

She hurried up the stairs.

I bent down to pick up my candle. What a mess—the crates were strewn about, absolutely in the way now, but I wasn't about to put them all back myself. I'd inform the housekeeper in the morning.

Movement caught my eye, and just in time I caught a wooden toolbox, precariously propped atop the metal barrel, before it tipped upon my head. I reached up to shove it back more securely but dislodged the barrel lid in the process. *Drat.*

As I stepped closer to restore the lid, I caught a whiff of something distinctly unpleasant. Sharp and rottingly sweet. Perhaps a mouse had died in there? No, the odor was too strong.

I stood on tiptoe and held the candle over the opening. The smell was even stronger now. My breath hitched at the sight of bare ankles, crossed, and feet shod in velvet, mono-grammed slippers. I recognized the monogram—a gold *W*, encircled in an embroidered ring of ivy. I had seen it on his cravat, cuffs, and the handkerchief wrapped around the gun that had killed Viola Templeton.

Barrett Ward was wedged in headfirst, curled in the pose of a sleeping child, and clearly dead.

CHAPTER 18

*T*he candle dropped from my nerveless fingers and plunged me in darkness. I sank to the floor, clasping my knees, taking slow breaths to calm my racing pulse. *Barrett Ward had been here the entire time.*

How had the police missed the body? Even as I considered the question, an answer presented itself. Once the gun had been found, Malvern's focus had shifted to determining the whereabouts of the guilty man who'd recently fled. The idea of another victim had never been a consideration.

What to do now? The storm made it impossible to get immediate help from the authorities.

Whatever was to be done, sitting here in a dark, cold cellar beside Barrett Ward's body wasn't it. I groped my way up the stairs, taking care to shut the door firmly behind me when I reached the corridor. We didn't want any stray kittens chased by young boys to discover what was down there.

I shook Cassie awake as gently as I could. "Cassie."

She sat up with a yelp.

"I'm sorry to disturb you, dear, but I need your help."

I explained my grim discovery as I reached for the skirt and shirtwaist that I'd taken off only a few hours before. I may as well be properly attired for whatever was to come next.

Ever the practical soul, Cassie got out of bed and quickly dressed as well. "How horrible, Pen! What are we going to do now? Fetching the police is obviously out of the question."

"I'm going to turn the problem over to Mr. Sanderson." The man professed a fondness for taking charge of things, after all, but given the way he'd reacted to the first body, I wasn't sure how he'd handle a second. "And Greta will need to know. Which means Flora will also learn of it. Beyond them, however, it's best if we keep this as quiet as possible."

Cassie nodded. "We don't want a panic on our hands."

"I'm concerned about Flora in that regard—she's rather high-strung. I hope you don't mind going up with me to break the news. You may need to settle her down." I had little tolerance for female hysterics.

"Yes, of course," she said. "I'm more worried about the children learning of it, though. It's fortunate you didn't find the body until the boy and Sally had gone."

Part of me wished I hadn't found Ward at all, but ignorance was an indulgence we could ill afford. There was a murderer among us.

In the end, our circle of knowledge came to include Leonard as well, as Sanderson needed assistance in extricating the body. Although two days had passed since Ward had died, apparently the chilly cellar had slowed the passing of *rigor mortis*, so the job was a difficult one. I had not shared that detail with Cassie, who prudently elected to remain on the ground floor to monitor the hallway in case our activity drew someone's attention. Greta and Flora—not in hysterics, thankfully—gathered a few supplies stored in the cellar that might be required for the next day. The cellar door would be kept padlocked until the police could be summoned.

Then we made another discovery—Viola Templeton's jewels were tucked in Ward's bathrobe pockets. Not sure what to do with them, we left them there for the police, then decorously draped Ward's body on a table in the cellar and locked the door behind us.

We gathered in the kitchen to shake off the chill of our gruesome task. Cassie and Flora tended the stove to get the kettle going. It was too early for the cook and her assistant to be up, though that would be soon.

Leonard brushed off his trousers and rolled down his sleeves. "I hate to leave the poor fellow down there like that."

Sanderson made a face. "Let's hope it won't be for long."

"It shouldn't be," Greta said briskly. "The station master promised a coal delivery in the morning. We'll ask them to take word to the police station. Unless we can dig ourselves out first."

"We have another problem on our hands," Cassie said. "Who killed Ward? Was it the same person who killed Miss Templeton?"

Leonard shrugged. "Ward wasn't shot as Miss Templeton was. He was struck on the back of the head."

"This is very confusing," Flora said, setting cups of steaming tea in front of us.

"I've been giving it some thought," Sanderson said, "and the different manner of death supports my theory."

"Indeed?" Leonard asked. "And what theory is that?"

"That Ward killed Miss Templeton, as we have supposed, but then he in turn was killed to avenge her death."

Greta raised a skeptical eyebrow. "Who could be so certain that Barrett killed Viola? And be so overcome by vengeance as to take his life?"

"John Davis," I answered promptly, which earned me a black look from Sanderson. I'd stolen his dramatic moment.

"Davis?" Greta's incredulous tone made her voice louder.

"Yes, of course," Sanderson said. "He and Miss Templeton were lovers, you know."

I blinked in surprise. Sanderson was more discerning than I'd given him credit for.

"What if Davis found Miss Templeton dead in her room just after it happened?" Sanderson suggested. "Perhaps he had come to her bedroom for a late-night assignation—"

"Sir," Leonard interrupted indignantly, "there are ladies present. The woman to whom you refer is dead and cannot defend herself. Choose your words carefully."

Sanderson inclined his head. "Of course. Let us say that, for whatever reason, Davis found her dead, went to sound the alarm, and encountered Ward. Something triggered his suspicions that Ward was responsible—perhaps he came upon him lurking nearby, or he still had the gun in his hand...."

I folded my arms in disbelief. "And then what—Davis killed Ward, carried the body down to the cellar, and stuffed him in the barrel? What about the jewels?"

Flora's lips twitched. She watched Sanderson closely.

"I cannot think of every detail," he said defensively. "Maybe Davis somehow lured Ward down to the cellar and killed him there. And the jewels were taken as a distraction."

I pushed my teacup aside. My eyes felt gritty from lack of sleep, and this conversation was devolving into pointless speculation. I stood. "If you'll excuse me, I'm going to retire."

"Good idea," Cassie said.

Amid the weary chorus of good-nights as the others followed suit, I pushed through the kitchen door to catch a glimpse of a night-gowned Kay Finnerty beating a hasty retreat down the hallway.

I'd had the feeling Greta's tone had grown strident enough to attract notice. I was too tired to go after Kay. One could only hope that she would keep silent regarding what she'd overheard.

TUESDAY, MARCH 13

We awoke to a strange quiet, for a town of this size. No voices in the street, no horns, no sounds of machinery from the thread mill in the distance. Just the wind rattling the panes and the quarter-hour chimes from the church three blocks away.

Cassie went over to the window and drew aside the curtain. "It's stopped snowing, thank goodness. Come see."

The drift-riddled landscape held large, white lumps of unidentifiable objects, roofs with thick white caps, sweeping expanses where streets should be, and snow-draped, abandoned vehicles. Most of it was a pristine blanket, with narrow paths created by a few hardy souls—or foolish ones—who were determined to go out.

"Some of the drifts must be fifteen feet high," she said. "There's a lot of snow sitting on those roofs."

"The wind did its fair share of damage, too." I pointed to the torn awnings hanging down in front of the stores across the street.

Below, groups of men carrying shovels trudged through snow up to their knees, preparing to go at it again. I recognized several among them from Marlowe House. Greta was obviously determined to clear the walks so we could fetch the police as quickly as possible.

I noted the steel-gray sky. "I'm not sure the storm is quite over. Either way, it's going to take a while to dig out." I suppressed a shiver, the image of Ward's body fresh in my mind. I glanced over at Cassie, noting the hollows beneath her pale cheeks. She was thinking about Ward, too.

We dressed in our warmest walking suits and wool stockings. There was no predicting whether we'd get out that day, but best to be prepared.

A soft knock sounded at the door. A voice called, "Pen? Cassie? Can I talk to you?"

Cassie opened the door. "Kay! You look terrible—what's wrong?"

The young lady was clasping her hands together so tightly her knuckles were white. Cassie led her to a chair.

As she sat, her dark eyes held mine. "You were right. I didn't tell you the truth yesterday. And now with—with Barrett dead—" She choked off a sob.

Cassie started. "You know about that?"

"She overheard us talking in the kitchen." I quickly closed the door and sat on the bed. "All right, then—take a breath and tell us what you know."

"I saw something." She dabbed at her cheeks with a handkerchief Cassie handed her. "I'm not sure how important it is." She hesitated.

I motioned her to continue.

"It happened Saturday night, while everyone was at the play. Viola was sneaking up the stairs towards the fourth floor. And she wasn't limping at all."

Cassie and I exchanged a glance.

"I couldn't imagine what she was up to." Kay impatiently brushed ragged strands of hair from her face. "Or why she'd been feinting the extent of her injury. I had to know what was going on. I went up the other staircase…I even took off my shoes so no one would hear me." She ducked her head. "I felt like a wretched sneak thief."

"Then what?" Cassie asked.

"A short time later, I heard something break. Something large. I started to crack the stairwell door open when I saw Viola hurry out, toward the other set of stairs. She had something—a pouch, I think—in her hand."

"Did you follow her?" I asked.

Kay shook her head. "Someone else was coming up the staircase I was on, so I crept up toward the roof access and hid. I couldn't see from that angle, but I could tell the tread was heavier, like a man's."

That must have been Leonard, coming in search of me. The staircases were unusually active that evening.

"I slipped away once he had moved on," she finished.

"Did you say anything to Miss Templeton?" Cassie asked.

Kay grimaced. "I wasn't sure what to do. The players returned a short time later, and then there was the party... I couldn't ask her with all those people around. I decided to wait until morning."

"That's why you volunteered to bring her breakfast tray," I said.

"Yes. But then—well, you know the rest. Is that helpful? Honestly, that's all I know."

"You didn't tell the police, I assume?" I asked.

"Once they suspected Barrett, it seemed pointless to malign her. No one wants to speak ill of the dead."

Speak no ill of the dead—an investigator's biggest obstacle.

After seeing Kay out, I closed the door and leaned against it, rubbing my temples.

"I'm asking the same question as Kay," Cassie said. "Was that helpful or not?"

"At least it clarifies the motive," I said. "Someone was after the counterfeit plate, and the lady was killed in the process."

"Not many people knew the plate existed in the first place." Cassie ticked off the list on her fingers. "Flora, Greta, Sanderson, Rose, Leonard, you, and me. And the gang of counterfeiters. Perhaps they hired another intruder."

"How would someone from the outside know she had it?" I countered.

Cassie bit her lip. "I have no idea. I'm also puzzled by her motive for taking the plate at all."

"I've been considering that," I said. "I believe she wanted a hold over Greta Marlowe."

"Why?"

"You heard the reason yourself, remember? Rose told us that Greta was responsible for the breakup of Ward and Miss Templeton. Miss Templeton was undoubtedly nursing a grudge."

Cassie gave a slow nod as she considered it. "She did express bitter feeling towards the woman."

"But the question remains—who could have known Miss Templeton had the plate?"

"Maybe the person responsible didn't know it for a fact, but *surmised* that she had it," Cassie said. "After the attack, you spoke with Greta, Flora, and Sanderson about Miss Templeton as a possible suspect. Did you speak to anyone else?"

"Perhaps Leonard, but we can certainly leave him out," I said. "Who would want the plate badly enough to kill for it?"

"I doubt either Flora or Greta cared about the plate anymore. Besides, Sanderson was guarding them both that night."

I nodded my agreement. "If you think about it, the only person here at the hotel who wanted the plate quite badly was Daniel Sanderson. But he wouldn't need to murder her to get it."

"True," Cassie said. "He could simply request an official search. You never explained why he didn't do that the day he arrived."

"He was ordered by his boss at the prosecutor's office to recover it discreetly and avoid publicity. It was only at the eleventh hour that he'd planned to call the police and authorize a search of everyone's belongings before we left."

She grew quiet.

"What is it?" I asked.

"He would need to show identification for that, would he not? Have you ever seen it?"

"His identification?" I thought back. "No…just a business card. But Frank's telegram said—actually, all it said was that a man was coming to take over the case. Frank didn't name him or describe him in the message. But Sanderson's name was on the deposition orders Flora signed."

"Sanderson must have shown his identification to Lieutenant Malvern, surely?"

"Maybe. I don't know." My thoughts swirled with new possibilities. "My distinct impression at our first meeting was that Sanderson had been in frequent communication with Frank. How would that be possible if Frank wasn't the one who sent him?"

Cassie leaned forward in excitement. "What did Sanderson say when you first met?"

"He was certainly knowledgeable about the case, and about the circumstances that brought him here." I grimaced. "He insisted that a *firm hand* was needed—his hand, of course, in order to protect Flora—" I broke off, remembering his exact words.

And now her life has been put in danger…evidenced by the second-story man breaking in.

Second-story man. I had not detailed our intruder in my telegram to Frank, nor had I related the particulars to Sanderson. How would he have known, when not even Frank had?

A chill pricked my neck. Unless Sanderson himself had hired the would-be thief.

And when the plan had been thwarted? He'd come himself.

Was he in league with the counterfeiters?

"What is it, Pen?" Cassie asked anxiously.

I shook myself. "It's time I have a chat with the man." I went over to the dresser, extricated my double-barrel derringer, checked that it was loaded, and tucked it in my skirt pocket.

Cassie's eyes widened. "You need your gun for a *chat?*"

"Best to be prepared."

I pulled the door open to see Leonard Frasier standing there, hand raised to knock.

"Ah! Good morning." His eyes crinkled as he smiled beyond me, toward Cassie. "I noticed you two weren't in the dining room, so I came to see if you'd care to join me for breakfast. Probably the only bit of peace we'll get today, once the police return."

I shook my head. "I have something to take care of first." Recalling the covert handholding I'd witnessed at the sing-along last night, I added, resisting a wink, "You and Cassie go on without me."

Cassie, with a glance down the corridor—no one there—hissed, "I will not leave you to deal with that man alone, Pen. He could be dangerous."

"What's going on?" Leonard asked.

His expression darkened as I explained why Cassie and I thought Sanderson may not be the man he claimed.

"I must speak with him immediately," I finished. "You were downstairs—is he at breakfast?"

"Not yet. Only Pierson and the Chaffees so far. Oh, and I just passed Flora as she was heading down. Greta and Sanderson can't be too far behind."

Calling out a possible murderer was not something I cared to do on an empty stomach, but with the sidewalks being cleared, I didn't want to risk him escaping. And this certainly wasn't a conversation for the dining room.

I straightened my shoulders. "I'm going up to the fourth floor, then. I'll catch up with you later."

"You shouldn't do this alone. I'll go with you," Leonard offered. His glance flicked over to Cassie. "Why don't you wait for us downstairs?"

My friend put her hands on her hips and glared up at him. "Do you believe I'd be content with munching toast and sipping tea while you two are confronting a would-be murderer? I'm coming with you."

Leonard took a startled step back. I hid a smile. Childhood friends or no, he had a lot to learn about Cassie. Better to know what he was getting into sooner rather than later.

"We'll all go," I said.

CHAPTER 19

Sanderson and Greta had just stepped out of the fourth-floor suite.

Greta's expression brightened at the sight of us. "The day looks promising for us getting out, thank goodness. We should be able to summon the police soon."

"Before we do," I said, "I have a few questions for Mr. Sanderson. Shall we return to the suite, where we can all sit down and be comfortable?"

"I'm afraid now is not a good time, Mrs. Wynch." A smile tugged on his lips as he tried to side-step me.

"On the contrary." Leonard blocked his path. "Now is the perfect time."

Sanderson frowned. "What's going on? Stand aside, sir."

Cassie went around us all and opened the doors.

"Flora is waiting for us downstairs," Greta objected.

"You're welcome to go on ahead, Mrs. Marlowe," Cassie said. "Pen's questions are for Mr. Sanderson particularly."

Greta lifted an eyebrow. "Indeed?" A small smile tugged at her lips as she observed the discomfited Sanderson. "Well then, I'll stay, for a little while."

Leaving Leonard to deal with the man—really, how did I

manage without him before? I was positively spoiled now—I followed Cassie inside, Greta close behind.

∾

"I must protest this high-handed behavior," Sanderson complained.

We were ensconced in Greta's living room—Cassie and I upon the divan, Greta in a nearby rocking chair. Sanderson sat next to the writing desk. Leonard remained standing beside the hearth, arms folded and expression watchful.

I felt the reassuring weight of the gun in my pocket. Fortunately, the fellow had given no indication of desperation. Yet. "Some issues have arisen that require us to confirm that you are who you claim."

He scowled. "Don't be absurd. You know who I am."

"You neglected to present me with legitimate identification that you are, in fact, Daniel Sanderson, assistant district attorney for the City of New York," I said. "If you would produce something official to that effect, the matter will be settled, and we can all go down to breakfast."

Greta leaned forward. "Do you mean that he might *not* be the assistant district attorney?"

"It's a possibility," I answered. I turned to Sanderson. "Well?"

"I—I lost it on my way here," he stammered. "But I assure you, I am who I say."

I shook my head. "You were very convincing, I must admit. You knew a great deal about the counterfeiters' scheme, and you spoke knowledgeably about the missing plate."

"How could he have done so without being from the prosecutor's office?" Leonard asked. His brow cleared. "Unless he's one of the counterfeiters?"

"I wondered that myself," I said. "However, his affect is

too polished to be a regular associate of a gang of roughs. He also understands the workings of a prosecutor's office. I'd say he works there in some junior capacity. Perhaps as a clerk. Someone the gang pays to tip them off when the authorities are close to cracking down on their operation."

Sanderson stayed silent, but perspiration beaded his brow.

"'Tip them off,'" Greta repeated. "You mean the warning note Flora intercepted?"

"Exactly," I said. "The one intended for her husband. Who better placed than someone within the prosecutor's office to know that arrests were imminent?"

"Well, he didn't do such a great job of warning him," Greta said sarcastically.

I watched Sanderson fidget with his watch chain. "The ringleader of the scheme must have been angry when Humphrey Richards wasn't warned in time to escape. I imagine threats were made unless you mitigated the damage that had been done. And what would that involve—recovering the missing plate? Silencing Flora?"

Greta's eyes widened in alarm.

"This is pure fantasy." Sanderson's voice was hoarse.

I pressed on. "Working in the prosecutor's office meant you could watch for incoming telegrams. That's how you would have learned I'd been hired to escort Flora to New York to testify. You knew you'd have to act quickly to get the plate. Tell me, how did you know she had it? Did her husband tell you?"

Greta waved a dismissive hand. "Humphrey would never talk to the police or someone from the district attorney's office. Flora told you that."

"You forget," I said to her, "Flora's husband would have known this man was working for the same gang. Of all the men in the prosecutor's office with access to jailed prisoners, he'd be the *only* one Richards would talk to." I wondered about the others, the potential witnesses, found dead in their jail cells. Had he been responsible? I suppressed a shudder.

Greta scowled. "Did he hire the man who broke in? The one with the knife?"

I nodded. "In order to get the plate back without becoming personally involved."

"This is outrageous," Sanderson snapped. "Where is your proof?"

"Merely suspicion, I grant you. But certain items are telling in retrospect. Our first conversation in the parlor, for example. You took me to task for risking Flora's life at the hands of what you termed *a second-story man*. I had shared nothing so specific about our intruder in my telegram to Frank. Nor would that have been a ready assumption. Most intruders are of the smash-and-grab variety. Skilled second-story men are not at all common." I didn't volunteer the fact that I myself had not anticipated that development until it was nearly too late.

All eyes fixed upon Sanderson, who shifted uncomfortably.

Greta pursed her lips. "And when the hired henchman was incapacitated, he had to come himself?"

"I can't be certain he knew I'd shot the intruder," I said. "I didn't put that in my telegram to Frank, either. However, my message obviously worried Frank enough to send word to the district attorney's office that more help was needed. Sanderson was no doubt monitoring office communications closely. He would have inferred that something had gone wrong. Unless the fellow himself had sent word?" I asked Sanderson.

His eyes flickered, but that was all.

"Your boss never saw the message, did he?" I went on. "You must have replied to Frank yourself, pretending to be him, saying you would send a man to take charge of protecting the witness. No doubt you asked Frank to inform me as well."

"And then he came here to search for the plate," Leonard prompted. "A daring step."

"It's true the scheme carried risk," I said, "but he had enough knowledge to pass himself off as a government official and enlist my help."

"Very clever," Cassie said.

"He grew impatient, however, and made an aborted attempt to search your suite on his own." I glanced at Greta. "One of your footmen chased him off."

Her lips quirked. "Well, that's something. I was beginning to wonder how effective they were."

"In the end, he had to content himself with waiting for me to find it," I continued. "Neither of us expected Viola Templeton to attack me and take the plate. Unfortunately, she put herself in more danger than she realized."

Greta blinked in surprise at first, then her forehead smoothed in understanding. "Viola—yes, of course," she murmured. "Something to use against me. How did she know about the plate to begin with?"

I made a face. "After Sanderson's arrival and conversation with me—and then you, Greta—he noted afterward that Miss Templeton had been lingering nearby as the two of you left the parlor. It's impossible to know what she may have overheard." That had been Thursday. It felt like ages ago.

"Ah yes—that was when you passed him off as Mr. Frasier, the *theatrical agent*." Greta's tone dripped with sarcasm.

Leonard gave a snort that he unsuccessfully tried to turn into a cough, which I ignored.

"Sanderson asked me for help in creating an alias," I said, "ostensibly because his name was on the deposition documents and would have been recognizable to you." I watched Sanderson. No reaction. "You played a cunning game, convincing me you were a guileless fellow who couldn't even come up with a cover story."

Even after Miss Templeton's death, he'd played his part

well, I reflected, pretending to be concerned for the where-abouts of the counterfeit plate when the police arrived, pleading to be allowed to assist in the search. But he'd had it all along. We'd find it in his belongings, I had no doubt.

"Is there an actual Daniel Sanderson who is the assistant district attorney?" Cassie asked.

"Presumably," Greta said, "as the name was on the papers Flora had to sign."

I looked over at Sanderson. "What is your real name?"

He shrugged, an amused smile touching his lips.

Greta shifted impatiently. "Even if you decline to explain yourself to us, sir, you shall be obliged to do so by the police."

"He killed Miss Templeton, then, to get the plate?" Leonard asked.

"I'm not sure his original intention was to kill anyone. He had no expectation of being caught. The first part of his plan, slipping out of the suite after Flora and Greta had latched their inner doors for the night, went smoothly. After all, who watches the watcher? It was a handy alibi. Then, once he was confident Miss Templeton was asleep, he expected to search quietly for the plate, take it away with him, and no one the wiser."

I watched him fiddle with the desk blotter, his expression a neutral mask. "Did she awake to find you in her room?"

He made no answer.

"Deliberately or not," Cassie said tersely, "it made no difference to poor Miss Templeton in the end."

I barely noted her point, valid though it was. My attention was entirely upon Sanderson. "She fought you when you tried to smother her, didn't she? You had to shoot her then. Luck was in your favor when the boiler masked the sound."

"But how did Ward's death come about?" Leonard asked.

"I can only think that Ward surprised him somehow," I said, "though I have no idea why Ward would have returned to Miss Templeton's room at that hour."

"Quite a lot of coming and going at odd hours," Cassie said dryly, "even for theater people."

Greta scowled.

"This is outrageous," Sanderson said airily. "If I am the culprit you claim, feel free to search my belongings. I do not have the plate."

I stiffened. That was to be my next step. Was this a bluff?

I heard the rustle of skirts behind us and the sound of the door closing. We all turned to see Flora crossing the foyer.

"That's right, Mr. Sanderson," she said acidly, "or whoever you are. You don't have the plate. *I* have it."

The silence seemed to stretch as we gaped at Flora.

"What are you doing here?" Greta asked.

That wasn't to be my first question of the young lady.

"I came back to see what was delaying you," Flora said. "I didn't expect to step into the middle of...this."

Finally, I marshalled my thoughts. "Sit down, Flora, and explain yourself."

She flicked an uneasy glance toward Sanderson as she sat in the other rocking chair across from Greta. "A noise woke me in the early morning hours before Viola was found. I opened my bedroom door, just a tiny bit, and saw him in the living room. That's where he's been sleeping, to make sure we didn't escape," she added caustically.

"I already told them about the arrangement," Greta said.

Flora gave a nod and continued, "He was fully dressed but in his stocking feet, bending over his valise to tuck something inside. Then he went back to his cot."

"What time was this?" I asked.

"Three o'clock or so."

"Then what?" asked Leonard.

"I didn't have a chance to be alone to search his case

before the police arrived," she said, "but when he was occupied with Lieutenant Malvern, I took a chance and found the plate beneath a couple of monogrammed shirts. I pinned it into my petticoat until I could find a better hiding place."

A daring move. "And you managed to leave the premises while the police were here," I said.

Flora narrowed her eyes. "I wanted it out of his reach, so I hid it in the theater. You'll never find it there," she added pointedly, glaring at him.

Other things were making sense—the change in mood between Sanderson and Flora that I hadn't been able to understand. I realized now that what I had witnessed was a shift in control. Sanderson had held all the cards and had carried himself with confidence—arrogance might be the better word—while Greta had feared for her dejected, cowering niece. But Flora had taken away his prize. I recalled Sanderson's uneasiness the morning of the snowstorm. Flora's demeanor had been the opposite.

"But why would you take it?" Cassie asked Flora. "Surely you must have realized he'd suspect you right away."

Flora shrugged. "But he couldn't outright accuse me of taking it, because that would mean admitting he'd killed Viola."

"You opportunistic little minx," Sanderson snarled.

I ignored the outburst and kept my attention on Flora. "You knew, then, that he killed her. And yet you said nothing."

"I needed something to bargain with," she said defensively. "I was going to offer him the plate in exchange for keeping me out of the witness box. I know the sort of men Humphrey associates with. Witnesses have a habit of dying before giving testimony. I didn't want to be one of them."

In the face of our silence, she added, "Besides, I wasn't *sure* he'd killed her, especially after Barrett went missing and the gun was found in his room."

"But when Ward's body was discovered last night,"

Leonard said, "you must have realized Ward wasn't responsible, and that this one"—he gestured contemptuously at Sanderson—"had killed them both."

Sanderson stiffened, and a desperate glint came into his eyes.

I drew out my gun and held it discreetly in the folds of my skirt. "All right, Mr. Sanderson—tell us what happened to Ward."

He was cornered, and he knew it.

Even as I wondered how to get him to confess, I realized Flora had mentioned another potential item of evidence—monogrammed shirts. Sanderson hadn't worn any such attire, but Ward had. I stood. "Well, then, we'll start by examining the contents of your valise. Some of Ward's shirts were taken to make it appear as if he'd fled. If you put them in with yours—where they would blend in—the monogram would show to whom they belong."

"Excellent idea," Leonard said enthusiastically.

A loud rumbling crash sounded across the street, along with a chorus of screams.

We dashed to the windows.

"Heavens, the roof of the boys' academy has collapsed!" Cassie exclaimed.

"The weight of the snow must have done it," Greta said.

Rapid movement snapped my attention back to our own problem. Sanderson—something gripped in his hand—was running toward the door.

Leonard stepped in his way, and I saw the flash of metal. The letter opener from Greta's desk blotter.

I lifted my gun and opened my mouth to shout a warning, but it was too late. Leonard, stabbed in the side, let out a groan and collapsed to the floor.

Just as I was trying for a clear sight line on Sanderson, he grabbed Greta, who had bent down to help Leonard.

"Not another step!" Sanderson dragged Greta toward the door, holding the now bloodied letter opener to her neck.

Flora, Cassie, and I froze. My gun remained pointed in his direction, but I dared not fire. Derringers aren't accurate. I might hit Greta.

"Mrs. Wynch," Sanderson said, though clenched teeth, "you will put the gun down and slide it over to me."

I hesitated. He pressed the blade into the folds of Greta's neck. She gasped.

"Do it. *Now*," he said coldly.

I took a breath to steady my pulse. "Why would I give you a better weapon?" I asked, fighting to keep the tremor out of my voice. At the edge of my vision, I saw Cassie crouched over Leonard. Please heaven he was still alive.

Sanderson hesitated, still clutching his hostage.

"You see how difficult it is," I went on, "to injure someone who isn't actively attacking you. Especially an old woman like Greta."

Even in her distressing predicament, Greta had the where-withal to frown at that remark.

"You don't want yet another death on your hands." I took a small, careful step toward them.

His grip flexed upon the blade handle. "I don't *want* to hurt anyone. Just...let me go."

Greta, face contorted in fear, squirmed in his arms. "Help me, please!"

My arm was struck sharply—by Flora—and the gun flew out of my hand. It discharged as it hit the floor. The bullet embedded harmlessly in a table leg.

Before I could retrieve the derringer, Flora kicked it toward Sanderson.

"There!" she cried. "Now let her go!"

"*Flora!*" Cassie exclaimed.

Sanderson swiftly pushed Greta away and picked up the derringer, which for the first time I wished was a single-barrel weapon. If he'd been out of bullets, I could have jumped him.

"Now"—he pointed the gun in my direction—"everyone —into the dressing room. Is he still alive?" he asked Cassie.

I held my breath, waiting for her answer.

She glared up at him. "For now."

"Him, too, then. Quickly."

As gently as we could, Cassie, Flora, and I picked up Leonard by his shoulders and feet and carried him to Flora's dressing room. Greta followed, dabbing at her neck with a handkerchief.

Once we were all inside, he checked the door lock for the key. "Ah, good."

"We're still snowbound," I said. "You won't get far."

He ignored that. "Make yourselves comfortable, ladies. I don't think anyone will come looking for you for quite some time." The door closed, the key turned in the lock, and his footsteps hurried away. We were plunged in darkness, the only light seeping through the crevices around the door.

"He's likely correct." Greta sighed. "The roof collapse is bound to occupy everyone's attention."

"I'm s—so sorry..." Flora choked, flinging herself in Greta's arms. "I—I just couldn't bear to have him hurt you!"

I was in no mood for Flora's histrionics. I groped my way to Cassie, who knelt beside Leonard. "How is he?" The sound of his ragged breathing made my heart constrict.

"He's still with us," Cassie said, "but oh, Pen, I'm so worried. We must get help quickly."

"I know. Stay calm. I'll get us out." I groped for the hair-pins in my chignon. What I wouldn't give for my lockpicks right now.

At least Greta's closet lock wasn't a complicated one. However, working in near darkness meant it took four bent hairpins and an interminable number of minutes before we were free.

Once I had the door open, Flora and Greta hurried for the stairs, yelling as they ran.

I lingered to check Leonard's condition. He was still unconscious. His pallor was alarming, as was the growing blood stain on his shirt. Cassie lifted her tear-streaked face. "I don't know if he'll make it."

"Stay with him. Flora and Greta are getting help."

"What about you?" She bit her lip at my grim expression. "You're going after Sanderson, aren't you?"

I blew out a breath. "I must."

"Alone? You're unarmed now."

I shook my head. "I'm not so foolish as that. I plan to recruit help." I touched her lightly on the shoulder. "Do what you can for him."

CHAPTER 20

$\mathcal{E}$veryone was outside, assisting at the calamitous scene of the roof collapse. I threw on my coat and boots and dashed outside in search of Chaffee among the clumps of people.

Greta and Flora were talking to one of the footmen clutching a shovel. I could tell by the fellow's wide-eyed expression that he was struggling to digest the entirety of it all.

"Fetch the doctor first," Greta was saying, as I approached, "before you go for the police."

I stopped the man as he turned to leave. "When you do talk to the police, be sure to tell them the murderer is at the theater. They must go there first to apprehend him, before they deal with the—um, discovery in the cellar." Ward wasn't going anywhere, but Sanderson was unquestionably intent upon escaping.

He blinked in confusion before turning to Greta. "Ma'am?"

"That's right," Greta said brusquely. "Be sure to tell them that."

With a quick nod, he hurried off.

"I'm looking for Chaffee," I said to Greta.

She pointed to a group of men farther up the block, currently helping two disheveled, plaster-dust-covered boys make their limping way out of the building.

With a shiver, Flora clutched her jacket closer to her petite frame. "What are you going to do?"

"Stop Sanderson," I said curtly. Which would have been unnecessary if Flora hadn't disarmed me, but recriminations now were pointless. "Where did you hide the plate?"

She hesitated.

"We're wasting time. Tell me *now*, Flora." My hand twitched in a restrained urge to slap her.

"It's in the recess of one of the footlights. I can't remember the exact one. The set of them along stage right." She bit her lip. "I *am* sorry for all the trouble I've caused, Pen. Be careful."

I walked away, too angry to acknowledge the apology. I stumbled along the narrow path carved in the snow as quickly as I could manage. "Mr. Chaffee!" I called.

He turned, as did two other men—John Davis and Nat Pierson.

"I need you all to accompany me to the theater," I began, then hesitated. None of them even knew about Ward's death. Explanations would take too long. "It's urgent. You'll just have to trust me. I can explain—somewhat—along the way," I added lamely.

Al Chaffee grunted, "We're needed here, Mrs. Wynch. There are still people trapped."

Davis gave me a quick, penetrating glance. He alone of the group knew who I was. "Give me the keys," he said to Chaffee. "I'll go with her."

Keys in hand, we turned back up the path. "Thank you," I said to Davis.

"What's this all about?" he asked.

"Sanderson is our murderer," I said tersely. "He's escaped

and heading for the theater. Is your gun still in Chaffee's office?"

"Sanderson? Who's that?"

I gritted my teeth at the layer of lies I had to peel away for this to make sense. "The man going by the name of Frasier, the talent agent."

"Ah. He isn't really an agent, I take it? And his name isn't Frasier?"

"That's right. His name isn't Sanderson, either, but I don't know his real name." At the sight of his confused expression, I added, "It's a long story. Now, tell me—is your gun still in Chaffee's office?"

"It should be. Al hasn't been back to the theater since the blizzard stranded us."

"We should retrieve that first, then." I thrust my tingling hands deeper inside my pockets.

"As long as you tell me what's going on."

Between huffing breaths and the wind in our faces, my account was by necessity a succinct one. He stopped short when I got to the part about discovering Ward's body.

"Poor Barrett," he murmured. "And here we all suspected him of killing Viola."

"No doubt that was our killer's intention. He was counting upon being long gone before the body was found. The storm interfered with that plan."

I concluded my account as we approached the Marlowe Theater. The snow hadn't been cleared here yet. There were deep tracks where someone had gone around to one of the side doors leading to the backstage area. It must be our quarry.

Even stepping in the tracks already made, it was slow going. I leaned against the wall to catch my breath as Davis fumbled with the keys.

I pointed to a broken window a few yards away, more snow dislodged beneath it. "That's how he got in."

Davis bit his lip. "Caution is called for."

That was an understatement.

"What's our plan?" he asked.

I could appreciate the methodical mind of the stage actor, wanting to choreograph our movements in advance. It was also wise to avoid conversing extensively within the theater, where we could be heard.

"After we retrieve your gun," I said, "we'll search for him. If possible, we'll sneak up on him and catch him unawares. If that doesn't work, I'll distract him with your gun while you disarm him."

Davis raised an eyebrow. "He's armed?"

I grimaced. "He has my double-barrel derringer, but there's only one shot left."

"What happened to the first bullet? How did he get your weapon to begin with?"

"Long story," I said wearily.

"You seem to have a number of those. All right, let's go."

I was grateful to have Davis take the lead in navigating the maze of back rooms and narrow corridors, as I was only familiar with the wardrobe room and Flora's dressing room. We could see our breaths in the cold, still air. We didn't dare turn on any lights. If they worked at all. From the looks of it, the entire town was without power.

Unmistakable sounds of furniture recklessly shoved aside in Flora's dressing room reached our ears. Obviously, Sanderson wasn't expecting anyone to come after him so soon. That was an advantage we had to preserve.

We crept toward the theater manager's office, thankfully on the opposite side from the dressing rooms. Davis muffled the keyring in his hand as he unlocked the door. We slipped inside and closed it softly behind us.

My eyes were adjusting to the gloom. Davis groped in Chaffee's top desk drawer, extricated the medium-frame, double-action revolver, and handed it to me. "Careful," he whispered, "it's loaded."

I brought it over to the window and unlatched the top break to check the chambers. Yes—fully loaded and ready to go. I snapped it shut.

He was watching me closely. "You're familiar with the Smith and Wesson," he murmured.

I shrugged. Not really. But there are only so many ways one can design a revolver.

The sound of approaching footsteps sent us to our positions—Davis beside the hinged side of the door and I behind the desk.

The door opened. I held my breath, gun ready, waiting for Davis to pounce upon him.

Instead, I heard a soft exclamation, then Sanderson's voice. "Davis? What are you—stop right there! Put up your hands."

Still crouched, I peeked around the corner of the desk to see Davis, hands meekly raised. Time for the alternate plan.

"What are you doing here?" Sanderson demanded. "Who sent you?"

Davis shrugged as he took a step back, no doubt to give me more room. I should have been insulted the fellow didn't trust my aim. "I'm just here to retrieve my gun," he said nonchalantly.

"Huh?"

That was my cue. I stood. "Sanderson."

Startled, he swiveled sharply away from Davis and faced me, my derringer gripped in his hand. Davis jumped him.

I flattened myself against a file cabinet, hearing the wood splinter at my shoulder as the gun went off. Our furniture had suffered grievously lately.

But now—*no more bullets*.

I tugged on the chain of the desk lamp but nothing happened, drat it—how quickly one forgets—so I was obliged to call out, "Give it up, Sanderson! The police are on their way."

At least, one would hope.

～

At last, Lieutenant Malvern, four policemen in tow, came hurrying up the path that Davis had cleared after we'd securely tied Sanderson to an office chair in Chaffee's office. I was keeping an eye on our prisoner—who wouldn't say a word and refused to even look at me—while also watching for their arrival.

I breathed a sigh of relief, stepped out into the corridor, and called, "In here, Lieutenant."

Malvern, scowling beneath the brim of his snow-dusted police cap, gestured to the men to tuck away their billy clubs. He poked his head into the office, saw Sanderson, turned back to me, and asked, "Anyone else with you?"

"Mr. Davis—he's retrieving the counterfeit plate. Flora says it's hidden away in one of the footlights."

"Indeed? Before I talk to him"—he inclined his head toward Sanderson, who glared in return—"you'd better fill me in on what's going on at the hotel. All I know is we have another body and an injured man who requires a doctor, but I was directed to come here first in pursuit of this fellow."

"Has the doctor gone to take care of Mr. Frasier?" I shivered, no doubt from the bitter temperatures—not sentimentality. Absolutely not.

"You can rest easy on that, ma'am." He gestured to one of his men standing nearby, whom I recognized from Sunday's visit. "Keep an eye on the prisoner. Leave him bound for now."

"Yessir."

After the patrolman had gone inside, Malvern led me

farther down the hall, out of earshot of the office. "It seems a great deal has occurred since I left the hotel Sunday evening."

"We would have contacted you as soon as we found poor Mr. Ward last night," I said, "but the storm made it impossible."

He nodded. "Let us start at the beginning, then. I want to know how an assistant district attorney becomes a murder suspect."

"That would require that he be an assistant district attorney to begin with," I retorted. It had been a wearying day, and Malvern's tone sorely tested my patience. "Did you ask for his identification when he told you who he was?"

Malvern blinked. "But you vouched for him, and he showed a card—well, *ah*, no. I did not."

I softened my tone. "It would be unfair to fault you, Lieutenant, as I had a similar lapse. Sanderson used intercepted communications and inside knowledge of the prosecutor's case to fool me as well. It wasn't until I found Ward's body and had time to think through it all that I realized something was off about the man." I proceeded to outline my deductions and the subsequent confrontation with Sanderson that had ended badly, particularly for Leonard.

Though not fatally so, I prayed.

"Sanderson—or whoever he really is—has admitted to nothing outright," I finished, "so there are particulars we don't have regarding the murders of Miss Templeton and Mr. Ward."

"His attack and flight constitute an implicit admission of guilt," Malvern said. "I'll have no problem taking him into charge. We'll proceed from there and get the rest of what we need. Once telegraph service is restored, we'll be able to establish his identity."

I hoped that would be soon.

Malvern stood. "In the meantime, I'll see if I can glean

anything from him. Those bindings appear rather, um, unconventional—what are they, exactly?"

I smiled. "Rick-rack trimming, left over from Flora's gown.
Surprisingly sturdy."

His lips twitched. "Indeed. Well, they should be feeling
rather uncomfortable by now—"

"Found it!" A dusty-kneed John Davis hurried down the
corridor toward us, waving an equally dust-covered velvet
pouch in triumph. "Wedged in the second-to-last recess of
footlights."

"I'll have charge of it, thank you." Malvern reached out a
hand. "Now then, though I am grateful to you both, we'll take
it from here." He gestured to another policeman who stood by
the door. "The sergeant will escort you safely back to the
hotel. Go carefully—the snow has started up again."

EPILOGUE

SATURDAY, MARCH 18

*I*t took another three days for the town to dig out from the storm. Several buildings had suffered structural damage—the boarding school wasn't the only roof collapse—but finally, life was returning to normal. Power and telegraph lines were restored to much of the town, primary thoroughfares and fire hydrants were cleared, businesses had re-opened, and coal and food deliveries had resumed.

Most importantly, the trains were running.

The Pierson Players had left us yesterday, with the intention of salvaging their Philadelphia tour.

Flora had not gone with them. She remained at Marlowe House, waiting to learn if she would still be required to give testimony in New York.

Malvern had paid us a visit two days after Sanderson's arrest to explain.

"I've been in communication with the prosecutor for the counterfeiting case," he began, settling his pocket tablet on his lap after ushering Flora, Greta, and me into comfortable chairs in the parlor. "Humphrey Richards' trial is being post-poned because Lachlan's actions have muddied the waters. There's a great deal more evidence they must sort through now."

"Lachlan?" I asked. "That's his name?"

"That's right." He glanced down at his notes. "Charles Lachlan. A clerk for assistant district attorney Daniel Sanderson—the real one—who was completely in the dark as to his employee's criminal activities." He sat back with a sigh. "It's the old story—Lachlan has expensive tastes and needed money. He started informing for the Morrow Gang last year. When things went awry, he was in a heap of trouble with them, and—well, you know the rest."

Flora's clasped hands relaxed slightly. "Does this mean I won't have to give testimony against Humphrey?"

"The prosecutor isn't sure yet. He's inclined to think it won't be necessary. Lachlan's full confession has provided a lot of names and details—the district attorney's office never suspected the existence of a completed twenty-dollar plate, for example."

"Then why did they want me to testify, after I'd submitted a written deposition?" Flora asked.

He shrugged. "I didn't discuss that with him. I've given him this address as the best place to reach you, however."

"Quite right," Greta said, patting her hand. "She's welcome to stay here as long as she likes."

Flora pressed her hand in return before turning back to Malvern. "Am I in further danger from the Morrow Gang? I wouldn't want to risk Aunt Greta."

"Doubtful. The same cannot be said for Lachlan, however. He knows too much for their comfort. We've implemented extra precautions while he awaits arraignment here for the murders of Miss Templeton and Mr. Ward and the attack on Mr. Frasier. Eventually, he'll be sent back to New York."

Flora's blue eyes narrowed in disdain. "In manacles, I hope."

Malvern ignored the bitter remark. "How is Mr. Frasier faring?" he asked me.

"He's out of danger, thank heaven." Though Leonard had lost some blood, the knife had not hit a vital organ. The news had been quite a relief to us all. "The doctor says he'll fully recover. He'll be able to travel in a few more days."

Greta shook her head. "We've had to avail ourselves of Dr. Byrd's services quite frequently this past week."

The good doctor was on his way to becoming a regular at Greta's breakfast table.

Malvern stood. "I should be going. There's a great deal to be done."

I stood as well. "I'll see you out, Lieutenant."

Malvern retrieved his overcoat from the cloakroom. "Something else, Mrs. Wynch?" he asked, as I made no move to leave him.

"I was hoping you could tie up a few loose ends for me, regarding the deaths of Mr. Ward and Miss Templeton. Mere curiosity, I grant you," I added, as he rolled his eyes. "You say he made a full confession—I assume that included the murders as well?"

The policeman let out a noisy sigh. "Very well—I suppose you are entitled to an explanation." He gestured to a nearby bench, and we sat.

"You'd already surmised a great deal," he said, "but for simplicity, I'll start at the beginning. Everything stemmed from Lachlan's desperation to retrieve the plate."

I nodded. "And he'd come close to achieving his goal, with the second-story man he'd hired."

"He came closer still when you had it, then lost possession," Malvern added.

I grimaced at the memory. "How did he know Miss

Templeton was responsible? Even I hadn't been sure it was her, particularly after seeing Miss Finnerty's hand injury."

"Lachlan had eliminated Miss Finnerty as a possibility earlier."

I blinked. "He had?"

"He'd pilfered Mrs. Young's keys and searched Miss Finnerty's room while the party was still in progress."

So that was what the maid had been so frantic to find that night. And no wonder—the housekeeper was likely fit to be tied over such a loss.

"Lachlan planned to search Miss Templeton's ground-floor room next, but the lady retired for the night before he had the chance."

"So that's why he was in the library and how he came to overhear the argument between Ward and Miss Templeton," I mused aloud.

Malvern gave a nod. "That bit of information—along with you having heard it, too—proved useful to him later."

"It gave him the idea to implicate Ward as Miss Templeton's murderer."

Now it was Malvern who grimaced. "I regret being deceived by the ruse."

"Before we discuss how Ward came to be killed," I said, "tell me—did Lachlan intend to kill Miss Templeton all along?"

"He asserts not, and I believe him. Far easier for him to leave by the next day's train when nothing appears out of the ordinary. Lachlan's priority was to get back to New York with the plate."

And what of Flora, I wondered. What would have happened to the young lady along the route? We would never know.

"He obviously underestimated the difficulty of searching a room while its occupant slept," I observed.

"True enough. He said he'd found the plate in the bottom

of the wardrobe, got careless in his excitement, and bumped into a chair. As the lady awoke and took breath to scream, he tried to smother her with a pillow. She fought back quite forcefully."

"The torn fingernails," I said.

"We found scratches on his arms, by the way. When he saw he was losing the struggle, he groped for the gun in his pocket and fired."

I steeled my imagination from following that dark path and focused on my questions. "If Lachlan didn't intend to kill Miss Templeton, he certainly didn't plan on killing Ward. How did that come about?"

"Ward had returned to the lady's door and heard the shot."

No amount of noise from a defective boiler could prevent a wide-awake person right outside the door from hearing the gun. To Mr. Ward's great misfortune.

I frowned. "What was Ward doing there at such an hour?"

Malvern lifted a shoulder. "We can only guess. According to Lachlan, the man was clutching a slip of paper as he bent over Miss Templeton."

"Wait—a piece of paper?" I'd seen it, on the floor beneath the bed skirt.

I hope you'll forgive me.

Malvern nodded. "Yes, we saw the paper, though it made no sense at the time. There was no telling how long it had been there."

"Ward was leaving a note of apology under her door," I mused aloud.

"It would seem so."

"How was he struck from behind, if he surprised Lachlan?"

"Lachlan had just enough time to duck out of sight when he heard the door open. He hit Ward on the back of the head as the fellow was preoccupied with the lady."

"The brass lamp," I murmured.

"Yes, it's quite heavy. And he dared not fire the gun again, since the sound had brought Ward running. According to Lachlan, the single blow killed him."

I could only imagine what it had been like for Lachlan— not a professional killer and certainly out of his depth—to find himself in a room with two dead bodies to deal with. The pounding heart, the dry mouth, the wave of panic as to what to do next....

Then, finally, an idea to act upon.

"That's when he remembered the argument between Ward and Miss Templeton," I said.

"Yes. When he was assured no one else had been alerted by the disturbance, he concealed Ward's body in the barrel in the cellar."

"That couldn't have been easy, even though Lachlan is the larger man," I said.

He inclined his head to acknowledge my point and continued, "Then he planted the gun in Ward's dresser drawer and removed enough personal items to suggest Ward had fled."

"Putting the clothing in his own suitcase," I added. "Extra articles of male attire would hardly be noticed there, though when Flora mentioned monogrammed shirts, that got my attention. Ward was the only fellow I'd noticed with monogrammed clothing. And the safest place for the jewels, I suppose, was hiding them with Ward's body. But why take the jewels in the first place, if he was going to lay the blame upon Ward?"

"I put that question to him. Turns out it was a matter of sheer fatigue by that point, rather than deviousness." The policeman shook his head. "As you are no doubt aware, we're more likely to catch the careless criminals."

I stifled a snort. He'd very nearly missed catching this one. But I maintained proper ladylike decorum and refrained from pointing that out.

His mouth quirked. I had the sense he knew exactly what I'd been thinking. "The room was already in disarray," he went on, "and Lachlan was simply too tired after moving Ward's body to try to restore order to the room. He decided the appearance of a theft would add an extra layer of complexity, as if Ward himself had arranged it to look like a burglary gone wrong."

"It wasn't outside the bounds of probability," I admitted, "though for it to work, Lachlan had to leave town quickly, before Ward's body was found."

Malvern picked a speck of lint from his sleeve. "And the storm thwarted his plans."

Indeed it had.

"That's the gist of it." He tucked his hat under his arm as he stood. "If you'll excuse me, ma'am, I must be going."

Leonard insisted he was well enough to see us off at the train station.

He did seem much improved. There was a healthy brightness to his gray eyes and he didn't move as stiffly, though when he stepped aside for the porter to take our cases, I noticed a pained expression flicker across his brow.

The station was congested with eager travelers who were finally able to leave town. Amid the chorus of shouting porters, wailing children, and the sing-song calls of the soup-and-sandwich vendor, we felt the platform rumble as the loco-motive approached.

Leonard clasped Cassie's gloved hand in a lingering farewell—pinkening her cheeks in charming fashion—then turned to me with a gallant bow.

"Goodbye, Leonard," I said. "And thank you, again."

"Happy to be of assistance. Shall I say hello to your mother on your behalf?"

I lifted a shoulder. "I suppose."

"I'll take care to explain the current state of affairs to her. She won't try to pair us together anymore."

I gave a snort. "Her matchmaking days are far from over, but thank you, yes—that may help." After a pointed glance at Cassie, I asked mischievously, "And what *is* the current state of affairs?"

His neck flushed almost as pink as Cassie's cheeks. "You know?"

"I suspected." I winked. "I am a detective, after all."

He smiled at us both. "Cassie can explain better than I." And with a final wave goodbye, he left.

The crowd surged around us as the train slowed at the platform.

We stepped up to our railcar, Cassie slipping her arm through mine. "You're not angry, I hope? It was a surprise to us both. The night Leonard and I went out to search for Rose —well, that's when it became apparent."

How refreshing that something so wonderful had come out of such tragedy.

I squeezed her hand. "On the contrary, I'm delighted for you both."

And I meant it.

∾

THE END

AFTERWORD

I hope you enjoyed the story. While each *Chronicle of a Lady Detective* incorporates aspects of day-to-day life in the 1880s, this particular book necessitated in-depth research into the stagecraft and theaters of the period. If you're interested in learning more, I've included resources below.

In addition, the mystery's denouement employed an actual historical event—the Great Blizzard of 1888, which cut a swath along the East Coast extending from Maine to the Chesapeake Bay. The blizzard raged from March 11th to 14th, incapacitating trains, telegraph, and basic infrastructure across the cities and towns in its path. Even ships at sea were affected —two hundred either wrecked or foundered and one hundred sailors perished.

In the aftermath, public officials realized the vulnerability of their above-ground transit, telegraph and electrical lines and took steps to move them below ground. The first subway systems in Boston and New York City opened in 1897 and 1904, respectively. You'll find interesting sources about the blizzard below.

Thanks for reading!

~K.B. Owen, September 2022

≈

Select Primary and Secondary sources

ChroniclingAmerica.loc.gov
~~A digitized database of historic American newspapers. A lot of information on the Great Blizzard can be found through advanced keyword and date searches.

Connecticut History Online. "The Blizzard of 1888 - The Eye of the Storm: A
Journey into the Natural Disasters in Connecticut," 2012. *https://connecticuthistory.org/blizzard-of-1888-devastates-state/*
~~Wonderfully detailed account of the effects of the blizzard upon the area.

National Museum of American History, Smithsonian Institute: "The Blizzard of 1888." https://americanhistory.si.edu/blog/blizzard-1888
~~In-depth account of the impact of the blizzard upon major areas of the East Coast and the notable people (such as William Steinway) who were affected.

HathiTrust.org
~~A valuable resource for primary documents, including city directories.

Rader, Peter. *Playing to the gods: Sarah Bernhardt, Eleonora Duse, and the rivalry that changed acting forever*. New York, Simon and Schuster, 2018.
~~A fascinating look into the daily workings and interactions among female actors and their audiences of the period.

Roger Sherman House / *https://rogershermanhouse.com/2019/
09/02/george-b-bunnell-takes-control-on-may-1-and-from-that-time-it-
will-be-known-as-the-hyperion/*

~~The fictitious Marlowe Theater was loosely based upon
the Hyperion Theater in New Haven, CT (across from Yale
University). While the Hyperion no longer exists, this site,
along with articles from the historical newspaper archive,
provided useful details.

Special thanks to...

Thank you to Liz Colandene, Performing Arts Coordinator,
Workhouse Arts Foundation, for taking the time to give me a
tour of their theater and answer questions; Amy Shojai,
mystery author and theater performer, for her help with my
research; Melinda VanLone, for her fabulous cover art;
Kristen Lamb, for edits to the early pages; Kirsten Weiss, for
her developmental edits; Julie Glover, for her meticulous final
edits.

And my heartfelt *thank you* to my dear husband Paul, for
his love and unfailing support.

~KBO

EXPLORE MY HISTORICAL SERIES SET IN A 19TH CENTURY WOMEN'S COLLEGE

THE CONCORDIA WELLS MYSTERIES

*S*et in a fictitious 1890s women's college, this cozy-style series features Miss Concordia Wells, a young lady professor who cannot resist a little unseemly sleuthing when those she cares about are at risk. Who knew higher education could be…murder?

Start with:

*Dangerous and Unseemly, book 1. Winner of **Library Journal's** "Best Mystery of 2015: SELF-e"!*

"A fun historical whodunit with a delightful background of the early days of women's collegiate education." ~*Library Journal*

ALSO BY K.B. OWEN

THE CONCORDIA WELLS MYSTERIES:

Dangerous and Unseemly (book 1)

Unseemly Pursuits (book 2)

Unseemly Ambition (book 3)

Unseemly Haste (book 4)

Beloved and Unseemly (book 5)

Unseemly Honeymoon (book 6)

Unseemly Fate (book 7)

CHRONICLES OF A LADY DETECTIVE:

Never Sleep (#1)

The Mystery of Schroon Lake Inn (#2)

The Case of the Runaway Girl (#3)

The Secret of the Forty Steps (#4)

The Twelve Thieves of Christmas (#5)

The Case of the Reluctant Witness (#6)

ABOUT THE AUTHOR

K.B. Owen taught college English at universities in Connecticut and Washington, DC and holds a doctorate in 19th century British literature. A long-time mystery lover, she drew upon her teaching experiences in creating her amateur sleuth, Professor Concordia Wells and from there, Lady Pinkerton Penelope Hamilton was born.

kbowenmysteries.com
contact@kbowenmysteries.com

facebook.com/kbowenwriter2
twitter.com/kbowenwriter
instagram.com/kbowen_mysteries